2612 CHERRYHILL LANE

-2612-
CHERRYHILL LANE

—A NOVEL BY—
GLENN VO

NEW YORK

LONDON • NASHVILLE • MELBOURNE • VANCOUVER

2612 Cherryhill Lane - A Novel

Published in New York, New York, by Morgan James Publishing. Morgan James is a trademark of Morgan James, LLC. www.MorganJamesPublishing.com

ISBN 9781642798425 paperback
ISBN 9781642798432 eBook
Library of Congress Control Number: 2019951452

Cover Design by:
Rachel Lopez
www.r2cdesign.com

Interior Design by:
Christopher Kirk
www.GFSstudio.com

Scriptures marked NIV are taken from the NEW INTERNATIONAL VERSION (NIV):

Scripture taken from THE HOLY BIBLE, NEW INTERNATIONAL VERSION ®. Copyright© 1973, 1978, 1984, 2011 by Biblica, Inc.™. Used by permission of Zondervan

Morgan James is a proud partner of Habitat for Humanity Peninsula and Greater Williamsburg. Partners in building since 2006.

Get involved today! Visit
MorganJamesPublishing.com/giving-back

DEDICATION

For my wife,
whom I adoringly call "Squeaky."
For my daughter,
whom I lovingly call "Princess."
And for my son,
whom I affectionately call "Boy."

ACKNOWLEDGMENTS

········

First and foremost, I want to thank my Lord and Savior Jesus Christ, with whom all things are possible. *"Be strong and courageous. Do not be afraid or terrified because of them, for the LORD your God goes with you; he will never leave you nor forsake you"* (**Deuteronomy 31:6 NIV**).

Thank you to my wife Susan for always believing in me and for accepting me for who I really am—flaws and all. Your love and devotion to our family inspires me every day to be the best possible husband and father I can be. My day starts and ends with me thinking of you—always.

Thank you to my kids Kylie and Jackson for all the laughs, hugs, and kisses. And for the very important reminder that my most important job in their life is to always be their dad.

Thank you to my mother for the unconditional love that only a mother can show her child. And thank you, Mom, for the many years of sacrifice you showed our family so that we can all pursue our dreams.

Thank you to my Father for giving me the opportunity to have a better life in America.

Thank you to my sisters Brittany and An for always "having my back." No matter what was going on in my life, whether it be good or bad, your support for me never wavered. Both of you are true examples of what strong women should be.

Thank you to Hieu, Anissa, Elijah, Christopher, Meghna, Amanda, and Shakila for your unwavering support and continued friendship. I am blessed to have the very best friends in the world.

Thank you to David Hancock and the entire Morgan James Publishing team. You help make this dream a reality, and I look forward to many more collaborations in the future.

Thank you to Nick, Ethan, and Jennifer for your help editing and proofreading the manuscript. Your guidance and attention to detail helped make the writing so much easier!

And finally, a huge thank you to any family member, friend, colleague, or classmate that I had the privilege to meet during life's journey. Just know that you had a huge part of shaping my life, and for that I am eternally grateful.

ACT I

CHAPTER 1

C heers from both sides of the field mixed through the humid air as Jonathan McCalister, the quarterback of the Katy Tigers, surveyed the formation in front of his offensive line. The roars and chants reverberated in his ears as beads of sweat formed on his brow. The dense air made every movement much more strenuous.

He'd led the Tigers on a long drive from their own twenty-yard line and, now, they had only ten yards to go. They were down by four points. The Tigers needed a touchdown. It wouldn't be easy. It was the fourth quarter, and the clock had ticked down as Jonathan threw completion after completion and advanced the offense forward down the field. The scoreboard, high and bright in the balmy night air, illuminated by the Friday night lights, had the clock at ten seconds to go. The Tigers had just used their last time out. It was now or never.

The stakes were higher than just any ordinary game. This was, after all, Jonathan's last chance to win the state championship title. It wasn't his first rodeo—he'd brought his team to the state championship game every year—but this was his last chance to go home with a ring and his last chance to win the trophy for Katy High. He would surely go down in the Katy hall of fame if he could, somehow, score a touchdown on this next play.

"Down!" Jonathan shouted out. His mouth was dry, and his throat was hoarse. Nerves fluttered like butterflies in the pit of his stomach.

Jonathan was supposed to do a play-action pass. He would pretend to hand it off to the running back, who would feign a run down the middle, and then Jonathan would roll out to the right side where his receiver, a lanky boy named Peter Lunt, would be open to catch a pass in the corner of the end zone and put this contest to an end.

Linebackers jumped around in front of him, making adjustments to the defensive line by tapping the defensive linemen on their hips. The defensive coordinator shouted from the sideline. The middle linebacker looked over at him and then called out an audible.

"Pranty 19, Pranty 19!" The linebacker called out.

What does Pranty even mean?

The whole formation shifted to Jonathan's right. Immediately, somehow, Jonathan put it together.

They're going to blitz the right side. I can't roll out that way now.

"Nifty 42, Nifty 42!" Jonathan took a few steps back from the offensive line and lined up next to his running back. "Nifty" was an audible that changed the formation from a single back to a shotgun. The "42" was a play that meant that, if you were a receiver, you had to do whatever you could do to get open. The shotgun formation would buy him more time to get the pass off. Because the defense was blitzing, Jonathan knew the pass coverage wouldn't be too strong. Jonathan had built trust with his coach over the last four years, and his coach always let him call an audible. Jonathan, his coach would say, was a genius when it came to play calling. Before the defense could shift into zone coverage, Jonathan snapped the ball.

"Hut!"

The ball spiraled from between the center's legs into Jonathan's outstretched hands. Every player burst into action.

As Jonathan suspected, the defense blitzed the right side. The defensive backs were on man-to-man coverage, and the safeties dropped back to cover a pass into the end zone. Jonathan began to panic. Nobody was open. The defense was rushing in. He had a moment before he'd be on his back. One of the defensive linemen broke through. Jonathan whirled around and ran a few steps back as he felt the tug of the defensive lineman trying to tackle him by the shoestrings. He high stepped out of it and rolled over to the left, only to see another lineman running straight at him. With a quick sidestep, he juked to the right of the oncoming lineman and left him face down in the turf. There was no chance he was getting a pass off.

He started to sprint toward the end zone. Every defensive back broke their coverage and started to chase after him. They were closing in on him as he approached the end zone. Jonathan let out a battle cry as he leapt into the air and made contact with one of the defensive players rushing toward him. Jonathan spun over the player's back and saw the red turf of the end zone under him as he whirled through the air and landed upon it. The crowd seemed to let out a collective gasp before they broke into a deafening roar. He had scored the winning touchdown. The sidelines stormed the field as the tight end of the Tigers, an enormous boy named Steve Perry, picked Jonathan up and lifted him into the air. The team gathered around Jonathan as they jumped up and down and chanted triumphantly. The coach held back as he took off his soaking wet coat. Two players had dumped an entire cooler of Gatorade on him.

The bleachers chanted along with the players on the field. "MVP! MVP! MVP!"

Jonathan lifted two fists into the air and hollered victoriously. Utter ecstasy flooded from his chest to his arms and legs as he shouted out. From his perch, he could see his mother, father, and little sister waiting patiently on the sideline. They were participating in the chants as well, and Gabby, his little sister, was perched up on their father's shoulders as she strained to get a look at Jonathan. She was wearing a Texas University hat with her blonde hair pulled back into a ponytail that poked out the back. Jonathan's father had gone to Texas University to play football, and Jonathan had a full ride to play quarterback for them next year. Gabby, as she had told Jonathan at least a million times, planned to go there herself. "You have a long ways to go," he'd tell her. "You're only ten years old!" Along with the Texas University hat she was wearing, as always, her cheerleader outfit. She had made it herself and wore it to every game.

Steve put Jonathan down, and the team made their way over to the trophy ceremony that was forming in the center of the football field. The team gathered around Mayor Kean, the Mayor of Katy, as he began to speak into his microphone.

"Ladies and gentlemen, with great pleasure, I present to you the State Championship Trophy for the Katy Tigers."

Next to Mayor Kean was a man holding a large trophy in his hands—at least two feet in length—with an outline of the state of Texas at the top and under it, in large font, read "State Champion, 2012."

"I would like for Jonathan McCalister, as the Most Valuable Player, to come up to accept the State Championship Trophy."

Jonathan's teammates patted him on his shoulder pads as they nudged him forward. The path cleared between him and the trophy, and he jogged up to the front of the ceremony as cameras from every angle followed him.

"Jonathan McCalister, you played an excellent game today. It's my pleasure to give you the MVP trophy as well as the State Championship Trophy. Congratulations."

With that, somebody handed an MVP trophy to Mayor Kean and he passed it along to Jonathan. It was a silver, shiny football with the words "Most Valuable Player" imprinted upon it. With one hand, Jonathan held his MVP trophy and, with the other, he grabbed the State Championship Trophy. He lifted both into the air, the team let out a cacophony of yowls, and they all gathered around him for a team picture. The photographer snapped the picture as Susan Dowl, a well-known news reporter in Katy, approached Jonathan for an interview that would be broadcast to the whole town. She held the microphone up to Jonathan's mouth as her cameraman fixed an angle on Jonathan's face. His face was barely visible under all of the smeared eye-black, but his handsome features—dark green eyes, wavy blond hair, and prominent cheekbones—were nonetheless distinguishable.

Behind the cameramen, Gabby was beaming as she watched with her bright blue eyes and a big smile on her face. Rose and Jeff McCalister, their parents, were behind Gabby. Jeff, a stocky and well-built man, had an expression of pride as he nodded to Jonathan with his hand on Gabby's shoulder. Rose, a sleek brunette who seemed to never have aged, was smiling a sweet smile as she gave Jonathan a thumbs-up. Next to the three of them was Jonathan's girlfriend, Lacey Snow, with her long bleach-blond hair falling down to her shoulders. She was wearing Jonathan's varsity letter jacket. Her hazel eyes were glued to him as she twirled her hair and flirtatiously waved to Jonathan.

"Jonathan," Susan Dowl began, "This isn't your first award in any regard—you've been awarded the Player of the Year every year you've been a Katy Tiger—but this is your first time winning the MVP for the state championship game. How does it feel?"

"I can't even express with words how happy I am right now. We've been here every year, four times in a row now, and this is the first time we've finally won it. I'm happier that we finally got a championship win at last than I am about being the MVP. This was a team effort, for sure, and I couldn't have done it without my guys."

Susan smiled as she listened to Jonathan. When he was done with his answer, she continued, "Next year, you're going on to bigger and better games. You'll be playing Division One football, at Texas University, where your father has left a football legacy. What are your thoughts on playing football for your father's alma mater?"

"Honestly, Susan, it's the best thing to ever happen to me. I'm hoping to make it to the big leagues."

"Your statistics this year are better than ever. They're incredible. It's no surprise you're a five-star prospect. You completed 312 of the 428 passes you threw, threw 35 touchdowns, and passed for over 3,000 yards. Do you think this momentum is going to carry on and improve as you progress to the college level?"

"The sky's the limit, Susan. I don't think I'm slowing down any time soon." Jonathan was eager to get the interview over with. He wanted to talk to his family and Lacey. "I'm just glad to be here, to win the championship game, and to have my family to thank. I couldn't have done it without them."

"Jonathan, how about—"

Jonathan interrupted her. "Hey, Susan, it was great to talk." He nodded at her and walked around her to greet his family and embrace Lacey.

"MVP! MVP! MVP!" Gabby squealed in delight as she ran up to Jonathan and wrapped her arms around his legs. He kneeled down next to her and hugged her back.

"I'm so proud of you, Jon." Rose tousled Jonathan's hair as he hugged Gabby.

"I never won MVP." Jeff added, "That was an impressive performance. That last play was incredible."

"Thanks." Jonathan stood up and faced Lacey. She was hanging back. Jonathan's varsity letter jacket was too big on her, down to her knees, and he couldn't help but think about how perfect she looked to him right now. He couldn't help but think how perfect *everything* was right now.

"Hey, Lacey—" Jonathan started, but his voice was muffled by her lips as she jumped into his arms and planted a kiss on his mouth.

"Nice game, stud." Lacey whispered as she pulled away from his lips.

Jonathan smiled and held her in his arms, her legs wrapped around his waist, and went in for another kiss when Gabby interrupted.

"Ew! Gross." Gabby let out a dramatic gag and looked at the two lovers with disgust, "Get a ROOM."

Jonathan laughed. "Sorry, Gab." He put Lacey down and turned to his family.

"Listen, champ," Jeff said, "We've got a reservation at your favorite restaurant, that Tex-Mex place I can never remember the name of—"

"Chuy's," Rose interjected, "It's called Chuy's, honey."

"Right," Jeff continued, "We've got a reservation at Chuy's. To celebrate the win." He looked at Lacey warmly, "Invite Lacey, of course, as well as any other friends you want to invite."

Lacey smiled, rested her head on Jonathan's shoulder, and looked up at him affectionately. "I'll meet you there, babe. I'll tell Steve and Peter and everyone to come, too. I got to run home first, though." She whispered in his ear so that his family couldn't hear what she said next. "I got a surprise for you. Check your phone later." She winked and took her head off his shoulder and made her way into the crowd of people that was now dispersing in the middle of the football field. Jonathan watched as she walked away, his jacket too big for her, and sighed yearningly. He felt a kick on his calf and looked down to see Gabby looking up at him expectantly.

"Can I, Jonathan?" She asked.

"Can you what?" Jonathan realized he had tuned out when watching Lacey walk away.

"I want to go with you, doofus!"

"Go with me where?"

"I want to ride with you to Chuy's! Mom and Dad said I could." She looked over at Rose and Jeff. "Right?"

"That's right, honey." Rose murmured.

Jonathan smiled at Gabby. "Of course, Gab. Let me just change into some clothes and take a quick shower. Can you meet me outside of the locker room?"

"Yep!" Gabby squeaked and skipped off toward the school.

"We'll see you there, champ." Jeff patted Jonathan on the shoulder as he and Rose turned and made their way to the parking lot. Jonathan followed after Gabby.

CHAPTER 2

———— • • • ● • ● • • ————

Jonathan smiled as he sat in his 2002 Camaro Z28 under a full moon. The car was nearly ten years old and, while it looked like it was in perfect condition, it wasn't in the best condition on the inside. Jonathan washed it routinely to make its deep red hue shine, performed all the checkups on it—albeit not too extensively. He had inherited it from his late uncle who never took good care of it. It wasn't the safest car, but it was perfect in Jonathan's eyes.

The car engine revved loudly as Jonathan twisted the key in the ignition. Gabby sat beside him in the passenger seat. His father never let her sit in the front seat but, that night, Jonathan didn't care. He had just won the state championship game. He was going to go down in the history of Katy High School. He was going to go play ball at a Division I college as a quarterback and make his way into the NFL if he kept progressing. Everything was just perfect. Nothing could go wrong.

"I can't believe you flipped over somebody to win the game!" Gabby was excited. She always loved talking about football with Jonathan. "Did you know you were going to run that in all by yourself? Or were you trying to pass to someone?"

Jonathan put his hand on the back of Gabby's headrest as he craned his neck to look out the back window and reversed the car out of its parking spot. He shifted the stick into first gear and looked up at the bright yellow moon above.

"It just kinda happened, Gab. I was trying to pass it at first. In fact, at first, I was supposed to do a play-action pass," Jonathan explained, "but their linebacker called an audible. I don't know what 'Pranty' means—that's the audible he called—but I could tell they were going to blitz on the right side."

"How could you tell?" Gabby was bouncing up and down in her seat. "I don't know how you can always tell this sort of stuff. It's crazy how smart you are when it comes to football."

"I could tell because all of the linebackers were really close to the line, and all of the defensive linemen shifted to the right."

"And you knew they'd blitz just because of that?"

"I guess so, yeah." Jonathan opened his window as he pulled out of the parking lot and onto the road. The fresh air felt refreshing to Jonathan as the crickets chirped outside. The lights from the stadium polluted the night sky and put a veil over the stars above. The moon was as bright as ever, though.

"So what'd you do? Did you call an audible?"

"Yeah. I called a Nifty 42."

"A Nifty 42!? But they were blitzing!" Gabby knew the Katy Tigers playbook as well as Jonathan did. "Weren't you afraid they'd sack you?"

"I almost did get sacked." Jonathan looked over at Gabby only to see her staring back at him eagerly. She was still bouncing up and down in her seat. "Put your seatbelt on, Gab."

"But you didn't! Cause you're the best!" Gabby thrust her hands in the air and let out a jubilant yowl. "MVP! MVP! MVP!" She reached into her purse and pulled out her iPod. Gabby scrolled down to one of her favorite songs on the Creedence Clearwater Revival's greatest hits album. She connected her iPod to the sound system and cranked up the volume.

"Bad Moon Rising" began to play through the car speakers as Jonathan's phone pinged. He looked down to where it was, nestled in the cupholder, and saw an unopened message from Lacey.

Gabby began singing along. She loved that song.

He reached for his phone and opened it to see a text from Lacey.

I can't wait to see you later. I told you I got you something special. ;)

Lacey had sent a suggestive picture of herself. Jonathan excitedly began to type back and took his eyes off the road.

Gabby stopped singing and gasped. "Jon! Look at the road! It's against the law to text and drive. They taught me that at school!"

"I've got it under control, Gab." Jonathan struggled to type the letters. He kept misspelling words as he switched between looking at his phone and looking at the road.

"Jon!" Gabby shrieked. "Watch out!"

Jonathan looked over at Gabby and saw her frame silhouetted by two bright, yellow headlights. Headlights brighter and yellower than the moon above. The lights grew brighter and brighter as they came closer and closer in what felt like an eternity. Jonathan stepped on the gas pedal in a desperate attempt to rocket out of the way. He had run a red light, and the bright headlights were those of an oncoming eighteen-wheeler truck going at least forty miles per hour. The truck blared its horn as Jonathan's Camaro narrowly evaded it.

Thank God.

Jonathan's rush of relief quickly waned when he noticed a large oak tree right in front of him. They were driving right into it. He slammed on the brakes, but it was too late.

CHAPTER 3

— •‧•●•‧•• —

Jonathan's legs throbbed. Everything was black. A beep sounded with every beat of his heart. The air smelled stale. He could hear a TV commercial playing.

What's going on?

Jonathan opened his eyes. He immediately noticed the blanket draped on top of him was flat, as if his feet weren't under the blanket. After a few moments, he realized his feet actually *weren't* there. Panic surged through him. He shot up and tugged on IVs sticking into his arms, trying to rip them out, to no avail. He was in a hospital. And his legs were gone.

"Jon! You're awake!" The voice of his mother startled him. She was sitting in a chair next to him. They were in a small, windowless room. A TV was mounted on the wall at the foot of the bed playing a commercial for some carpet cleaner.

"Mom? What's going on?" Jonathan's voice cracked, and nausea began to overcome him as he realized the gravity of the situation. He had no legs. He was in a hospital.

"You were in a car accident about two weeks ago. After the big game. On your way to Chuy's. You crashed into a tree on Cherryhill Lane." Rose reached for Jonathan's hand. He retracted it aggressively.

"Where are my legs?"

"They had no choice but to amputate your legs. It was the only chance to save your life."

"Where's Gabby?" He stammered. He looked around the room expectantly, as if he'd find her in there alongside him, somehow hidden in the closet-sized room.

"Gabby didn't make it, Jon."

Despair flooded through Jonathan as if the IVs were injecting it into his veins.

"What?" He thought he had misheard her.

"I'm sorry."

Jonathan was at a loss for words.

"Her funeral was last week." Rose furrowed her brows with tears forming in her eyes. "You've been in a coma since the accident."

Gabby . . .

"Where's Dad?" Gabby was the light of Jeff's life. If anyone could feel worse about the accident than Jonathan, it would be him.

"Your father has had a tough time coping with the accident," Rose said as she caressed Jonathan's forehead dotingly. "You know how he is. He's locked himself up in the house. He doesn't want anyone to see him in such a vulnerable state."

Jonathan brushed Rose's hand away from his forehead and covered his face with his palms. The nausea was getting worse and worse as he wrapped his head around reality.

This must be a bad dream.

"I'll go get the doctor and let them know you're awake." Rose stood up and made her way to the door. The death of Gabby was tragic, surely, but Rose was relieved that the accident in front of 2612 Cherryhill Lane hadn't taken both of her children from her. The doctors had put Jonathan in a medically induced coma at first. Then they said he was progressing enough that they could pull him out of it, but she was still relieved that he was awake and talking with her. It had only been two weeks, and while she knew he would have to stay in the hospital for some time, at least he was alive. That's all that mattered to Rose.

* * *

Rose fetched the doctor, who introduced himself to Jonathan as Dr. Grady. Dr. Grady asked Jonathan to slowly sit upright to see how he felt. When Jonathan did this, he felt dizzy and the nausea he was already feeling grew. After a few seconds of trying to fight the dizziness and nausea, it only felt worse, so Dr. Grady had him lie back down.

"Can you move your arms and legs?" Dr. Grady asked after Jonathan lay back down. Jonathan felt a surge of anger when Dr. Jones asked that question.

I have no legs. How can I move them?

Jonathan bit his tongue and moved his arms and the stumps of his legs. They felt heavy, and Jonathan felt much weaker than usual, but he was able to move them.

"We've got to get a scan of your brain," Dr. Grady explained, "to monitor your brain injury."

"Brain injury!?" Jonathan had no legs, and that was bad enough, but to have a brain injury too?

"We had to put you into a medically induced coma because of your brain injury. It would have been a lot worse if we hadn't. But the fact that you can move your arms and legs is a good sign. The area of the brain that controls movement of the arms and legs is often affected by brain injuries like this. So, if you can move your arms and legs, there's a very good chance the brain injury isn't too severe."

Jonathan was speechless. Rose sympathetically watched her son react to Dr. Grady's news. He was ghostly pale and looked faint.

Dr. Grady let the silence sit for a moment before speaking again. " We've got to get you comfortable moving around first, though, so we will need to wait until we can get your dizziness and nausea under control. We can't put you in the MRI machine if we don't. Once you're comfortable, we'll put you in a wheelchair and bring you over."

"How long do you think he'll be in the hospital?" Rose asked.

"At least a few weeks," Dr. Grady replied. "We've got to do some physical therapy to get his body strong enough to continue from home, we've got to start a treatment process for him to begin to adjust to the amputations, and we've got to make sure he's fully functioning mentally. I know in the movies they make it seem like you wake up from a coma one day and you're up and running the next day, but the reality is that it takes some time. We'll do our best to make sure it's a speedy recovery. It could have been a lot worse. You're lucky to be alive." With that, Dr. Grady smiled at Jonathan and Rose and left the room.

* * *

Word spread that Jonathan was awake and progressing slowly. A little over a week later, Rose began inviting his friends and family to visit him. That's when Lacey first visited him. She held his hand and kissed his forehead and told him she loved him, but her words rang hollow. He was emotionally numb. His friends also came and went, all offering condolences and words of support, but Jonathan felt numb to their sympathies, too. He was surrounded by balloons and Hallmark cards that wished him to get well soon, but he felt like everyone he knew was pitying him.

Everyone *was* pitying him, except for his father. His father, Jeff, never visited. Rose showed up every day. And, every day, she'd make an excuse as to why Jeff didn't make it, mostly suggesting his father wasn't ready to leave the house. Jonathan wasn't buying it, though, and felt abandoned by his father. But Rose would sit and read for a few hours to give Jonathan company. They didn't speak much outside of a brief hello and the daily excuse about why Jeff didn't make it, but Jonathan didn't want to be alone, so he appreciated Rose being there with him. He felt grateful for his mother's love, although he wondered where his father was and what the real reason was that he wasn't coming to visit. Despite feeling abandoned by his father, Jonathan never brought it up to Rose, just feigning acceptance of whatever excuse Rose gave.

Two weeks later, after an MRI showed Jonathan's brain injury wasn't severe, he was transferred to a transitional care hospital to continue his rehab. There, Lacey visited him for a second time. Jonathan couldn't help but feel worse when she visited. Rose had just left when Lacey knocked on the door.

"Come in," Jonathan called out.

Lacey creaked the door open and shut it behind her gently as if she was trying not to make a sound. She walked over to the end of the bed and looked at Jonathan with a mixed expression of sorrow and guilt.

"Well, look who's showed up," Jonathan said. He didn't only feel abandoned by his father; he felt abandoned by Lacey, too. She was his girlfriend. He thought she'd be eager to see him and make sure he was okay. But she had only come twice in three weeks. If she were in this state, he'd visit her every day.

"Sorry, I've just been so busy with school," Lacey replied, but Jonathan didn't believe her. She had already been accepted to Texas University, where Jonathan once had a full scholarship lined up to play football. Why would she be busy with school if she already got into college? The truth was Lacey didn't visit him often because it hurt her to see him like this.

Jonathan shrugged it off. He was too apathetic to inquire. "I'd be busy with school, too, if I was still going to college."

Lacey couldn't hide the surprise she felt when Jonathan said that. She expected he'd still be going to Texas University with her even if he couldn't play football. "You're not going to school?"

"No. I can't play football anymore. There's no scholarship lined up now. The doctor says I've got to take some time off from school, anyway, to make sure my brain is functioning fully, or else I might struggle with concentration and memory."

"So I'm going to school all alone?"

Jonathan was irked by her selfishness. Didn't she understand his situation? It was unfair of her to guilt-trip him when he was already feeling so despondent. "Are you serious? Your boyfriend is lying in a hospital bed with no legs and a brain injury, and all you can do is guilt-trip him because he can't go to college with you anymore?"

"How are we going to be together if I'm at school all the way across the state without you?"

"It's only a few hours. You can drive."

"I can't be living the college experience if I've got to commit to traveling to you. I don't want to be held back."

Jonathan was hurt. "Held back by me?! I can't believe you. What am I to you? A burden?"

"Listen, Jon," Lacey said, with tears forming in her eyes. It genuinely pained her to say what she was about to say. "You're going through a lot right now, I understand that, and if I'm going to be in college across the state, I'm not going to be able to be there for you. I can't offer the support you need. I've got my whole life ahead of me, and I need to move on. So do you."

"You're going to abandon me just like that?"

"You're a fighter, Jon, and you'll be able to handle it. I know you will. I just can't handle it. This is all too much for me. I'm sorry." Lacey turned around and walked out the door as tears began to stream down her cheeks.

Her final words to him echoed in Jonathan's head. He wasn't sad, though. He felt more anger than anything. He felt angry at her for texting him. He felt angry for her abandoning him in his time of need. He felt angry at his father for not ever visiting him. And he felt angry at God for letting such a horrific accident happen, robbing him of everything he thought he was called to do on this earth and taking Gabby's life at such a young age. There was a lot of anger he was experiencing, and he didn't know who he could possibly confide in. His life was in ruins, and he had no one by his side but his mother to help him get through it.

The next day, when Rose came to visit, he was surprised to finally see his father with her for the first time. Seeing his dad gave him a short-lived positive boost, which he desperately needed after Lacey broke up with him. The positive feelings quickly subsided when Jonathan realized his mother had dragged his father in to see him.

"Where have you been, Dad?"

Jeff glowered at Jonathan. It was a menacing look that Jonathan thought he would never see from his own father. "I've been mourning your poor sister, Jon."

"And I'm not mourning? Is Mom not mourning? We're a family. We're supposed to stick together when tragedy strikes. You've been completely ignoring me. You've abandoned me. I have no legs—"

"Look at you," Jeff said. He was scowling at Jonathan with utter furiousness in his glare. Jeff walked up to the foot of the bed. He crossed his arms with a look of contempt on his face as he looked at Jonathan. "Your sister is DEAD! She's gone! And all you can do is talk about your legs. We got the accident report. We know what you were doing. We saw the text. You couldn't be an idiot by yourself. You had to drag Gabby into this!"

Jonathan didn't know what to say. Dread festered inside of him as he realized his dad blamed him for Gabby's death. Jonathan was already blaming himself. He needed his dad to support him. He needed someone to confide in. Not this.

Jeff continued. "Now, I wake up every morning knowing that my little girl is gone. That I'll never get to hear her laugh. I'll never get to see her smile. I'll never get to watch her grow up. I'll never get to walk her down the aisle and dance at her wedding. And I'll never get to see her start and raise a family. I only have you. And you're the reason she's dead."

Tears started to pour down Jonathan's cheeks. His lips quivered as he stuttered between gasps.

"Dad—"

"What, Jon? Have you got something to say? Are you sorry?" Jeff's voice was rising to a shout. "I don't think sorry is gonna cut it. You killed your sister. You ruined your dreams. You've ruined my dreams. You can't play football anymore. Say goodbye to that scholarship to Texas University. I don't have my little girl anymore. You'll never see her again." Jeff grasped the bar at the end of the bed and shook the bed frame. "What have you got to say to that?!"

Jonathan couldn't muster up an answer. He was shaken to his core. His thoughts pulsated into a headache. One thought kept running through his head over and over.

Gabby . . .

"Answer me!" Jeff was livid.

Jonathan stared at his father in disbelief. He couldn't utter a word.

Jeff dashed around the side of the bed, up to Jonathan, and slapped Jonathan in the face.

"Jeff!" Rose shouted. "How dare you!"

Jeff turned around and marched out of the room. Rose ran after him. The door slammed behind them. Jonathan had never felt so alone. He froze, not even rubbing his face where he had been slapped. He was bewildered. He could taste the salt of his tears as they ran down his face.

ACT II

CHAPTER 4

· · • • ● • • · ·

J onathan stared out the window as Professor Hoffpower droned on in his monotone voice. Jonathan fidgeted in his wheelchair, rolling the wheels back and forth, staring out the window. Right outside the window was a large sign that read "Central Texas University College of Liberal Arts" and a bunch of students playing a pickup game of football in the courtyard.

Almost two years had passed since Jonathan first arrived at Central Texas University. Five years had passed since he woke up from his coma to learn Gabby was dead, he had missed her funeral, and his dream of playing quarterback for Texas University was shattered.

Next to the sign was Dominic Viana, jumping up and down and waving his skateboard in the air, trying to get Jonathan's attention. Class would be over in a minute or two, and Dominic—Jonathan's personal assistant—was eager to bring Jonathan to a renowned physical therapist named Dr. Jackson Bui. Dr. Bui was known for helping amputees adjust to life without limbs. Visiting Dr. Bui was a big step for Jonathan. He had a bad experience with prosthetics four and a half years ago and fell deeper into despair. He had all but given up on ever living without a wheelchair, but Rose had persuaded him to try again. She assured him Dr. Bui was the best of the best, and things would be different this time.

Jonathan didn't know it, but Dominic had some news he had been keeping from him, as well. Dominic was nervous to break the news, trying to pick the perfect time to cue Jonathan in given his fragile emotional state. Dominic thought after the appointment with Dr. Bui would be a good time. Dominic didn't want Jonathan to be distracted going into the appointment. He would tell him after.

Jonathan nodded to Dominic to let him know he saw him. He then tapped his wrist, as if motioning to a watch, and put up his pointer finger as if to say, "One moment."

Professor Hoffpower cleared his throat loudly causing Jonathan to return his gaze to the front of the room. Jonathan's heart jumped when he realized that Professor Hoffpower was looking right at him. Jonathan sheepishly ran his fingers through his hair and pretended to take notes.

Professor Hoffpower stayed silent for a moment, glaring at Jonathan in disappointment. Jonathan could feel his glare. Finally, he broke his silence, "Alright, class, that about wraps it up. See you Tuesday. We'll be reviewing for the final. I recommend you all start studying tonight, though."

Jonathan was already prepared for the final, though. Professor Hoffpower bored Jonathan out of his wits, but Jonathan was a smart kid and had done all the work. Political Science, his major, came easily to him. He hoped things would get more challenging when he got to law school. Right now, things were too easy.

Jonathan waited patiently for the other students to clear the doorway and tucked his wheelchair behind the last group of kids to create a barrier between him and Professor Hoffpower. Professor Hoffpower always wanted to talk to him after class, it seemed, and Jonathan wasn't ever in the mood for it. Spit would fly out of Professor Hoffpower's mouth whenever he said the letter P, and the smell of his breath always turned Jonathan's stomach. He gave him the same spiel every time they talked. He would also inevitably try to get Jonathan to shave his beard, get a haircut, and wear something other than sweatpants and T-shirts. "You need to look like a gentleman," he'd tell Jonathan. "You're such a smart, handsome kid. You don't play the part."

Jonathan especially didn't want to talk to Professor Hoffpower that day because he'd probably give him the typical "get a haircut" spiel plus a lecture about paying attention in class, since he caught Jonathan watching the pickup game and engaging with Dominic out the window. As soon as the crowd of students dwindled, Jonathan speedily wheeled out the doorway, keeping his chair hidden behind the students until it was too late for Professor Hoffpower to interrupt him. He followed the crowd out into the yard and made his way over to Dominic.

"'Bout time, man," Dominic called out as Jonathan rolled toward him, "I've been waiting here for like three minutes."

"Shut up, dude, I'm learning all about public law. Stuff's *intriguing,*" Jonathan said sarcastically. "You almost got me in trouble with Bad Breath Hoffpower."

"That guy scares me," Dominic replied. "I don't know if it's his caterpillar eyebrows or how he combs his hair over his bald spot. For some reason, he gives me the creeps."

Jonathan let out a laugh. Professor Hoffpower was balding badly and tried to hide it with a combover that consisted of three hairs gelled over the shiny knob of his noggin. His eyebrows were wild and basically connected in the middle of his forehead. It looked like a furry caterpillar was inching across his face whenever he gesticulated and moved his eyebrows around. It was gross. Fortunately, he rarely gesticulated, because he was so boring and monotone. Usually he'd just talk without any expression whatsoever.

Jonathan was relieved class was over. He only had the next class on Tuesday and the final. Then he'd be done with this year and going on to the fall semester of his junior year with new professors. He wasn't exactly excited, though. More relieved. He never bounced back from the two days in the hospital when Lacey dumped him and his father berated him and blamed Gabby's death on him. Nothing had been really exciting for him since then, and Dominic was basically his only friend. All they ever did was play video games, go to the gym, and toss the pigskin around.

"Let's roll." Dominic got behind Jonathan's wheelchair and gripped the push handles with both hands. He then threw his skateboard on the ground and stepped on one end of it to prop it up onto two wheels. Dominic loved pushing Jonathan when he had his skateboard with him. Pushing Jonathan while walking made him feel bad for Jonathan. It made Jonathan feel bad, too. But when Dominic had his skateboard, he would create a bit of a commotion and get some good speed snapping the skateboard onto the ground and rolling behind Jonathan, as if the wheelchair was an extension of the skateboard.

This time was no different. With the skateboard up on two wheels, Dominic picked up his foot, causing the side that was up in the air to snap down onto the ground with a loud crack. He stomped his left foot onto the middle of the board as soon as it hit the ground and pushed off the asphalt with his right foot, holding the push handles of Jonathan's wheelchair so they would take off together. It happened so fast, it seemed as if Dominic and Jonathan both took off with the crack of the board hitting the ground.

Jonathan chuckled. "It's funny how much faster we get around when you've got the skateboard." They began to accelerate down a sloped sidewalk as they made their way through the main courtyard of the campus. Usually it would take them around ten minutes to get to the student parking lot from Professor Hoffpower's class, but when Dominic had his skateboard, it took less than half the time. And as they sped down the sidewalk, Dominic would honk a horn he put on the wheelchair to warn people the speeding pair were behind them. They wouldn't slow down, either, and people often jumped out of the way to avoid getting run over. They developed a reputation around campus. The other students often nudged their friends, pointed at the pair, and laughed at two guys flying down a hill with a wheelchair and skateboard honking a horn and not stopping for anything. It used to annoy Jonathan when people laughed and pointed but, after two years, he had gotten used to it.

"Yo, Jon," Dominic raised his voice to get his words through the wind that was buffeting them as they gained speed. "Do you think we would still have become friends if your mom never put out that ad?"

"What do you mean?"

"Like, would we have met if I didn't see that ad your mom put out looking for someone to be your personal assistant? I mean, I was a sophomore when you were a freshman. What if we never hung out?"

"I don't know, man, why?" Jonathan replied.

"I'm just wondering." Dominic didn't know what to say, but he was starting to get emotional and overcome with sadness. He knew his days as Jonathan's personal assistant were coming to an end. They had become close friends in the years since Jonathan had come to Central Texas University, and with Jonathan entering his junior year, it meant Dominic was entering his senior year. When they first met, Jonathan was reluctant to get any assistance, but his mother insisted. He didn't like feeling helpless, he'd say. He was still reeling in emotions from the accident and losing his football scholarship, too bitter to even play video games for the first few weeks of school. He was always upset about something. Even now, he was often upset about something, but he had warmed to Dominic. It was hard to earn his respect, but Dominic had done it.

"You sound all sentimental, man," Jonathan replied. "You good?"

"Yeah. I'm good."

Their roll began to slow as the slope of the sidewalk flattened and turned into an incline. The student parking lot was in sight. Up front, in the handicap spot, was Jonathan's handicap-accessible van. Dominic jerked the wheelchair to a halt, applied the brakes, and popped his skateboard on two wheels again. He grabbed the other end, picked up the board, and tucked it under one arm. Like he typically did as they approached the parking lot, he released the brakes and let go of the push handles, letting Jonathan roll himself to the van. While Jonathan had fun with Dominic skateboarding behind him, he insisted on pushing himself at other times. He didn't want any help. He was still stubborn like that.

The two of them made their way over to the van. As they approached it, Jonathan tossed the keys to Dominic. Dominic caught them and pressed a button on the keys that lowered the ramp so that Jonathan could wheel himself in.

Jonathan looked at a lake through the trees that flew by as he and Dominic drove along the highway. Country music softly played on the car radio. Jonathan felt nervous about the appointment with Dr. Bui, and Dominic felt nervous about delivering the news after the appointment. Both of them were so busy thinking about what they were feeling nervous over that neither of them spoke for most of the ride, until Jonathan broke the silence.

"What's the name of this place, anyway? And why is this guy supposed to be so great?"

Dominic knew all about it because he had gone over the details with Rose. Jonathan had spoken to Rose, too, but he had a lot fewer questions and less interest than Dominic. Jonathan saw this as more of an obligation than an opportunity. He didn't want to go to another physical therapy session after his experience with his first physical therapist, Dr. Austin, which was downright demoralizing.

Dominic, on the other hand, was excited about what this could mean for Jonathan. He had been urging Jonathan to try prosthetics out for the past two years. So, when Rose told Dominic about Dr. Bui, he was full of questions and enthusiasm. He even did some research on his own after he spoke to Rose.

"It's called the Calvary Performance Institute. The guy who both founded it and runs it is Dr. Jackson Bui. He works with a lot of amputees, mainly war veterans, and helps them to get prosthetics that work and feel comfortable. World-class athletes come to train here. I don't know why he's the best of the best, but he's really good at what he does."

"The last time I tried a physical therapist, to get prosthetics, was a disaster," Jonathan said as he stared out the window unenthusiastically. "It was this dude named Dr. Austin. He just yelled at me and made me feel worse about myself. I . . ." While his mouth was moving, his mind traveled back to the past. All of a sudden, he was in the room with Dr. Austin during his last visit again.

Jonathan sat in a chair, taking an elastic sock called a shrinker and an elastic bandage off the stump of his right leg. The shrinker and the elastic bandage were supposed to help control swelling, reduce phantom limb pain, speed up the healing process, and assist in shaping his amputated legs. Once he got them off, he started putting on his temporary prosthetics. Dr. Austin impatiently stared at him with his piercing blue eyes. "C'mon, Jonathan, it's not that hard," he said. "We don't have all day." Maybe Dr. Austin thought he was pushing Jonathan with tough love or something but, to Jonathan, it just came across as him being a jerk.

Jonathan had to start with temporary prosthetics because his legs were still swollen from the amputation. It had only been a month since the accident and, as Dr. Austin explained to Jonathan when they first met, "It could take months to get your long-term prosthetics. We can't fit them until the swelling has gone down, the surgical incision has healed, and your physical condition has improved." Jonathan was doing all he was told to do to get the swelling to go down and get familiar with prosthetics, but Dr. Austin's attitude wasn't helping. Jonathan already didn't feel like himself anymore. He was void of motivation, and all Dr. Austin did was tear him down with condescending remarks and angry energy.

Once Jonathan got the temporary prosthetics on, he stood up from the chair and tried to walk. Dr. Austin held on to one of his arms to help him balance.

Jonathan didn't like the foreign feeling of the prosthetics. They were hard to walk in but, with Dr. Austin helping him balance, he was able to walk a few lengths across the floor.

"Alright, Jonathan, let's try to walk without my help."

Dr. Austin released his grip. Jonathan could only take a few steps before tripping on his own prosthetic leg and falling to the floor.

"Jonathan," Dr. Austin barked, "do you want to be in a wheelchair for the rest of your life? C'mon!"

Jonathan couldn't take it. He had had enough. He took the prosthetics off his legs and threw one of them at Dr. Austin. "I'll stick to the wheelchair, you jerk," he retorted.

Jonathan shook his head and snapped back into the present. He continued what he was saying. "I ended up just throwing the prosthetics at him and telling him I'd rather stay in a wheelchair than go through what he was putting me through. I never went back. I'm not too excited about going to another one of those guys right now."

Dominic felt sympathy for Jonathan. He couldn't imagine how tough it would be to be in his situation. He knew all about the accident, the death of Gabby, and the shattering of Jonathan's dreams as a football player. "Your mom was really adamant about you meeting Dr. Bui. She said he's a miracle worker. He's one of the best in the world, and he's right here in Waco. It'd be silly not to give him a try."

Jonathan didn't respond. Silence passed between them for a few seconds.

"Do it for your mom, Jon. She really wants this."

Jonathan nodded. His mom was the only person who had stuck with him throughout the whole ordeal following the crash in front of 2612 Cherryhill Lane. His dad didn't speak to him. His girlfriend dumped him. Even to this day, Dominic was the only friend he ever confided in. And he only had one friend other than Dominic, a guy named Tom Dawson. But he wasn't close enough with Tom to confide in him like he did with Dominic. The least he could do to repay his mom for all her support was to get through one appointment with this supposed "miracle worker" physical therapist. "You're right," he replied. "I owe her this much."

The rest of the ride passed in silence. Central Texas University was located right outside the town of Waco, Texas, and the Calvary Performance Institute was in Waco, so the ride wasn't long at all. It took no more than ten minutes before Dominic pulled into the large parking lot of the Manh Training Center where Calvary Performance Institute was located. The building was an enormous rectangle mostly made of glass windows.

In large red letters above two large double doors was a sign that read "Calvary Performance Institute."

"Well, this must be it," Dominic said, as he pulled into one of the few parking spots available. Usually there was only one or two handicap parking spots where he and Jonathan went, but here there were dozens of handicap parking spots. All but four were taken.

"There must be a lot of people in there," Jonathan observed. "How is he helping everyone at once?"

"I don't know, man. He's probably a very busy man, and he's probably got a whole staff of physical trainers. He said he's going to work with you directly, though."

Jonathan was confused.

Why would Dr. Bui want to work with me directly when he's got world-class athletes and war veterans to attend to? What makes me so important?

As Jonathan wondered why Dr. Bui was going to work with him directly, Dominic got out the car and pressed the button to lower the van's ramp. Jonathan wheeled down the ramp once it was lowered, and the two of them headed to the large double doors under the Calvary Performance Institute sign. Dominic opened one of the doors for Jonathan, let him in, and then followed after him. There were at least fifty people bustling around in the lobby. Jonathan's attention was drawn specifically to one man. He had no legs, like Jonathan, but he was walking around in prosthetics that Jonathan had never seen before. They looked like upside-down question marks.

"What are those?" Jonathan asked, as he pointed at the man with the peculiar prosthetics.

"I don't know," Dominic said, "I think—"

Suddenly a voice sounded from the left of them. "Those are running blades." Jonathan and Dominic turned to see a petite Asian woman with silky black hair tied back into a ponytail, a white collared shirt with a blue pen in its front pocket, a black skirt that went below her knees, and white stilettos. She was about five feet away from them, next to the double doors, and holding a clipboard.

"Oh, uh," Jonathan said, "thanks."

"Are you here for an appointment? Are you possibly Jonathan McCalister?" She smiled sweetly to reveal a row of pearly white teeth.

"I am, yeah. Are you Dr. Bui?"

"No," she said, "my name is Emily. I'm here to give you a little tour of the facility and to bring you to Dr. Bui." She took the blue pen out of her front shirt pocket, jotted something down on the notepad stuck to her clipboard, and looked up. "Come right this way." The click of her heels hitting the linoleum floor mixed in with the rabble of everyone in the lobby as she walked through the crowd of amputees. Jonathan and Dominic followed after her and got within ear-shot as she began giving them a tour of the facility. "If you look this way"—Emily pointed at two large glass double doors to the right of the lobby—"you'll see the entrance to the athletic center. We'll go in there first." She made her way to the double doors and clicked a little button on the wall beside it, which opened the doors. Jonathan and Dominic wheeled in behind Emily as she entered the athletic center.

The entrance to the athletic center led to a balcony that overlooked a track surrounding a basketball court. To the right of the track and basketball court, divided by a large net, was a soccer field. There were people with running blades running around the track, people wheeling around the track in wheelchairs that looked like tricycles, people in wheelchairs playing basketball, and people who had one leg and elbow crutches playing soccer.

"This is where world-class athletes come to train," Emily said. "Some of the people on the track and basketball court are on Olympic and Paralympic teams. The team training in the soccer field are some of the US players for the Amputee Football World Cup."

"Wow," Jonathan murmured.

Emily turned around and walked back to the door they entered through. "Follow me," she said as she clicked a button to open the door.

Dominic and Jonathan followed after her. She pointed to a door on the oppo-site wall of the lobby. "That's the door to the rehabilitation center. I'll show you that next."

As they walked to the door to the rehabilitation center, Dominic tapped Jonathan on the shoulder. "Look to your right, man. There's a whole wall of people Dr. Bui has helped."

Jonathan looked to his right and saw a tall and wide wall with a sign at the top of it that read "Always Thankful." Under that sign were pictures of military veterans who had gone through rehab programs at Calvary Performance Institute. Jonathan could tell they were military veterans because at the bottom of each picture a deployment date was listed plus the rank of the person and a notation of whether they were an airman, marine, sailor, or soldier. Many of the veterans in the pictures were standing next to a muscular Asian man with thick, wavy hair. Jonathan assumed that was Dr. Bui. They all had prosthetics, and most of them were smiling from ear to ear. Jonathan scanned every picture he could as he wheeled his way over to the rehabilitation center.

When they got across the lobby, Emily pressed the button to open the doors to the rehabilitation center. Dominic and Jonathan followed her in. The doors led to another balcony. This one overlooked what appeared to be a gym full of work-out equipment. People with prosthetics were working out on elliptical machines. Others were practicing walking with an elbow crutch on one arm and a physical therapist on the other. Some weren't in prosthetics at all. They were lying on mats catching balls tossed to them by physical therapists or lying on tables with pulleys wrapped around the stubs of their legs doing some sort of resistance exercises.

"This is the rehabilitation center," Emily explained. "Many of the people here are athletes or veterans working to become comfortable with their prosthetics. We have a staff of physical trainers who help them to do just that. You'll be working with Dr. Bui directly, however, in his own studio. You're lucky to have such a priv-ilege." Emily smiled at Jonathan, but he was still too confused to smile.

Why am I being singled out to work with Dr. Bui?

"Come, it's time to meet Dr. Bui." Emily pressed the button to open the doors. The three of them headed out of the rehabilitation center and back into the lobby. Emily then led Dominic and Jonathan to an elevator to take them to Dr.

Bui's office on the second floor. Dominic and Jonathan followed Emily past some cubicles where people were diligently working on computers. The cubicles were too high up for Jonathan to get a look into them, so he couldn't tell exactly what the people were doing, but he caught a glimpse of someone who looked like they were working out the physics of various prosthetic limbs using some sophisticated software program.

Dominic said what Jonathan was thinking as they passed by the cubicles. "This place means business, huh?"

"Yeah," Jonathan said. "Kind of intimidating."

Emily either didn't hear them or ignored them and kept on walking, taking a right turn, down a short hall and through a door with a sign on it that read "Consultation Room." She held the door open for Dominic and Jonathan and they passed through the door. This time, there was no balcony overlooking a sports or fitness facility, only a desk, two chairs, and a wall of windows overlooking a river.

"Dr. Bui will be with you shortly," she said as she exited the room.

Jonathan looked around the room and noticed a bunch of plaques and certificates showing off Dr. Bui's credentials on the walls, including a doctorate degree in physical therapy from Washington University in St. Louis, Missouri.

Dominic followed Jonathan's gaze to the doctorate degree. "I don't think too many physical therapists have doctorate degrees," he remarked.

"Dr. Austin had a doctorate degree. That didn't work out so well for me."

"C'mon, Jon, cheer up," Dominic urged. "It'll be different this time."

Jonathan kept surveying the plaques and certificates on the wall. He couldn't deny that Dr. Bui's credentials were impressive. He just hoped his personality would coincide with Jonathan's personality or else it would be a reboot of Dr. Austin. Jonathan didn't want that in the slightest.

Suddenly, the door opened. Jonathan turned to see the man he saw in the pictures on the wall full of rehabilitated veterans. He was just as muscular as he looked in the pictures, and his hair was just as thick and wavy, too.

"Hey," Dr. Bui said excitedly. "I'm Dr. Bui. It's a pleasure to meet you, Jonathan!" He walked up and shook Jonathan's hand, gave him a half hug, and then did the same to Dominic. "I'm guessing you're Dominic?" Dr. Bui asked, as he gave Dominic a half hug.

"I sure am," Dominic said.

"It's a pleasure to meet you, Dominic." Dr. Bui had an energy that reminded Jonathan of the motivational speaker Tony Robbins. He seemed enthusiastic and outgoing, the opposite of how Jonathan had been since the accident. "Jonathan, my man!" Dr. Bui continued. "Your mother told me all about your story. I know about the trauma you've been through. I know about the struggles you had during physical therapy with Dr. Austin. Don't worry. We're going to take good care of you here."

While Jonathan liked Dr. Bui's energy, he felt a little betrayed by his mom. He didn't feel comfortable with her telling people his story. It was something deeply personal to him. The only person he ever told his story to was Dominic.

"I want you to know I'm different," Dr. Bui continued. "I have a passion for this like you've never seen before. I've worked with veterans who have had horrific injures and hopeless circumstances. I feel as though God has put me on this earth to do one thing: help people like you. Are you ready to walk again, Jonathan?"

People like me?

Jonathan felt a bit offended. He felt like Dr. Bui was pitying him. Did he think he was in hopeless circumstances?

"I don't know, Dr. Bui. This facility seems like it's the cream of the crop. I don't know if I can afford such luxurious physical therapy." Jonathan knew his mom would pay for it, and his family definitely had the means to, but Jonathan didn't want to be a financial burden to his family. There was no doubt in Jonathan's mind that working with Dr. Bui would be expensive. "I think it's best if—"

"Jonathan," Dr. Bui interjected, "I'm offering this *pro bono*."

Jonathan was even more confused. It was confusing enough that Dr. Bui wanted to work with him one-on-one, but the fact that he was willing to do it for free made Jonathan extremely confused and slightly suspicious. "Why?" Jonathan asked.

"I believe your rehabilitation can be a story that inspires others. Especially athletes who have gone through career-ending injuries."

Jonathan thought about all the amputees and paraplegics training in the athletic center. Their injuries weren't career-ending. They were still athletes, only shifting their careers in light of their new disabilities. Anger roared inside Jonathan's belly. "Career-ending?!" he asked with his voice raised almost to a shout. "How about *crippling* injury?!"

"I didn't mean to offend you—"

"C'mon, Dom, let's get out of here." Jonathan wheeled past Dr. Bui and out the door.

"Wait, Jon!" Dominic called after him. Jonathan ignored him and wheeled down the hallway back toward the elevator. Dominic looked at Dr. Bui, who had a look of sympathy on his face. "I'm sorry, Dr. Bui."

"It's okay," Dr. Bui said with a sigh. "Be a good friend and get him to come back later so he can move forward with his recovery. It'll change his life."

"Uh, sure," Dominic replied as he walked out of the consultation room and after Jonathan. Jonathan was fuming, moving as fast as he could to get out of the facility. He was going too fast for Dominic to walk alongside him, so Dominic just let him go on ahead. Jonathan waited impatiently for Dominic at the van, rocking his wheelchair back and forth to vent some of the anger he was feeling. Dominic didn't say anything as he pressed the button to lower the ramp and hopped in the driver's seat. After a few minutes of silence on the way home, Jonathan finally voiced the source of his frustration to Dominic.

"I'm just a marketing tool and charity case to him," he said. "One of his many patients in *hopeless circumstances* for him to play savior. He just wants another picture to hang on the wall and story to tell to get more high-priced patients. He doesn't care about helping me. He just cares about how I can help him."

"That's not true, Jon. He's trying to help you. I think you should reconsider his offer."

"I deserve this wheelchair, man. I don't deserve to be walking around, prosthetics or otherwise. I just want to move on with my life."

"This is how you move on with your life. What do you mean you don't 'deserve' this?"

"*I'm* the reason I'm in this wheelchair. *I'm* the reason my football career ended before it really even got started. I did this to myself. Even worse, I killed my little sister. *I'm* the reason she's dead. If she can't walk, why should *I*? I don't deserve to be in prosthetics. I deserve to be confined to a wheelchair."

"That's not true, man!" Dominic was sincere, and Jonathan could hear it in his voice. "You should go back to Dr. Bui. Give him a chance."

"Whatever. I'm good." Jonathan didn't want to talk about it anymore. "As my friend, I'm asking you not to push this. I've made my decision."

Dominic conceded. He knew what to say to make Jonathan feel better. "Alright, fine, let's just grab some pizza and chips and head back to your apartment to hang out."

He was even more nervous to deliver the news he'd been avoiding, at that point. Jonathan already felt crushed, clearly, and he knew he might make him feel even worse. Unfortunately, Dominic knew he had no choice.

"Fine."

* * *

Nostalgia flooded through Dominic as he and Jonathan made their way down the corridor to Jonathan's apartment with pizza and chips. Jonathan's handicap-accessible apartment building was located on campus, and his apartment was at the end of the hall on the first floor. Every day, after classes, Dominic would make his way down this hallway with Jonathan excited to play video games or just chill out. It always evoked positive emotions because that meant the stresses of the day were handled and he was heading to hang out with his buddy Jonathan.

Jonathan wheeled ahead of Dominic and waited for him next to the door. The two entered the apartment to the familiar scent of Jonathan's ocean breeze air freshener. Jonathan's apartment was basic, with only a living room, bathroom, simple kitchen, and one small bedroom. The living room took up at least 70% of the space. It was a wide area with plenty of room for furniture. But the only furniture that mattered to Dominic was a large leather couch across from a big flat-screen TV. Behind the TV was an enormous window that spanned almost the entire outside wall. Shafts of light shot through the window blinds. Jonathan undid the blinds to unveil a beautiful vista of the pond his apartment overlooked.

I'm gonna miss this place, Dominic thought.

CHAPTER 5

—————————— •••••••• ——————————

"**D**ude, you're kidding me!" Jonathan shouted at the TV. "How is that even possible?!"

"I'm a crack shot. That's how." Dominic laughed as he added another mark under his name on the piece of paper he and Jonathan used to keep tally up their wins. Dominic and Jonathan had a competition every night over who got more wins in whatever game they were playing. They usually played either Halo, a first-person shooter game, or Madden, a football game. That night, it was Halo.

"I was behind a wall, dude."

"You're just mad because I'm better than you." Dominic smiled as he continued to mash the buttons on the video game controller.

"I'm sick of losing. You got me tonight," Jonathan conceded, as he put down the video game controller. "Are you going to the gym tonight?"

"Yes, I am," Dominic replied. "Tom could use our company."

Tom Dawson, a mutual friend Dominic and Jonathan met during Jonathan's freshman year, was a graduate football assistant and the head personal trainer at the school's gym. Dominic and Jonathan went to the gym together three nights a week. Tom had been working the front desk for years when Dominic and Jonathan met him. They'd always talk with Tom for a few minutes when he worked the front desk. Tom thought it was nice to have someone actually recognize him rather than grunt as he scanned their pass.

Tom knew who Jonathan was as soon as he saw him, even under all the scruff. He was a college football assistant, after all, and Jonathan was once a five-star prospect. The game-winning play during the championship game and his full highlight reel nearly went viral on YouTube. And everyone who knew about Jonathan McCalister also knew about the accident. Tom and Dominic stood out to Jonathan because they were two of the very few people who never brought it up to him. Most people exchanged pleasantries and either expressed sympathy or asked how he was doing. Not Tom and Dominic. They focused on the present and future with Jonathan. Once, Tom asked Dominic whether or not he should tell Jonathan that he recognized his face and Dominic told him not to. "I don't think he wants to remember that part of his life anymore," Dominic told Tom.

Even when Jonathan helped Tom analyze scouting reports for new recruits, or organize offensive plays for the offensive coordinator of the football team, Tom played dumb. He pretended he had no idea Jonathan was once a football star known for his genius play-calling abilities. He would just take his advice and compliment his football knowledge.

"Yeah, I'll head over with you," Jonathan responded to Dominic's invitation to head over to the gym and help Tom. "Football season is starting soon. I'll bet you anything he's watching game tapes and sifting through scouting reports as we speak."

"No doubt."

The Halo theme song played faintly as Jonathan wheeled his way over to a closet behind his couch to grab his gym clothes. Dominic, still in his chair, cleared his throat.

Here goes, Dominic thought.

"Listen, man," Dominic began. "I've been meaning to tell you something."

"What's up?" Jonathan asked as he threw his gym clothes into a duffel bag and turned to look over at Dominic. Dominic's gaze was resting on the floor as if he had some bad news.

"I got into law school."

Jonathan felt relief. He was anticipating bad news. "That's great, man! Congratulations. We'll both be lawyers. Maybe we can run a firm together one day," Jonathan joked. He threw the duffel bag around the back of his wheelchair. "C'mon, man, let's go." He started to make his way to the door.

"Yeah, it's cool and all, but it means I won't be able to be your assistant anymore. I need to resign after this week."

Jonathan stopped. The words seemed to echo throughout the living room and bounce around in his head. "What?! I thought you weren't leaving until next summer. I thought you'd stick with me through graduation."

"I'm leaving for Boston right after graduation, man. I need to spend more time with my girlfriend before I go."

"So you're just going to abandon me? To spend time with your girlfriend?!" Jonathan felt betrayed. Dominic was his best friend. He didn't think he'd just leave him in the dust with less than a week's notice.

"We can still hang out, man. I just can't be with you all the time. I just can't be your personal assistant anymore."

"No, I see what's going on. Your girlfriend is more important than our friendship," Jonathan said dejectedly. He was more depressed than angry. Everyone had abandoned him. Lacey, his father, and now Dominic. He had nobody left.

"That's not true at all, man! I just spend so much time with you that I never have time to hang out with her. We can still hang out."

"Get out, man." Jonathan retorted. "Just leave. Go be with your girlfriend."

"Jon—"

"I said get out!" Jonathan yelled as he opened the door.

Dominic was confounded. "Why are you overreacting, man?! It doesn't have to be like this."

"Get out!" Jonathan shouted.

Dominic jumped up, grabbed his bag, and walked out the door.

CHAPTER 6

· · • • ● ● ● • · ·

Rose McCalister called Jonathan at least once a week to check on him. Since his father wouldn't speak to him after the accident, Rose took it upon herself to make sure Jonathan still felt loved by at least one of his parents.

Jonathan didn't like being called every week, though. His mom's attempt to make him feel loved just made him remember that his father wouldn't speak to him. He'd usually tune out by the third question or so and just say, "Yeah," and "Uh-huh" until the conversation ended. This week, her call came the night before his falling out with Dominic, so he thought he wouldn't hear from her for a while. The only people who called him regularly were his mother and Dominic, so when his phone started buzzing just a few minutes after Dominic left, he was caught a bit off guard. He didn't want to talk with either of them, so he ignored the buzzing.

As Jonathan sat there, he fought the urge to punch a hole in the wall or pick up his TV and throw it out the window. Dominic, like everyone else, had abandoned him. But he wondered whether he had overreacted to Dominic's resignation.

Next to the phone was the piece of paper he and Dominic used to keep score. With his phone on the third or fourth buzz, Jonathan looked over at the phone, noticed the piece of paper, grabbed it, ripped it up into shreds, and threw the shreds onto the floor next to him. Feeling a little guilty about whether he had overreacted with Dominic, he picked up the phone to see if the call was from

Dominic. But it wasn't. It was his mother calling again, just one day after her last phone call.

I really don't want to talk to her right now.

He cupped his face in his palms and stifled a scream as the phone went to voicemail. Within seconds, the phone started buzzing again.

Fine.

Jonathan picked up the phone with a hostile tone, "What, Mom? You called yesterday. Why are you calling again today?"

Rose ignored his hostility. "Hi, honey, I heard about what happened with Dominic and Dr. Bui. I'm sorry."

"How'd you hear?"

Rose paused with a deep breath before tentatively replying. "Dominic called me."

Anger flared up in Jonathan. Was Dominic going behind his back to tell his mommy on him, now?! But he didn't respond to Rose.

A few moments passed before Rose continued. "He's worried about you, Jon. He's still your friend. You've got to understand."

Again, Jonathan didn't respond.

Rose hesitated. Another ten seconds of silence passed. She even checked her phone to make sure Jonathan hadn't hung up. When she saw that he hadn't, she broke the silence. "I'm going to put another job ad out there for a new personal assistant."

"I don't need a personal assistant, Mom. I'm not helpless," Jonathan retaliated, "I'll manage just fine by myself."

"Jonathan, I love you very much. I'm looking out for you. You need to stop pushing me away."

Guilt crawled up Jonathan's spine. His mother was the only person who hadn't abandoned him, he realized. Dominic wasn't the last person he had left. His mom was.

"Sorry, Mom."

"It's okay, sweetie." Rose said warmly, "I'm going to reach out to the counselor's office and get some help finding a new assistant for you."

"Okay."

"Hang in there, Jon."

With that, she hung up. Jonathan sat in his living room with an overwhelming sense of loneliness.

A new personal assistant? What if I don't get along with them?

Dominic would be hard to replace. Jonathan and Dominic got along right from the start. Dominic was able to look past Jonathan's dejected personality and cheer him up. Any other person might have thought Jonathan was just a boring, bitter person. But Dominic didn't. He got Jonathan to open up. Now, Jonathan feared his replacement wouldn't be able to do the same. They might not play video games, know how to throw a football, or go to the gym.

CHAPTER 7

・・●●●・・

Samantha Reid sighed as she opened the door to the locker room of Dr. Angela Johanssen's zoology lab. It was going to be a long day for her. She had been in the library all morning studying for her summer classes' final exams, and it was time to put on personal protective equipment to get ready for her part-time job.

For nearly two years, Samantha had been a student assistant in Dr. Johanssen's zoology lab. Her job was to take care of the lab mice and geckos. She didn't earn much, but she made enough to pay her rent at her two-room apartment she split with her best friend Kylie Tran. Kylie also worked the same job at the zoology lab. Their idle chatter would make time go by faster when they were feeding, cleaning, and handling the mice and geckos.

Samantha walked to her locker, opened it up, and took out a pair of nitrile gloves, her lab coat, her mask, a hairnet, and shoe covers. As she tied her wavy blonde hair back into a bun, the voice of Dr. Johanssen startled her.

"Hey, Sam," Dr. Johanssen said.

Samantha jumped and whirled around. "Hey, Dr. Johanssen! You scared me!" Samantha laughed and put her hand on her chest as if it would slow down her heart. Her half-finished bun flopped down to the nape of her neck. She expected Dr. Johanssen to be in the lab, but she wasn't even dressed up to be in the lab. She was wearing scrubs without any personal protective equipment on.

43

"Sorry," Dr. Johanssen said with a polite laugh. "Where's Kylie?"

"She should be here soon. We were studying in the library all day, and she had to finish something up." Samantha began to fix her bun. "You know how tough premed can be, especially now that summer classes are coming to an end and we're about to start finals. We've got to take summer classes if we want to graduate early, though, so no complaints here!"

"Oh. Okay," Dr. Johanssen replied. "Don't put your PPE stuff on yet. I've got to talk to both of you."

Kylie walked into the locker room in the midst of Dr. Johanssen's last sentence. She tilted her head curiously as she stood behind Dr. Johanssen and heard her last sentence. "Talk about what?" she interrupted.

Now it was Dr. Johanssen's turn to be startled. She cringed, hunched her shoulders up in surprise, and flexed her fingers. She eased and turned to Kylie. "Hi, Kylie," she said, "Could the two of you come with me to my office?"

Samantha and Kylie exchanged an anxious look and followed Dr. Johanssen to her office.

Samantha had never been in Dr. Johanssen's office before. Her office was at the end of the long hallway where the lab animals room was, but Sam never had a reason to go there. Every day she worked, she just went from the locker room to the lab and back. As they entered, Samantha was surprised to see the number of books Dr. Johanssen had collected. They lined the walls almost like wallpaper. There were about four shelves on each wall, and each shelf was filled to the brim with books, with even more books piled on top of the shelves. They were perfectly organized by subject matter and author. Most of the books didn't pique her interest because she was studying to become a pediatrician and not a zoologist. But she was impressed with the volume of books in the collection.

"Please, take a seat." Dr. Johanssen gestured at the two seats in front of her desk.

Samantha and Kylie each took a seat. Samantha felt cramped in the tiny office space, as if the books surrounding her on all sides were going to fall on top of her. Dr. Johanssen walked around her desk and sat. Samantha looked down at her desk and saw a wide array of tiny skulls. She couldn't discern what animals the skulls belonged to, but they creeped her out. She loved animals but didn't like to see them as dead, inanimate ornaments.

"What's going on, Dr. Johanssen?" Kylie asked innocently.

Dr. Johanssen folded her hands and put them on the desk. "Listen, girls," she said, "there have been some serious budget cuts to the lab that are going to take effect in the spring." She closed her eyes, took a deep breath, and slowly opened them back up as she prepared to deliver the news. Samantha and Kylie held their breath as they waited for her to speak. Finally, she spoke. "I'm going to have to cut any paid student assistants." Samantha and Kylie stared silently. They both knew what she would say next. "I'm going to have to lay you off, girls. I'm so sorry."

Samantha couldn't afford to lose her job. She prided herself on being financially independent after growing up in the shadow of her father, Dan Reid, a successful businessman. She also needed Dr. Johanssen's recommendation to get into med school and fulfill her lifelong dream of becoming a pediatrician.

Kylie was the first to respond. "What about the mice and geckos? Who's going to take care of them?" Samantha could relate to Kylie's concerns. They had named each animal and were very fond of them. They were like pets to them.

"We're hoping to get volunteers to take care of them from now on." Dr. Johanssen sighed. She obviously didn't like that she had to cut Samantha and Kylie from the lab. "Don't worry, Kylie, they'll be okay."

Samantha jumped in. "Can't we be those volunteers?"

Dr. Johanssen creased her forehead as if to think about it for a few moments. "I suppose," she said at last, "but you know that means you're volunteering? Which means I can't pay you?"

"That's fine, Dr. Johanssen," Samantha responded, relieved that she would continue her relationship with Dr. Johanssen with the hope of earning a letter of recommendation. She didn't even consider whether or not Kylie wanted to be a volunteer, but she was happy when she looked over at Kylie to see her smiling and nodding her head.

Kylie must need her recommendation as much as I do, Samantha thought.

"Alright, then," Dr. Johanssen smiled, "I'm glad to still have you two on board. You can go ahead and get your gear on. I'll see you girls in the lab."

Samantha and Kylie stood up and walked out of the office, ready to start their shift.

CHAPTER 8

N ow that her job at Dr. Johanssen's zoology lab wasn't going to pay the bills, Samantha knew she had to find a gig to replace her lost income. The last thing she wanted to do was ask her dad for a handout. He would happily send her money, but for someone as fiercely independent as Samantha, it wasn't an option she would consider. She was high school valedictorian, earned a full academic scholarship, and was thriving at Central Texas University without any financial help from her family. She was determined to get into—and through— med school that way, too.

The first place she knew to look was the job board by the career services office. The board was full of flyers for odd jobs. There was always a plethora of jobs available. She wasn't worried about finding a job. The only question was whether she would find one she liked.

Right after her first shift as a volunteer, Samantha told Kylie she'd meet her back at the apartment and headed to check out the job board. The sun was setting as Samantha made her way over. A brilliant palette of colors fused in the clouds above. She was too focused on the task at hand to notice the beauty above her, however.

Samantha got to the job board as a counselor was pinning a new posting to it. It was a simple black and white piece of paper with the words "PERSONAL ASSISTANT NEEDED" across the top. Under the capital letters was a salary listed at fifteen dollars an hour. Intrigued, Samantha approached the posting. Below the salary was a phone number and job description.

Jonathan McCalister, a junior at Central Texas University, is looking for a personal assistant to help with day-to-day activities. He is confined to a wheelchair and looking for somebody to drive him from place to place in his handicap-accessible van, help him reach objects he cannot reach, plus various other tasks.

Samantha took out her phone and called. After two rings, a sweet voice answered.

"Hello?"

"Hi, I'm calling about the job posting for a personal assistant for a Mr. Jonathan McCalister?"

"Oh, that was quick!" The woman responded with a light laugh, "I'm Rose McCalister, Jon's mom. Whom do I have the pleasure of speaking with?"

"My name is Samantha Reid. I'm a premed student looking for a job. The wage is $15 an hour, I understand?"

"Yes, Samantha, that's correct. I'll need to know your availability and schedule in order to discern whether you'll be a good fit for the job. He needs help going to and from classes, and if you're unavailable at those times, then I'm afraid it won't work out. You also need to have a driver's license to drive his van."

Back and forth the exchange went until, finally, Rose and Samantha both felt Samantha was a perfect fit. Rose especially liked that Samantha was a volunteer at the zoology lab. It showed her Samantha had empathy and a good work ethic.

"Before I hire you, it's important for you to understand that Jonathan has been through a lot. He's experienced a lot of trauma. He needs someone who will encourage and support him. And he needs someone who will not give up on him."

"I won't give up on him, Mrs. McCalister, I promise. And I will provide tremendous encouragement and support."

With that, Samantha was Jonathan's new personal assistant.

CHAPTER 9

—————— ·•·•●•●•· ——————

Jonathan woke up to a knock at the door. He knew who it was. His mom had called him yesterday only about fifteen minutes after telling him that she was going to find him a new personal assistant. The new girl, Samantha Reid, was apparently the sweetest thing that ever walked this earth. Rose raved on about her to Jonathan, to the point where he tuned her out for a good ten or fifteen minutes. All he took away from the conversation was that his mom really adored her, and Miss Reid would come by first thing in the morning. And he wasn't thrilled his new personal assistant was going to be a girl. It wasn't a glamorous job, and some of the things he asked Dominic for help with were a bit embarrassing.

"One minute," Jonathan called out, as he hopped off his bed and into his wheelchair. He didn't even take a moment to gussy up in the mirror before opening the door. When he opened up the door, the first thing he noticed was how beautiful and uplifting Samantha looked as she stood in front of him smiling.

"Hi! Are you Jonathan?" Samantha quipped.

Jonathan rubbed his eyes and immediately regretted not at least pausing to see what he looked like before opening the door. He was stunned by her beauty. She had arched eyebrows above long eyelashes. Her long blonde hair fell down over her tanned, bare shoulders. Her pink lips looked softer than rose blossoms. She wore a floral top that didn't cover her collarbones and a pair of tight white jeans that accentuated her slender body. She had blue eyes that were the color of a tropical ocean.

"You. Can't. Be. Samantha?" Jonathan had a hard time getting those four words out, almost stuttering them. He was speechless.

"I *am*! Samantha Reid. I'm excited to meet you!" She reached her hand out to shake Jonathan's hand, but he was still catching his composure and just stared back at her.

"You aren't right for this job," he blurted out, his shock turning to annoyance at his mother. She was too pretty. Too delicate. They'd have nothing in common, he assumed. He couldn't play video games with her. He couldn't go to the gym with her. He couldn't chill out and be himself with her. He shut the door in her face.

Samantha knocked loudly on the door. "Your mom felt I'm the right person for this job." She paused. "And, you know what? I need this job, and I'm here to help. I'm also very persistent." She waited for Jonathan to open the door. When she realized he wasn't going to open it, she knocked again and then let out a loud sigh. "I'm staying no matter what you say. I'm getting paid by the hour, so I can do this all day!" Even her persistence was cute and peppy, Jonathan learned.

After a few more minutes, Jonathan cracked the door open. Sure enough, there she was casting a "told you so" smirk right back at him.

I'm not going to get rid of her.

"Do you play video games?"

ACT III

CHAPTER 10

·•·•●•••·

Samantha couldn't believe it when Jonathan asked her to play video games. She had never played a video game in her life. Steven, her little brother, always played video games—mostly sports games—and when they were younger, he'd always try to get her to play with him. He wouldn't leave her alone, unlike their older sister, Scarlett, whom he never even asked because she was so girly she wouldn't even go to the Pop Warner football games he played in.

Samantha and Steven got along well. She would go to his football games all the way until she left for college. She'd also often pretend to be interested in the video games he was playing, even though she never actually played. She just said for him to play by himself and sat with him, reading, studying for school, or talking with him. It was great bonding time for her and her brother. But she had *no* interest in playing video games.

Now, here she was. She had a door slammed in her face only to be cracked open a few minutes later. And the key to the door being opened and her getting invited in was to play video games.

"I've never played before," Samantha conceded. "But I'll give it a try!"

A few moments passed as Jonathan processed the response. Then, without saying a word, Jonathan rolled backward and opened the door for Samantha to come in. She was pleasantly surprised by the view of the lake but taken aback by how messy the living room was. Clothes were strewn across the floor in multiple piles, leftover pizza crusts were sitting on the coffee table, and she didn't see a single book other than the required textbooks stacked on an end table next to the couch. Samantha immediately recognized the textbooks as being for Political Science courses.

"Sorry about the mess," Jonathan said when he noticed the look of shock on Samantha's face as she looked around the room. "It's usually a little bit cleaner than this."

Samantha smiled politely. She doubted it was usually cleaner than it currently was. Jonathan didn't come across as a neat freak. He hadn't shaved in at least a week and clearly hadn't brushed his hair that morning. She could tell he was in good shape—his toned upper body filled out his T-shirt—but he looked like he hadn't showered in days. Under all the scruff, though, she had to admit to herself that he was quite handsome. He had deep green eyes that showed a lot of pain behind them, wavy blonde hair, and a sharp jawline.

Maybe, with the proper encouragement and support, he could clean himself up and let others see how handsome he is, Samantha thought. *The beard isn't too bad. It just looks like a really scruffy five o'clock shadow.*

Samantha was admiring the dimple on his chin when he looked up at her and made eye contact for the first time since the staredown in the hallway. Both of them looked into each other's eyes for a moment, awkwardly, before Jonathan broke the silence.

"So what do you want to try to play?"

"I don't know. What video games do you have?"

"I've got Halo and Madden. That's it."

"Oh, I know Madden. My little brother, Steven, plays it all the time."

"Then let's play Madden." Jonathan handed Samantha a controller as he turned on his TV and Xbox.

The controller felt foreign in her hands. She fidgeted with the thumb-sticks. "How do I play?"

"Well, first off, do you know how football works? Like, do you know the rules of the game?"

"Yeah, I do," Samantha chirped. "I went to every one of my brother's football games from Pop Warner through high school."

Jonathan took his gaze off of the TV and looked at Samantha with piqued interest. "Your brother plays football?"

"Yeah, he's a wide receiver. Why?" Samantha was confused as to why Jonathan seemed so interested in her brother being a football player. Samantha had no clue that Jonathan was once a football player himself. Rose never told her what trauma Jonathan had gone through or that it cut short a football career.

As she asked Jonathan about his interest in her brother, she noticed a black-and-white picture on the wall behind him. The picture showed a football player kneeling down with arm guards on his arms, the number 42 on his jersey, and a house behind him. It was just an ordinary picture, but it looked like it was taken fifty years ago. It definitely wasn't taken with a modern camera.

"I don't know," Jonathan replied. "Just wondering."

"Do you like football?"

What a dumb question, Samantha thought. *Of course he does.*

"Yeah."

Samantha pointed at the picture of the football player. "Is that a relative of yours?"

"No."

"Who is it?"

"Gerry Bertier."

Samantha ran her fingers through her hair nervously. "I shouldn't have even asked." She looked down to the floor. "I don't know any football players. I have no idea who Gerry Bertier is."

This isn't getting off to the best start, she thought.

"Not many people know who he is. Don't worry about it."

Samantha breathed a sigh of relief. She looked up from the floor and into Jonathan's verdant eyes. He was smiling warmly at her. "So, who is he?" she asked, with energy she hadn't shown since she first introduced herself in the hallway.

"Have you seen the movie *Remember the Titans*?"

"No. I don't really watch movies."

"I bet your brother has seen it. You should watch it sometime. It's a relatively true story about a high school football team. Gerry Bertier was one of the main characters in it. He was the captain of the football team." Jonathan looked out the window at the lake as he spoke. "He was a really good football player, but he got paralyzed because of a car accident."

Samantha blinked. Silence filled the air. She didn't know what to say but suspected there was a connection to Jonathan's trauma. But she didn't want to pry, so she just froze.

Jonathan kept staring out the window. After twenty seconds or so, he sighed. "He went on to win gold medals in the Paralympics for discus throw and shot put."

"Oh," Samantha said. "That's impressive!"

Awkward silence filled the air again. Jonathan wanted to impress Samantha, but he hadn't got off to the best start. *Do you want to play video games?* he thought to himself. *Really, man? What were you thinking?!*

Samantha felt a similar frustration. She wanted to get their relationship off to a good start, but this was awkward, at best. She needed this job and could easily be fired at any point if Jonathan didn't feel like they connected well enough. He could easily find a new personal assistant. But she promised Rose she wouldn't give up, so she wasn't going anywhere unless Jonathan gave up on her.

Both of them broke the silence at the same time.

"So how do I—" Samantha began.

"Do you want to—" Jonathan started.

Both of them stopped their question midsentence.

"Sorry," Samantha said. "You go."

"How about we go for a walk instead?" Jonathan stammered. "I mean, like, a stroll or something? There's a sidewalk that goes around the pond. We can take a lap around and get to know each other more. I don't want to make you play video games."

"Sure," Samantha replied with a smile, "Let's do that."

CHAPTER 11

$\bullet\cdot\bullet\cdot\bullet\bullet\bullet\cdot\bullet\cdot\bullet$

The air was crisp and slightly chilly for a summer morning, without a cloud in the sky, as Jonathan and Samantha made their way along the sidewalk surrounding the lake. Samantha had initially tried to push Jonathan along, but he refused. He didn't want to look helpless to her. The only time he liked to be pushed was when Dominic was riding his skateboard simultaneously, anyhow. That was fun.

"Everyone must still be sleeping," Jonathan said. "It's just us out here, nice and quiet."

Samantha nodded as she walked alongside him. "It's Saturday, after all. People are probably hungover after partying last night."

"Do you party?" Jonathan asked, not knowing what to make of Samantha. She was mysterious to him. With her looks, he couldn't get a read on her. He was sure she could do whatever she wanted but wasn't sure if she was a partier, straightedge, a teacher's pet, an athlete, or what. All he knew was that she was the prettiest girl he had ever laid his eyes on. He desperately wanted to impress her. He didn't care anymore about video games, playing catch, or going to the gym with her like he did with Dominic.

"No. Heavens no! I don't really get the party scene and don't really get along with people who party." As soon as she finished the sentence, she worried she might have offended Jonathan. The way he looked when he answered the door and the state of his apartment made a party lifestyle a real possibility. She didn't want him to think she wouldn't like him if he partied. "I mean, I don't *usually* like people who party. That doesn't mean I dislike *everyone* who parties."

Jonathan laughed. "Good thing I don't party anymore."

"You *used* to party?" she asked.

"Yeah, before the accident," his voice cracking with emotion as he said *accident*.

Samantha didn't ask him what he meant by "the accident." She wondered if "the accident" was what put Jonathan in a wheelchair but was afraid to ask. Maybe it was what Rose meant when she said he had been through a lot of trauma. Maybe her instinct about the connection to the Gerry Bertier picture was right. But she didn't want to ask. She figured she'd know in due time, so she quickly changed the subject.

"So, do you go by Jonathan or Jon?"

"Jon's fine."

"Okay," Samantha said, "you can call me Sam if you want."

"Okay, what do you do for fun, Sam?"

"I'm not too much fun. I'm a total nerd, actually. My life consists of volunteering in Dr. Johanssen's zoology lab and getting the grades I need to get into a good medical school."

"What's Dr. Johanssen's zoology lab like?"

Samantha felt a tinge of affection for Jonathan. She could tell he was really making an effort to befriend her. "It's so cool. I love animals and get to work with the lab mice and geckos. I feed them and everything, so it's pretty awesome. Plus, I get to do it with my best friend, Kylie. She's premed, too, and volunteers there with me. She wants to be a veterinarian. I'm sure she'd love to meet you! She's great!"

"Sorry, but I don't think I want to meet her."

Jonathan often frustrated himself with his lack of confidence since the accident. He didn't like making new friends or meeting new people. He couldn't fight the thought that everyone was taking pity on him because he was in a wheelchair. He was sure nobody genuinely wanted to be friends with him. Why would they waste time being held back by a guy in a wheelchair, having to wait for elevators, call ahead for special accommodations, and avoid activities most people love because you can't really do them with a guy in a wheelchair?

"I'm not really sociable."

"You seem sociable to me," Samantha countered. "We're getting along just fine. I'm really glad you opened the door."

"Yeah, well, we're going to be spending a lot of time together. So, I really don't feel like spending the rest of my college life miserable. I might as well be cordial."

Samantha felt slightly offended but understood what he meant. It'd be a long few semesters if they didn't get along. They'd be spending a lot of time together, after all. "Don't you want to make friends?"

"Not really. I just do my own thing, mostly." Jonathan felt frustration rising in his belly. He wanted to impress Samantha, but there was no way he was going to do it if he stayed as closed off as he was.

I've got to try, at least.

"If you really want me to meet her, I'll meet her," Jonathan said. "We probably won't get along too well, though."

"I bet you'll get along great," Samantha replied happily. "She's really nice."

"What do you and Kylie do together other than take care of lab mice and geckos and study?" Jonathan quipped, "You've got to have *some* fun."

The pair had almost made their way around the lake.

"Well, next week, we're running in a 5K charity event that benefits the local children's hospital," Samantha said. "It's called Race for the Kids 5K. I guess that's one way we have fun. What about you? What do you do, other than video games, to have fun?"

Jonathan's cheeks flushed with embarrassment. He didn't want Samantha to think he just stayed in his room all day and played video games, although that's basically what he did. "I, uh, I go to the gym."

"So you exercise? You should come to the Race for the Kids 5K with me and Kylie!"

"Seriously? Look at me. I'm in a wheelchair. I can't do a race," Jonathan said dejectedly, "I'd just slow you two down."

Jonathan rarely backed down from a challenge but didn't want to embarrass himself in front of Samantha by failing to complete the race or forcing her and Kylie to slow down out of pity. A 5K, he knew, was a little over three miles. He assumed it would be hard to go three miles in a wheelchair when he had never tried to go a long distance before. All of his classes were located in nearby buildings, so he never had to wheel himself more than a mile a day. He wasn't in any rush when he traveled that mile, either. A race was all about being in a rush. And he also knew a guy in a wheelchair would stand out like a sore thumb. He didn't want that attention.

"They have races for people in wheelchairs if you don't want to compete alongside Kylie and me." Samantha wanted to cheer him up. He seemed like such a dispirited person. She wondered if he had always been like this or if the "accident" had made him lose hope and confidence.

"I'll think about it." Depression settled in Jonathan's chest. He didn't think he had made a great first impression with Samantha. He had never felt so lame as he did after he told Samantha how he wasn't sociable and wouldn't participate in the race.

She must think I'm the lamest guy ever. There's no way she's even slightly interested in me.

But that wasn't Samantha's impression of Jonathan. She knew Jonathan had been through a lot in his life. For someone who had suffered a lot of trauma, she thought he was pretty friendly and personable. And, once he warmed up to her, she really enjoyed their time together, even if they started out on the wrong foot. He was still a bit closed off and dejected. But they just met, so she knew it would take some effort to get him to open up to her. She was sure she could get Jonathan McCalister out of his shell and help him fulfill his potential.

First things first, she thought. *He needs a haircut, a shave, and nicer clothes.*

CHAPTER 12

························

After their lap around the pond, Jonathan told Samantha he was going to go to the gym, and they parted ways. She said she'd see him on Tuesday after they both took their finals. Before going to the gym, Jonathan retired to his apartment and gazed out the window at the pond for a while. The depression that had settled in his chest at the end of the walk was growing. His conversation with Samantha made him realize how depressed he really had been and how much he'd closed himself off from life.

He hadn't felt that sad in a long time. It was like he was stuck in a hole he couldn't climb out of. The sky above him was blue and beautiful, but it felt to him like a blue dot miles up from the rut in which he was trapped. Every attempt to get out of the sadness, to get out of the hole, was futile. He clawed his way up only to find his thoughts back to focusing on Gabby, which caused him to lose his grip, fall back down, and feel even more pain as he hit bottom again. The thought of Gabby felt as if an immense wave crashed down on him, knocking him down whenever he attempted to pull himself up.

It wasn't an epiphany to Jonathan that he was still depressed. But talking with Samantha reminded him that he wasn't helping himself get out of the rut he had been in since the accident. The rut, as he called it, was how he described being antisocial and closed off. As he stared out at the pond, the painful memory of the accident returned . . . the headlights growing brighter and brighter. The horn blaring. The deafening sound of metal crunching as the car wrapped around the oak tree at 2612 Cherryhill Lane. He felt guilty about it every day and had learned to stifle the memory into the depths of his mind. He tried not to think about Gabby, but he remembered her sweet, smiling face every time he looked down at his amputated legs. They were a constant reminder that he ruined his football career, took his little sister's life, and destroyed his relationship with his dad, all because he couldn't refrain from texting Lacey back after she sent him that picture.

Jonathan's depression had been much worse in the past, but it was still constant. He hit bottom shortly after arriving at Central Texas University, just before he became good friends with Dominic. During that time, he seriously considered taking his own life. He even knew exactly what he would do. There was a busy highway by the campus, and Jonathan's plan was to roll himself onto the highway in the middle of the night when nobody could see him before it was too late. He even prepared to do it one night and wrote a letter to his mom letting her know the pain of being alive was too much. But when he started writing about Gabby, the sight of her name on that paper made him break down in tears.

After a long cry, he decided that it wasn't fair to his mom, leaving her childless. He knew his mother would blame herself for Jonathan's suicide, and he didn't want to leave her feeling that way. He also thought it wasn't fair to Gabby, either. She had always supported him, and Jonathan knew she wouldn't want him to take his own life. Although he wasn't a strong believer in God, he liked to think Gabby was up in heaven looking down on him. She would want to protect him. She wouldn't want him to take his life. So, he ripped up the letter and started his slow return to normalcy, never again thinking about killing himself after that.

But he still hated thinking about the accident and continued to battle depression. He would always call up Dominic when he started thinking about the accident. Dominic had a way to help him take his mind off of it. But Dominic wasn't around anymore. He didn't want to call Samantha. She wasn't his friend yet, and he didn't feel comfortable opening up to her about the accident. He was glad she hadn't asked about it earlier when he let it slip out.

I guess I'll just go to the gym and see Tom.

Jonathan grabbed the gym bag he had packed the night he and Dominic had a falling out. He locked the door behind him, wheeled down the hallway, and out into the courtyard. There, he started a stopwatch app on his phone and started to make his way to the gym. The gym was only a few buildings over from his apartment, but Jonathan would always time himself on how long it took him to get there. It was a quirk that stoked his competitive spirit.

Jonathan had two notebooks. One notebook was for working out, which is where he recorded how long it took him to get to the gym and his workout routines. The other was for writing. Jonathan was a voracious reader and excellent writer, but he hid that part of himself from others. He locked all his books and notebooks in a cabinet in the corner of his room—with the exception of the workout notebook, which he kept in his gym bag at all times. The only time he'd take out his books and writing notebook was before going to bed. He'd write poetry and journal entries and read a wide array of genres. His favorite two books, which he had read over and over again, were *Great Expectations* by Charles Dickens and *To Kill a Mockingbird* by Harper Lee. He had read *To Kill a Mockingbird* when he was in eighth grade, and it was the first book he really enjoyed. After he read that, he started to read more. His dad Jeff encouraged it, as a reader himself, and he would recommend books to Jonathan. Jeff's favorite book was *Great Expectations*. Jonathan had fond memories of *Great Expectations* because it was the first book his dad recommended to him, and it started a tradition between the two. Now that Jeff hadn't talked to Jon in years, those memories were even more special. Jonathan longed to have more of those conversations with his dad.

As Jonathan raced to the gym, he laughed aloud at the fact that he was, in fact, *racing*, even if it was racing only against himself. He had told Samantha he couldn't race because he was in a wheelchair, but here he was, sure enough, racing. It felt good to laugh. The depression that was overcoming Jonathan in his living room was subsiding, and he was looking forward to talking with Tom and getting his mind off the fallout from the accident. He was also nervous but excited about seeing Samantha on Tuesday. Maybe he'd tell her he'd do the race after all.

Jonathan slowed his roll as he approached the main door to the gym. According to the stopwatch, he had gotten there in one minute and twelve seconds. He took out his notebook and jotted the time down.

Not bad. I get faster every day.

Usually, he went to the gym with Dominic, who helped him open the large, heavy, glass door to the gym. Jonathan knew he was going to struggle to open it himself. He strategized for a few moments how to open it, until he noticed a gray "push to open" button three feet to the right of him. He rolled up to the button, pressed it, and the door slowly opened. *That was easy.*

Once the door opened, Jonathan wheeled himself in with haste, afraid the door would suddenly swing shut and crush him before he could get through. He made it, found the elevator, and took it to the bottom floor, where he would meet Tom. When the elevator reached the bottom floor, the doors opened, and Jonathan felt a rush of joy to see Tom working the front desk. Sometimes he wasn't there in the mornings. And when he *was* there, he often was training someone.

"Hey, Tom," Jonathan said as he rolled over to the desk. "How's it going?"

"What's up, Jon!" Tom replied without taking his eyes off the screen of his laptop. He looked away from the screen for a moment to write something down into a playbook. Once he got the thought down on paper, he looked up at Jonathan. "Honestly, man, I'm not doing too hot."

"What's wrong?"

"I've just got a lot on my plate right now." Tom said with a tone of exasperation, "Coach Gustaffson has tasked me with getting the new quarterback, Elijah Baines, up to speed with the playbook. He's a great athlete, and he's got a lot of raw talent, but he's not learning the plays no matter what I do. I'm watching his high school game tapes to see what plays are similar, so I can start with the plays that are similar to what he's already familiar with. It's just hard because his high school ran a Wing T offense, and here, we run an Air Raid offense. So, he's used to having to learn more running plays and fewer passing plays. We have tons of passing plays, and he's really struggling to learn them."

Coach Red Gustaffson, the offensive coordinator of the Central Texas University Stallions, was a tough, stocky man with a shiny bald head and a thick handlebar mustache. He was Tom's worst nightmare and notoriously unforgiving with his players and coaching staff. Tom reported directly to Coach Gustaffson.

"Football season has already started, though, hasn't it?" Jonathan asked.

"Yeah. The practices have. Our first game is on August 29th."

"So you have until this Thursday to get him caught up on the playbook!? That's ridiculous!"

"No," Tom said, "he's a freshman, and he's red-shirting this year to give him an extra year of eligibility. When Coach Gustaffson learned that Elijah was having a hard time learning the college offense, he red-shirted him. So, he can practice with the team, but he can't play in the games."

Jonathan nodded along as Tom spoke. "Maybe I can help," Jonathan suggested.

"Sure, man, I mean he's here at the gym right now," Tom responded. "Maybe you can talk to him. Everything I say to him goes in one ear and out the other. He just grunts whenever I try to explain a play to him. He's more concerned about his physique than he is about learning our playbook. I *need* him to learn the playbook, or my coaching career will be over before it even starts."

"Alright," Jonathan said, "where is he?"

"He should be over by the dumbbells. Here, let me introduce you."

Tom paused the game tape he had been watching, got up from his chair, and walked around the desk. Jonathan followed Tom toward the dumbbells. There were a few people near the dumbbells, but Jonathan was able to immediately identify Elijah because of his shirt. It was red and white—the school colors—and had the words "Central Texas University Stallions" on the back. He was doing biceps curls with a pair of thirty-pound dumbbells and grunting with each rep and gazing at himself in the mirror. Jonathan sighed. He hoped Elijah wasn't a typical meathead jock. But he certainly looked like one at that moment.

"Hey, Elijah," Tom said.

Elijah moved his eyes from his reflection in the mirror and to Tom's reflection. He put the dumbbells back, gave Tom a fist bump, and then looked at Jonathan. Elijah seemed to measure Jonathan with his eyes as he looked him up and down. After a slight hesitation, he fist bumped Jonathan.

"This is Jonathan," Tom said to Elijah.

Elijah didn't hear Tom because he was wearing headphones. Once he noticed Tom's lips moving, he took out the headphones. "What'd you say, Tom?"

"This is Jonathan."

"Oh. Nice to meet you, Jonathan."

Jonathan nodded. "Nice to meet you, too, Elijah. What're you listening to?"

"'God's Plan,' by Drake," Elijah replied. He noticed Jonathan had a pair of headphones dangling out of his pocket. "What do you listen to? What's on your playlist? I need to get some new tunes to work out to. Mine are getting stale."

Jonathan pulled his phone from his pocket and handed the headphones to Elijah. Elijah put Jonathan's headphones on, and Jonathan pressed play. The first song that played was "Life Goes On" by Tupac Shakur. Elijah began to bob his head as he listened.

"I like this," Elijah said. "It's some old-school stuff, ain't it?"

Jonathan smiled. "It's Tupac, man. He was the king of old school."

"What song did you put on?" Tom asked Jonathan.

"Life Goes On."

"That's a classic. Classics like that never die. Neither do their messages," Tom said.

Elijah kept bobbing his head as he continued to listen. "It's got a positive message, man. Kind of like 'God's Plan.' I mean, 'God's Plan' doesn't have a positive message in its lyrics, but have you seen the music video?"

"Nah, man. I've heard the song," Jonathan replied, "but I never watched the video."

"It's dope," Elijah said. "Drake was budgeted like a million bucks by his label for the music video, but he took all that money and gave it away instead and filmed himself doing so. The music video is just footage of him changing people's lives by giving them money, food, and other things with the cash he was supposed to have used for the video."

Elijah and Jonathan hit it off immediately. The two chatted for a few minutes while Tom just stood there quietly nodding along. They began to talk about football. When they realized they both shared the same favorite NFL team, the Cowboys, the two got lost in a conversation about the upcoming season. They discussed what they thought about how they'd do next season, what players they liked the most, and what players they liked the least. Tom wasn't sure what Jonathan was doing, though. He didn't see how chitchat about the Cowboys would help Elijah learn the playbook. But Jonathan had a plan.

"You two should come and chill at my place," Jonathan suggested. "We can hang out, play some Madden, and talk ball."

Tom was desperate to teach Elijah the playbook and figured it would be much easier to do so when he wasn't admiring himself in the gym mirror. "I'm down. I say we do a tournament and the two people who lose have to split the cost for some pizza."

"I'm starving," Elijah said. "Let's do it."

* * *

"You've got to read the defense to know what audible to call," Tom said as he and Elijah sat in front of Jonathan's TV. "The Air Raid offense is all about calling audibles when you get to the line of scrimmage."

Jonathan was sitting in his wheelchair while Tom and Elijah sat on the couch and played each other in the first round of the tournament. Tom was trying to explain how an Air Raid offense operates while Jonathan flipped through the Stallions' playbook on Tom's iPad.

"The Air Raid offense isn't designed to always go downfield and vertically harass a defense. Oftentimes, it's a lot of horizontal plays," Tom explained to Elijah. "Your receivers stretch across the field, sideline to sideline, making incremental gains that advance your offense down the field slowly, pass after pass. It's a bit like a West Coast offense, if you're familiar with that but more pass focused. Also, some passes will go a lot deeper than they would in a West Coast offense."

Elijah nodded as Tom explained the offense to him. "How do I read the defense?"

Jonathan knew what to say here. "If the cornerbacks press up into your receiver, meaning they get up close and personal on the line of scrimmage, they're probably going to be playing man-to-man coverage. If they drop back from the line of scrimmage and don't chase after the receiver when the play starts, they're probably playing zone coverage. If they're playing zone, all you need to do is pass the ball when your receivers get into a gap between the defenders, who will each be guarding a spot on a field instead of a specific receiver. If they're playing man coverage, look for a favorable matchup and then pass the ball as soon as your receiver plants his feet to make a break away from the defender guarding him."

Tom joked, "Don't help him. I'm not paying for pizza!"

"I'm having trouble with the playbook, Tom. I need his help if I ever want to see the field."

"That's what I'm for! That's why we go over the playbook all the time," Tom said.

"Going over the playbook with you is boring, though," Elijah said. "No offense, but Madden is fun and simple."

"What's confusing about the playbook?" Jonathan asked.

"The fact that I've got to memorize all the different receivers' routes for so many passing plays. When I played in a Wing T, back in high school, I only had to memorize a handful of routes. Now I've got to remember like a hundred of them. Every receiver runs a different route in every play."

"It's not hard to memorize the routes they run in each play if you just take some time to review the playbook in a way that doesn't bore you," Jonathan said, as he sifted through the playbook on Tom's iPad.

"Reviewing the playbooks bores me out of my wits, though. There's gotta be a better way."

"Well, look at the play you just called in Madden. You knew the 'four verticals' play meant all your receivers are going to go long. The four verticals play in Madden is the same play as the Hail Mary in the Stallions' playbook. If you can memorize that play in Madden, you can memorize the plays in the playbook."

"I guess Madden just captures my attention and focus better because it's a lot more fun than studying the playbook."

Tom was catching on and began to play along. He purposely lost his game with Elijah so he could put all his attention on teaching Elijah the playbook through playing Madden. Tom would show Elijah the playbook and point out the similarities between the Madden playbook and the Stallions' playbook. Then, when Elijah chose a play in Madden, Tom would quiz him on what the play was called in their playbook. Tom offered to pay for the pizza in appreciation of Jonathan's strategy. When the pizza came, Jonathan kept on talking about the playbook with Elijah, and they built a bond that was quickly blossoming into a friendship.

Jonathan was having a lot of fun with Tom and Elijah. He especially liked going over the playbook because it took his mind off of thinking about the accident or how he thought he appeared lame to Samantha. It brought him back to football, something he was really good at.

After a few hours, though, the fun came to a stop. By that point, Elijah had left. It was just Tom and Jonathan playing Halo.

"Where's Dom, man?"

Jonathan winced at the question. He still felt guilty and thought he had overreacted when Dominic told him he had to resign as his personal assistant. Dominic had yet to contact Jonathan, and Jonathan was too stubborn to be the bigger man. To be fair, though, it had only been a few days. But Jonathan hoped that they'd reunite before Dominic left for law school.

"He had to resign as my personal assistant," Jonathan replied. "He's going to law school in Boston after he graduates and wants to spend more time with his girlfriend before he leaves."

"Oh. Bummer, man."

Jonathan changed the subject before Tom could inquire more. "I have a new personal assistant now. Her name is Samantha." Jonathan wanted to add that he thought Samantha was really cute, but he didn't want Tom to hold it over him. Tom was the type to jokingly tease someone about things like that.

"Yeah?" Tom asked. "How's that?"

"It's alright. I don't know. I mean, I miss Dominic. I just met Samantha, and she already wants me to race a 5K with her and her best friend."

Tom looked at Jonathan excitedly. "You should do it, man!"

Jonathan sighed. He knew that Tom, as a personal trainer, would love the idea of Jonathan doing a 5K. He didn't know who else to confide in about it, though. He was still hesitant because he didn't want to embarrass himself, but he also desperately wanted to impress Samantha. "I don't know. I feel like I'll embarrass myself. I'll be the only person in a wheelchair, and Samantha and her friend will have to slow down to keep my pace. I'll have them coming in last."

"Don't be so negative. You'll kill it," Tom said confidently as he mashed the buttons on his controller.

Jonathan wanted Tom to tell him that he should do it because he never did anything memorable. But he figured Tom had no idea he was basically a recluse who did nothing with his life but play video games and go to the gym.

This can be the first step to get out of my rut.

"Yeah. I guess I'll go.

CHAPTER 13

— •••●●●•• —

Jonathan felt a touch of regret as he sat in Professor Hoffpower's class and looked out the window at the large Central Texas University College of Liberal Arts sign. Last time he was looking out the window at that sign, Dominic had been standing outside next to it waving at him with a skateboard.

Samantha wasn't waiting for him there. She was waiting for him in the hallway. He had seen her pacing back and forth outside the door, flipping through a stack of flashcards and murmuring to herself and glancing through the window at Jonathan every once in a while as he took the final exam. By this time, he had finished the final but still sat there pretending to review his answers. He didn't want to go out into the hallway just yet. He was nervous about telling Samantha he would do the Race for the Kids 5K. He wasn't sure why he was nervous. He just was.

Before the accident, Jonathan never got nervous talking to girls. If anything, he was cocky. After the accident, though, Jonathan didn't have any interest in talking to girls. Sure, he wanted to find a girl, fall in love, settle down, and start a family. But he didn't think he had a chance. He had no legs. He couldn't dance anymore. He would never be tall enough to kiss or hug a girl unless she bent down. And, to Professor Hoffpower's point, he looked like a scrub.

He felt especially embarrassed to talk to Samantha that day. He hadn't shaved in days. His hair was a scraggly mess. And he dressed like he was wearing pajamas. He wanted to shave the night before in preparation for seeing Samantha, but his beard was too thick to use a razor, and he didn't have clippers or an electric razor. Usually he borrowed Dominic's electric razor, but Dominic was no longer around. He also wanted to get a haircut the weekend before but never ended up going. And he wanted to dress up a bit for Samantha but didn't have clothes to wear other than sweatpants and T-shirts. Back in high school, he dressed like an Abercrombie & Fitch model, but he no longer had the confidence to pull off that look.

I can't hide in here forever.

Jonathan grabbed his exam and wheeled himself to the front of the room. He put his final exam on Professor Hoffpower's desk and turned around to head out the door before Professor Hoffpower could talk to him, but he was too slow.

"No handshake?"

Jonathan gulped. He slowly turned around, wheeled around the desk, and held out his hand with an insincere smile. Professor Hoffpower held out his liver-spotted hand, grasped Jonathan's hand firmly, and shook up and down slowly.

"Thanks, Professor Hoffpower," Jonathan said, "It's been great." He then tried to pull away, but Professor Hoffpower held on securely.

"You've got a lot of potential, Mr. McCalister," Professor Hoffpower said quietly. "I know you'll go far. You just need to believe in yourself."

What's his obsession with me?

"Thanks, Professor Hoffpower," Jonathan replied, as he pried his hand out of the handshake. "Maybe I'll see you around."

"Please, Mr. McCalister, call me Jim."

Jonathan really wanted to leave. This was getting creepy. "Sure, Jim," Jonathan agreed. "I've got to get going." Professor Hoffpower released his grip, and Jonathan rushed out the door.

Samantha didn't seem to notice Jonathan as he approached her. She was whispering to herself as she studied from flash cards she was holding.

"Didn't you already take your final?" Jonathan asked.

Samantha stopped, turned her attention to Jonathan, and smiled. "I did. I'm just going through the answers to see if I got everything on the exam correct."

"You really *are* a nerd, huh?" Jonathan responded with a hint of humor.

"Always have been," Samantha replied cheerfully. "Have you thought about the Race for the Kids 5K? I'd really like it if you came along. Kylie said she really wants to meet you. You don't have to race. You can just come support us. It'd mean a lot."

"I have," Jonathan replied, as nerves started jumping around in his belly. He paused for a moment, mustering up the courage to speak, and took a deep breath. "I'll come."

Samantha's face lit up. "Really?" She was surprised but thrilled at the same time. "Like you'll race? Or you'll come?"

"I'll race," Jonathan said with an unexpected smile. He was happy to see how impressed Samantha looked. "When is the race, exactly?"

"It's tomorrow!" Samantha said excitedly, "We've got to get you signed up by five o'clock!" Samantha stuffed her flashcards into the side pocket of her backpack and took Jonathan's hand. "Come on, we don't have much time!" Jonathan didn't want to let go of Samantha's hand, but he needed two hands to move his wheelchair.

"Um, Sam," Jonathan said with a sheepish smirk, "I need both hands unless you want to just spin in circles for a while."

"Oh." Her cheeks flushed as she let go of his hand, "Sorry, Jon."

"It's okay. Let's go."

The two sped down the hallway, Jonathan following Samantha as she maneuvered between people and kept looking back to make sure he was keeping up. Jonathan was moving his hands as fast as he could to push the wheels of the wheelchair forward.

I guess this is good practice for the race.

They took turn after turn from one hallway to another until they finally reached the main lobby of the building. In the corner was a table with a drape that read "Race for the Kids 5K" and "Sign Up Now!" The people working the table had already started packing things up, as it was approaching five o'clock.

"Wait!" Samantha called out as she ran up to the table. Jonathan was right behind her. "He would like to sign up!"

Jonathan was afraid they would reject him because he was in a wheelchair. To his relief, the woman working the table smiled and took a piece of paper out of the bag that was being packed up. "Okay," she said. "He just needs to put his name on this paper and pay the fee, and he's all set."

Jonathan rolled up to the table and grabbed a pen to sign up. The list was long. A lot of people had signed up already. At the very top was Samantha's name, followed by Kylie's and then Dean Pilling. Unlike the rest of the list, those three names were all written in the same handwriting, which led Jonathan to assume Dean was a friend of Kylie and Samantha. Whoever wrote their names down had also written his.

Jonathan wrote his name at the bottom of the list, where there were a few spaces left, and held the paper and pen out to the lady who was working the table.

"I assume you have a racing chair for the event?" She asked as she took the pen and paper from Jonathan's hands. Panic surged through Jonathan because he had no idea what a racing wheelchair even was.

"I don't, ma'am, no," Jonathan answered nervously. "Is it required?"

"No," she said, "it's not required. It's just helpful. I know a place nearby where you can rent one, along with some gloves and a helmet. If you head there now, you'll make it in time before they close. You'd better get going, though. They close at six."

"What's the name of the place?" Samantha asked eagerly.

"The Competition Corner."

Samantha and Jonathan rushed off to his apartment, grabbed the keys to his handicap-accessible van, and then rushed to the student lot to drive to The Competition Corner. This was Samantha's first experience with a handicap-accessible van, so she had no idea how to get the ramp to lower. She looked around for a few moments on the van's dashboard but couldn't figure it out. Eventually she realized there was a button on the keys to lower the ramp.

While she was trying to figure that out, Jonathan waited patiently and plugged the address of The Competition Corner into the map app on his phone. They had plenty of time to get there. It was 5:10 p.m. and the shop was only fifteen minutes away.

Once the ramp was lowered, Jonathan wheeled into the passenger-seat area. The seat was removed so Jonathan could sit up front. He locked his chair into place while Samantha settled into the driver's seat. Once settled, Samantha pulled out and they were on their way.

Samantha had never driven a van before. She was used to riding around in her Mini Cooper, which was much smaller, so the wide turn radius of the van took some getting used to. Jonathan navigated her with his map app as she drove. They exchanged idle chit chat throughout the ride.

While waiting for a red light to turn green, Samantha's phone pinged. She reached into her pocket and pulled it out to check who was texting her. It was Kylie, asking her how she thought she did on her exams. Before Samantha could respond, Jonathan snapped at her.

"Put your phone away!" The harshness of his tone surprised Samantha.

"Okay, one second, let me just text Kylie back," Samantha said. She started to type back to Kylie, telling her that she thought she did well on her exams, when Jonathan ripped the phone from her hands. "Hey—" Samantha started, but Jonathan cut her off.

"I said put your phone away!" Jonathan put her phone in the cupholder between them. The image of the phone nestled in the cupholder reminded Jonathan of his accident. His phone was in the cupholder of his 2002 Camaro Z28 when it pinged to let him know he received a text.

If I hadn't reached for it . . .

Anger at himself roared inside him like a fire. He immediately directed that anger at Samantha to get rid of it. "Why would you text and drive?!"

"I wasn't! We're at a red light! I wasn't—" Samantha stumbled over her words, "I wasn't texting and driving!" She was stunned. She didn't expect such an intense reaction. She didn't expect a reaction at all. She texted at red lights all the time, and people never got upset with her about it.

"You're at the steering wheel. You're driving the car. You were texting. Therefore, you were texting and driving."

"But we're stopped—"

"Listen, I have no tolerance for texting and driving. If you want to be my personal assistant, and if you want to drive me around, you can't text or talk on the phone when you're driving. I've got zero tolerance for it."

Samantha was confused. She wasn't driving. They were stopped at a red light. She had no idea why Jonathan was reacting so strongly. She wanted to tell him he was overreacting, but she didn't want to upset him any more.

Well, there's strike one, she thought.

For the rest of the ride, nothing but silence passed between them. Initially, Samantha had been excited to go shopping for rental equipment at The Competition Corner. She thought they'd bond a little in the experience. Now she was afraid she had gotten on Jonathan's bad side and that it was going to be an awkward experience.

After a short while, they arrived at the store. It was a small building on a main road sandwiched between a sushi restaurant and a coffee shop. The neon lights on the front of the store blinked and some of the letters weren't lit up, so instead of "The Competition Corner," the sign read "The Com_et_tion Corn_r." Samantha pulled into a handicap spot right in front.

Jonathan broke the silence that had been held in the car for the last ten minutes or so. "Rock star parking," he said. Samantha laughed politely to reciprocate his attempt to fix the awkwardness they both felt since the texting incident. She clicked the button on the keys to lower the ramp, and Jonathan rolled onto the pavement.

"How are we going to pay for the rental?" Samantha asked as they made their way to the entrance of the store.

"Don't worry about it," Jonathan said. Last night he had called his mom to tell her about the race. He hadn't told her he needed to rent anything, because he had no idea at the time. But she was so excited and happy he was racing Jonathan was sure she'd lend him any money he needed. His father was a successful lawyer. Expenses like this weren't a problem.

Samantha opened the door for Jonathan, and he rolled in. Nobody was in the shop except for a small man with round glasses and a goatee. He was standing behind a counter on the left wall of the store. He had been scratching at the countertop, bored out of his mind and just waiting for the clock to hit six o'clock, when the two entered. His head perked up and he immediately made his way toward them. "Hello there," he greeted them, "welcome to The Competition Corner! My name is Paul. What can I help you with?"

"We're looking to rent some wheelchair equipment for a race tomorrow," Samantha responded.

"Certainly," the man said. "What sort of equipment do you need?"

"We've got nothing," Jonathan answered. "So, basically we need a racing chair and whatever else people in wheelchairs usually rent for a race."

"Okay. So you need a racer chair, a helmet, and some gloves. That can be arranged. We just need to get you fitted." The man beckoned for Jonathan and Samantha to follow him and started walking toward the back of the store. There were bikes, oars, surfboards, snowboards, and a multitude of other sports equipment hanging on the wall. On the ground, under all that, were four large tricycles with wheels that looked like Viking shields. They were the same types of chairs Jonathan had seen on the track when he was touring the Calvary Performance Institute. Jonathan was surprised when the man pointed at the tricycles and said, "Alright, here they are."

"These are the racer chairs?" Jonathan asked. "They look like tricycles!"

"These are, indeed, racer chairs," the man replied.

"Alright. Let's go with the yellow one," Jonathan said.

For the next thirty minutes, the man adjusted everything on the yellow chair to Jonathan's liking while Samantha watched and asked questions like, "What does the 'camber' mean?"

The man was happy to answer the questions because it let him demonstrate his expertise. "Good question," he replied. "The camber is the angle of the wheel. It helps with stability and makes sure the chair won't tip over when turning. We usually have the wheels cambered somewhere between eleven and fifteen degrees, so riders don't bump their upper arms on the fenders."

Once the chair was customized, the man recommended some gloves and a helmet. Samantha picked up the chair and brought it out to the car while Jonathan paid the rental fee for the equipment. Jonathan met her outside after paying for everything.

"Do you mind if I pop into that sushi place to get some dinner?" Samantha asked Jonathan as he wheeled himself out the door with the helmet and gloves on his lap.

"I'll come with you. My treat." He wanted to apologize to Samantha for snapping at her on the drive over. Buying her dinner would be a good start, although he didn't even like sushi.

"Okay," Samantha replied with a smile. "Thanks."

CHAPTER 14

— ··•◦●◦•·· —

"**A**re you sure you don't want sushi," Samantha asked as they sat in the tiny restaurant. Nobody else was there, and the only sound they could hear other than each other's voices was the squeak of a ceiling fan.

"I'm sure. I'll just have these potstickers for now," Jonathan said. "I'm not too hungry, to be honest. And I'm not a big fan of sushi."

"Okay," Samantha murmured as she sopped a piece of sushi in soy sauce with her chopsticks and brought it up to her mouth. "Sushi is my favorite food of all time—other than my grandma's home cooking, of course."

"Where are you from?" Jonathan asked.

Samantha popped the sushi into her mouth and chewed thoughtfully. Once she swallowed, she replied, "I'm from Southlake, right here in Texas. I was born and raised in Texas."

"I'm from Texas, too," Jonathan said. "I grew up in Katy."

"The only time I've been out of Southlake was to come here to Waco for school. What's Katy like?"

"It's a big football town." Jonathan's gaze shift uneasily as his thoughts returned to his time as a Katy Tiger. "You said your brother plays football?"

"Yeah," Samantha said as she reached for another piece of sushi. "His name's Steven. He's a junior in high school."

Jonathan paused in his inquiries for a second, struggling to get a potsticker to stay on his chopsticks. He wasn't familiar with chopsticks and was having trouble getting each potsticker from the bowl to his mouth. He finally got one on the chopsticks, but as he brought it up to his mouth with a shaky hand, it fell onto the table. With a sigh, he continued asking Samantha about her life. "Is he your only sibling?"

Samantha frowned when Jonathan asked that. She didn't like talking about her older sister because everyone always talked about Scarlett when Samantha was growing up. Scarlett was the picture-perfect southern belle whom everyone admired. She got everything handed to her because of her natural beauty and charm while Samantha had to constantly try to achieve things to prove her worth. Scarlett was talked about enough.

"No. I've got an older sister. Her name's Scarlett."

"Do you get along with Scarlett and Steven?"

"I get along with Steven," Samantha said between bites of sushi, "but Scarlett's in her own world. I guess we get along, but she's really girly and pretty and successful and my mom's favorite and everything. She's a bigwig advertising executive, and—like my mom—a beauty pageant winner. When we were growing up, all the guys wanted to marry her, and all the girls wanted to be her friend."

Samantha fidgeted with her chopsticks as she spoke. "I guess I live in her shadow more than I get along with her. My mom thinks I live in her shadow, too."

"You can't be living in her shadow," Jonathan insisted. "You're beautiful, you're going to be successful, and—"

"Please," Samantha interrupted, as her cheeks turned beet red. Being called beautiful always embarrassed her. Jonathan caught her off guard. She wasn't sure how she felt about him saying it other than embarrassed, so she quickly changed the subject.

"Let's talk about your family. Do you have any siblings?"

Jonathan flinched. "I did," he said with downcast eyes. "Not anymore, though."

Samantha immediately felt guilty for asking the question. "I'm so sorry, I didn't know—"

"It's okay," Jonathan said. "I had a little sister. Her name was Gabby."

Samantha felt even more guilty for asking the question when she noticed his demeanor changing. Talking about Gabby was clearly painful for him. Samantha didn't want to ask what happened to her and was starting to understand what

Rose McCalister had meant when she told Samantha Jonathan had been through a lot of trauma. What seemed like a minute of silence passed while Samantha tried to formulate a response.

"I got in a car accident with Gabby in the car," Jonathan continued, "because I was texting and driving like an idiot."

"That's why you got so angry with me when I was texting earlier," Samantha deduced. "I'm so sorry. I had no idea. I completely understand why you reacted the way you did."

That's what he meant when he mentioned the accident as we walked around the pond, she thought.

"No, I shouldn't have gotten so angry with you. I just get angry when I think about texting and driving because it reminds me that it's my fault Gabby's dead."

"It's not your fault, Jon." Samantha had no idea what else to say. "Accidents happen."

She reached across the table and grasped Jonathan's hand. He let her hold it.

"It is my fault," Jonathan repeated, with tears forming in his eyes. He had become a pro at keeping his tears in check, but right then it was particularly difficult. He was ashamed of himself to show weakness like that in front of Samantha. He didn't want to come across as weak. He wanted to impress her. With a deep breath, Jonathan stopped himself from crying. He looked up at Samantha, almost sniffling, expecting to see her looking at him with pity. Instead, she was looking at him with sympathy and compassion and holding on to his hand tight.

Jonathan cleared his throat and straightened his posture. "Look, I don't want to talk about it anymore. Just know I'm sorry for snapping at you."

"It's okay, Jon. I totally understand. You don't need to apologize."

Jonathan changed the subject.

"So what time is the race tomorrow? And what does Race for the Kids even mean? What kids are we racing for?"

"I'll be at your apartment at eight o'clock sharp," Samantha tried to sound as cheery as possible to cheer Jonathan up. "The race starts at nine, but we should be there at least fifteen minutes early, and it's about forty minutes from your place. Make sure you get some breakfast in you so you have energy."

Samantha let go of Jonathan's hand. "We're racing for kids at the local children's hospital. The race is a fundraiser for them."

"Oh," Jonathan said as he pushed his blond locks off of his face with the hand that Samantha had held. "Do you do these 5K charity events often?"

"Yeah," Samantha replied. "I've done a few. Helping kids get the medical attention they need means a lot to me. It's why I want to go to med school and become a pediatrician." Samantha picked up the last piece of sushi with her chopsticks and held it in front of her mouth. "What do you want to do? I saw Political Science books in your living room. Is that your major?" She popped the sushi into her mouth and chewed while awaiting Jonathan's response.

"Yeah. Political Science is my major," Jonathan said. "I want to become a lawyer but don't have a cool reason to like you do."

"You'll find a reason to be a lawyer. You'll find your purpose. God has a plan for everyone."

Jonathan was surprised to hear Samantha mention God. He had no idea she was religious. "I hope you're right," he replied.

CHAPTER 15

———— •·•●•●•·• ————

Jonathan couldn't get a good night's rest. He was too worked up with equal parts anxiety and excitement about the race. He had never competed in an actual race and had never used a racing chair. The racing chair looked like a tricycle, and the mechanics of it seemed totally different than the mechanics of his regular wheelchair. The only reason he was doing the race was to impress Samantha. He had developed a huge crush on her, and he wanted her to like him back. It was the first time he had felt this way about a girl since Lacey.

By sunrise, Jonathan had barely caught a wink of sleep. But as the sun began to rise, Jonathan opened the blinds on his window to enjoy the sunrise over the pond. For a few minutes, he just stared at the sun ascending into the sky and admired the orange, yellow, and blue colors reflecting off of the resplendent pond. The whole time, he could not get Samantha's encouragement off his mind. *God has a plan for everyone.* Those six words had stuck with him since Samantha said them. He wondered why God would have a plan for him to get in a horrible car accident that killed Gabby and took both of his legs. Wouldn't God want Gabby to live a long and fruitful life? Why would God take her? Wouldn't God have wanted him to achieve his full potential on the football field? Why would God rip his dreams away?

While he couldn't answer those questions, Jonathan left open the possibility that God had a plan. Maybe Dominic got into law school and resigned as his assistant because God's plan was for Jonathan and Samantha to meet. Jonathan decided it was hard to think there wasn't a God with a plan when the world was full of beautiful sunrises like the one he was enjoying at the moment.

It was now seven o'clock in the morning, and Jonathan had an hour to spare before Samantha would be knocking at his door. Samantha had told him to get breakfast before she arrived, so he put on a pair of sweatpants and a dry-fit shirt to be ready for the race and then rolled to the cafeteria to grab an omelet. The cafeteria was empty, so he ate quickly at a table in the corner and then returned to his apartment to wait for Samantha. As he waited, he pulled out his writing notebook and scribbled out some poetry about what he was feeling after pondering whether God had a plan for his life.

Like a wingless bird waiting to land,
Like an hourglass without any sand,
I'm a man who can race but cannot stand.

Immediately after he wrote *cannot stand*, Samantha knocked on his door. "Coming!" He shut the notebook in the cabinet, locked it, and opened the door to see a smiling Samantha wearing black leggings, yellow tank top, and yellow headband.

"Are you ready?" she asked excitedly.

"Yeah," Jonathan said. "Let's do this."

The pair headed out to the student parking lot, got in the van, and began the long drive to the race.

"You don't need to hang back with me and match my pace," Jonathan said as they drove along the highway. "I'll just slow you down."

"That's nonsense," Samantha said. "I'm wearing yellow to match you as we race, anyway. So, you've got no choice. We're a team, and I'm going to be next to you, even if it means I have to sprint the whole time."

"Trust me," Jonathan replied, "you won't have to sprint. You probably won't even break a sweat."

"I saw you in the hallway, after your final, when we were going to get you signed up for the race. You were fast. Why do you think you'll be so slow? Have some faith in yourself."

Jonathan knew she was right. On his races to the gym, he went faster than he did when he was rushing down the hallway with Samantha. He'd probably be able to keep up with all the other runners, but he didn't want to embarrass himself if he couldn't. He wanted to set Samantha's expectations low so she'd be impressed when he did keep up.

A few minutes of silence passed between them when Jonathan asked a question that had been on his mind since the day before. "So, who's Dean Pilling?"

"Dean? He's a friend. Well, sort of a friend. He's more of a study buddy. He's in a study group with me and Kylie. How do you know about Dean?"

"I saw him on the list when I signed up for the race. He was up top, below you and Kylie, and whoever wrote his name also wrote your name and Kylie's. It was the same handwriting. I assumed he was a friend of yours, and you all signed up together. I'm guessing I'll meet him at the race?"

"Yeah," Samantha said. "You'll see him there."

Jonathan wasn't the only one racing to impress Samantha, apparently. Dean Pilling was, too. During their latest study group session, Dean overheard Samantha talking with Kylie about Jonathan. Samantha told Kylie that after getting to know Jonathan, she thought he was really sweet and invited him to the race. Kylie said she really wanted to meet Jonathan. Dean interrupted by pretending to care about the cause the race supported and asked if he could join them. They readily agreed, thinking he really did care about the kids. But the truth is Dean became jealous listening to Samantha talking about Jonathan and had different intentions.

For the rest of the ride, Jonathan and Samantha didn't talk much. Jonathan put on the radio and switched to the country station, and Samantha immediately sang along. Jonathan laughed as Samantha sang each song without missing a single word, as if she had written the songs herself. Jonathan loved country, too, and also knew the lyrics to most of the songs. But he didn't have the confidence to sing along. Samantha wasn't the best singer but was having fun with it, and Jonathan liked that. He liked that she didn't care about being off-key. Time went by fast as Samantha belted out song after song and Jonathan laughed along. When they arrived at the race, Samantha had pretty much lost her voice from all the singing.

Jonathan was surprised at how many people were there. A huge crowd was congregated under a big banner that read "Race for the Kids 5K." Most of them were in athletic wear with a white piece of paper with a number on it stuck to their torso. Others were in normal everyday clothes, clearly there just to watch. Jonathan had seen how long the list of names was when he signed up, but there seemed to be more people racing than there had been on the list. There were lots of kids, too.

"Are those kids from the hospital?" he asked Samantha.

"Some of them are," she answered. "The vast majority of the kids are too sick to leave the hospital, but those who are well enough are allowed to attend or even participate in the race. Most of the kids here are siblings of the kids in the hospital."

It wasn't hard to find parking. All the handicap spots were empty, which made Jonathan nervous. He would be the only person racing in a wheelchair. But he was committed to race, so he just kept his anxiety to himself. Once they parked, Samantha pulled out her phone and called Kylie.

"Hey," Samantha said when Kylie picked up. "Where are you and Dean?"

"We're by the starting line," Kylie replied. "It's under the big arch made of red and white balloons."

"Okay, we just got here. We'll see you soon."

Samantha pressed the button to lower the ramp and grabbed the racing chair as Jonathan rolled down the ramp and onto the pavement. Jonathan felt frustrated that Samantha had to carry the racing chair for him. He didn't want Dean and Kylie to think he made her carry it, but he couldn't wheel himself and carry the racing chair.

After a few minutes, Samantha and Jonathan found Kylie and Dean. Dean was standing next to Kylie wearing a haughty smirk as he glared at Jonathan through a pair of orange sunglasses. Samantha put the chair down and started to help Jonathan into it when Dean cracked a joke.

"Well, Samantha, it looks like you're going to have to work double to help Jonathan once you finish the race. Three miles in a wheelchair? He probably won't be able to do much for himself after that. Good luck."

If I could stand, I would punch you in your arrogant face.

Kylie gasped. "Shut up, Dean," she said as she smacked his chest with the back of her hand. "Don't listen to him, Jonathan. He's just mad because under all that scruff, you're better looking than him." She smiled at Samantha. "I can see why Samantha wants to spend so much time with you."

Jonathan smiled at Kylie's words, happy to hear that she approved of Jonathan. But he was still upset about what Dean said. He already didn't like him. "Nice to meet you, Kylie," he replied. He didn't even acknowledge Dean. He pretended to not care, but he was pretty bummed out and more than a little embarrassed. Samantha helped him into his racing chair and strapped him in.

A high-pitched voice sounded from behind Jonathan as he scooted around in his chair to get comfy. "Hey, can I try riding in that?"

Jonathan turned around and saw a little boy looking at Jonathan in his racing wheelchair as if it were a Ferrari. "I don't know if you'll fit in this one," Jonathan replied gently. "They set the size for an adult. But you can try my other wheelchair." The kid looked crestfallen. "I'm sorry, buddy. What's your name?"

The kid shuffled his feet shyly. "Diego. My name's Diego."

"How about you stand on the back of my wheelchair during the race, Diego?" Jonathan suggested. "We'll race as a team!"

Diego's eyes began to shine again. "Yes, please!" He jumped up and down excitedly.

Samantha felt a wave of affection for Jonathan at that moment. He had been the bigger man to Dean by not reacting and just made Diego's day by inviting him to stand on his wheelchair. She became even more excited when she found out that Diego was a patient at the children's hospital.

"Who are you racing for, Diego?" Samantha asked.

Diego went back to shuffling his feet shyly. "I'm racing for myself. And my friends at the hospital. I've been getting better, but the doctors say my friends are still going to be there for a long time."

"We can all race together," Samantha said warmly. "For you and your friends! How does that sound?"

Dean looked on with envy. Jonathan had impressed Samantha, clearly, and he looked like the bad guy.

Suddenly, a voice called out through a megaphone. "Ladies, gentlemen, and children, the Race for the Kids 5K is about to start! Everyone get to the starting line!"

"That's Meghna Angadi," Samantha explained to Jonathan. "She organizes all the events Kylie and I go to. She's awesome. She does lots of charity."

The racing chair felt awkward, but Jonathan was surprised by how fast it moved with the third wheel. It just felt weird because he was no longer sitting upright. In the racing chair, the rider had to hunch forward to grab a set of handles. Jonathan, being as athletic as he was, though, wouldn't have much trouble getting used to it. He was eager for the race to begin. Jonathan, Samantha, Kylie, Dean, and Diego all made their way to the starting line and situated themselves at the back of the crowd.

Diego was hitched on the back of Jonathan's chair. Jonathan was a little bit worried about having the extra weight of Diego on his chair, but he was determined to prove Dean wrong. He *would* complete this race, no matter what. And no matter how tired he was, he'd take care of himself after the race, too.

As they waited for the race to begin, Jonathan fidgeted with the handles of his wheelchair. As he moved them left and right, the front wheel followed. He hoped that the racing wouldn't be any more complicated than pushing the wheels and steering with the handles to turn. He didn't expect to be doing the race with a racing chair in the first place. He had envisioned he'd just be using his regular wheelchair.

With every second that passed before the race started, Jonathan began to doubt more and more whether it was a good idea to use the racing chair. He was unfamiliar with it and felt as though the likelihood of messing up was multiplied by using it. The last thing he wanted to do was mess up and crash in his wheelchair. He wouldn't just embarrass himself in front of Samantha. He'd also embarrass himself in front of Kylie, Dean, and all of the spectators. Even worse, he would probably hurt Diego, too.

Meghna Angadi's voice came over the buzz of the crowd gathered at the starting line again. The crowd came to a hush as she spoke the words they had all been waiting for. "On your marks! Get set! GO!"

"Let's do this!" Diego shouted from behind Jonathan's shoulders. Jonathan pushed with his arms as hard as he could to get moving. The wheelchair started to gain speed. At the same time, Samantha started jogging to match his pace. Kylie and Dean fell in right behind them.

Jonathan knew he wasn't going as fast as he could. He was only putting in half the effort as he did with his regular wheelchair and was going twice the speed.

Adrenaline started kicking in, and he wondered how fast he could go in an all-out push. But he didn't want to go faster for three reasons. He didn't want to leave Samantha behind. He didn't want to crash. And he wanted to pace himself so he could finish the race and prove Dean wrong. All three of these reasons were compromised when Diego began to demand for Jonathan to go faster.

"Faster! Faster!" Diego ordered between giggles of joy.

Jonathan pushed on the wheels faster and faster until they were passing person after person, eventually making it to the front of the pack with the crowd cheering on from the sides. He didn't go so fast that he left Samantha, Kylie, and Dean in the dust. He made sure he kept a pace at least Samantha and Kylie could keep up with. He didn't want to lose them in the crowd and also didn't want to come across as a show-off, although he was committed to finishing ahead of Dean. Participants and spectators cheered louder and louder as a jubilant Diego looked like a Roman on a chariot ushering his horse forward. Other kids ran out to the wheelchair as they saw it approach.

"Can I get a ride?" A ginger-haired boy with freckles asked as he panted alongside the pair trying to keep up.

"Sure," Diego replied. Jonathan came to a stop. Diego hopped off, and the ginger-haired boy mounted the back of the wheelchair. The boy threw his hands in the air and cheered gleefully as Jonathan picked up speed. Samantha and Kylie exchanged a look of adoration as Dean hid his envious stare under his sunglasses.

"Go, Jon, go!" Samantha called out as he sped forward.

For the remainder of the race, Jonathan stayed in the moment, forgetting about his fears of not being able to keep up with others or impress Samantha. It was perhaps the first moment of pure joy he experienced since the accident.

Samantha and Kylie laughed and cheered him on the entire race while Dean trotted behind the extravaganza sulkily with his head down. Kid after kid took turns hitching a ride while parents and spectators snapped pictures and rooted loudly for Jonathan.

As she laughed along with the kids riding with Jonathan, Samantha's thoughts went back to how embarrassed she was when Jonathan called her beautiful the day before. At the time, she didn't know how to react. Watching him enjoy himself as he brought joy to so many kids and spectators made her feel warm with affection for Jonathan. She had never felt that way about a boy before. She had crushes before and thought boys were cute. But this was different. This felt deeper. She wondered whether this was what love might feel like.

When they reached the finish line, they weren't nearly at the front of the race. All those starts and stops to give kids rides slowed them down quite a bit. In fact, they were amongst the last finishers. But Jonathan felt like a winner for the first time in a long time. He was surrounded by a posse of kids with Samantha, Kylie, and Dean in tow. The crowd gathered at the finish line and applauded as all the kids approached the finish line, together, with Jonathan and his wheelchair right in front of them, leading the way. Diego returned to the back of the wheelchair as he crossed the finish line. Once they crossed the finish line, the kids surrounded Jonathan, each smiling and cheering and asking for a high-five. Meghna Angadi emerged from the assembly and approached Jonathan as he gave a high-five to each kid.

"Hi," Meghna said. "I'm Meghna Angadi. I organize charity events and organized this race. I just want to commend you for being such an inspiration to both the kids and the adults who came. I've never seen such joy in these kids' faces before. Thanks to you, this will go down as the most memorable race to date."

"Thank you," Jonathan replied as Samantha came up behind him and placed her hand on his shoulder. She was beaming with pride. "I'm just here for the kids," he replied. While that was partially true, Jonathan failed to mention that his main motivation was impressing Samantha.

"I was wondering if you'd like to speak at one of my charity events," Meghna asked. "I'm organizing an event to celebrate unlikely heroes."

"I'm sorry, Meghna," Jonathan said. "But I've got to politely decline. I'm a horrible speaker." In truth, Jonathan didn't feel like a hero and didn't want that type of attention. Ever since the accident, the last thing he wanted was attention.

"Okay. If you ever change your mind, here's my card."

Jonathan accepted the card and she walked away. He turned to Samantha. "I'm glad you asked me to come. It was a lot of fun."

"I'm glad you came," Samantha replied. "You made those kids so happy. It made me really happy to see them so happy."

"Yeah that was awesome, Jon," Kylie said. "They loved you." Dean stood about ten feet away from them looking down at his phone.

"Thanks, Kylie. It was nice to meet you."

"It was nice to meet you, too," Kylie responded, adding in a hushed whisper, "Sorry about Dean. I don't know what his deal is today. He's usually not like that."

"It is what it is," Jonathan replied.

"We should get going, Kylie," Samantha said. "We need to return the racing chair and gear by noon."

"Okay, Sam, I'll see you later. Bye, Jon." Kylie smiled at Jon and then turned around to talk to Dean.

Samantha helped Jonathan into his regular wheelchair and they went to the van. Jonathan was exhausted and didn't say much. He just rested his head on the window and stared at Samantha while she drove to the store. His eyelids grew heavy as he admired her beauty.

Samantha's heart was fluttering. She was well aware that Jonathan was watching her with a dreamy gaze but couldn't summon the courage to look back at him and smile. She knew it would be obvious that she was falling in love. She wasn't ready for that, so she pretended to be unaware that Jonathan was gazing at her and kept her eyes on the road.

CHAPTER 16

———————— ··•••●•••·· ————————

"Why do we put them in this stuff?" Samantha asked Kylie as they rolled live mealworms around in a calcium and Vitamin D3 powder.

"It helps prevent metabolic bone disease," Kylie answered. "If Larry and Sandra only eat insects and plants, they'll have an imbalance in the levels of calcium and Vitamin D in their bodies. That will lead to metabolic bone disease. Since we only feed them mealworms and crickets, they don't get much calcium and Vitamin D. So, we roll the insects in this powder, and Larry and Sandra get the calcium and Vitamin D they need."

"Oh."

It had been a week since the race, and Samantha and Kylie were volunteering at Dr. Johanssen's zoology lab again. Larry and Sandra were Leopard Geckos they took care of.

"These things are gross," Samantha said as she dropped mealworms into Larry's cage.

"You've got that right," Kylie replied as she dropped a few mealworms into Sandra's cage.

"So, you've been hanging out with Jonathan a lot lately," Kylie said with a suggestive tone as the two moved on to clean the lab mice cages.

"Yeah, I mean I have to. It's my job."

Samantha sighed dreamily as she thought of him. She picked up Mickey, one of the lab mice, by the loose skin at the back of his neck, and placed him in a temporary cage. "It's pretty cool, though. It doesn't really feel like work. I really like spending time with him. He's really sweet. And it's a great opportunity for me."

Kylie raised an eyebrow as she picked up the other two lab mice, Tom and Jerry, and placed them in temporary cages. "He's really sweet? You like spending time with him? Ooh la la, Sam . . ." Kylie smiled and nudged Samantha with her elbow, "I think somebody has a crush."

Samantha turned red in the cheeks as she dumped wood shavings into Larry's clean cage. "I haven't had a crush on a boy in years. I barely know him. I mean, I know a little bit about him. But he's been through so much, and I have only seen the tip of the iceberg. He hasn't told me his whole story. I don't know how he lost his legs, or what his family is like, or anything like that. He's so mysterious."

"You've got to admit he's handsome under all that scruff," Kylie giggled. "I need a job as a hot guy's assistant!"

"Yeah, he's cute," Samantha admitted, turning redder by the second. "But he needs a haircut, a shave, and some new clothes. I want to be the one to help get him out of his shell. I don't know why. I just want to get him to really reach his full potential. I had to coax him into doing the race and meeting you, and look how awesome that turned out for him and the kids. He's got so much potential but is so secluded, and I don't know why. I don't know what his hobbies are other than playing video games and going to the gym."

"You should get to know him more and then—" Kylie grabbed Samantha's hand, noticing she was installing the water bottle improperly. Kylie grabbed the bottle Samantha had installed improperly. "Come on, Sam," Kylie said gently. "You're thinking about him, aren't you?"

"A bit," Samantha admitted. "A lot, actually. I think I do have feelings for him."

"Aw, young love," Kylie jested as she installed the bottle the right way. "He seems like a good guy. I approve of your crush."

* * *

While Samantha and Kylie were feeding the geckos and cleaning the cages, Jonathan was working out as Tom and Elijah were going over Elijah's performance in the scrimmages so far. The scrimmages happened once a week. Instead of a regular practice, the second-string offense played the second-string defense. Tom and Jonathan had just watched the latest scrimmage video, and Tom was offering advice to Elijah on what he could improve. Elijah was expressing his frustration with the play calling Tom had recommended. Jonathan was a few feet away doing shoulder presses.

"I feel like I'm not a good pocket passer," Elijah said. "This offense just doesn't feel right for me. The plays are all about planting your feet and throwing the ball. I'm more of a scrambler."

"An Air Raid offense is all about passing, Elijah," Tom argued. "That's why it's called an 'Air Raid' offense."

"Can't we choose plays where I can run the ball?"

"Elijah—"

Jonathan piped in to the surprise of both Tom and Elijah. They thought he wasn't paying attention. "To be fair, Tom, that's not a bad idea. Most of the big plays involving Elijah are a result of Elijah improvising and scrambling until someone gets open down the field. I think it'd be wise if you allow Elijah to use his athleticism in a pistol formation and read options."

Both Elijah and Tom went silent for a few moments. Tom nodded his head approvingly as he thought more about Jonathan's suggestion.

"What's a pistol formation?" Elijah asked.

"You don't know what a pistol formation is!?" Tom was astonished. "Don't you ever listen to me when we're going over the playbook?"

"We never did pistol formations in Madden," Elijah pointed out defensively. "And you know I can't focus when we go over that boring playbook."

"Calm down, you two," Jonathan said. "The pistol formation has the quarterback lined up four yards behind the center, rather than the seven-yard setback in a traditional shotgun formation. The running back then lines up three yards directly behind the quarterback. That's different from the normal shotgun where they are beside each other. The advantage with the pistol is the quarterback is close enough to the line of scrimmage to be able to read the defense but far enough back to give him extra time and a better vision of the field for passing plays. So it's very versatile, particularly if the quarterback is a threat to run the ball. It makes it tough for the defense to anticipate the play. The flexibility is enhanced by the read option."

"The pistol gives quarterbacks who are good on their feet the best of both worlds," Tom added. "You have the extra time and protection of a shotgun formation plus the running back spacing of an I-formation."

"Oh, okay, I like the sound of that," Elijah said. "What's a read option?"

"A read option is all about reading the defensive end," Jonathan explained. "If the defensive end is lined up outside of the offensive tackle, you hand it off to your running back—who will be right next to you, 'cause you'll be in the shotgun formation. If the defensive end is lined up inside of the offensive tackle—or if they chase after your running back when you go for the handoff—you fake the handoff and run it yourself."

"How do you have so much knowledge about football, Jonathan?" Elijah asked. "It's impressive. There's no way you know all that from Madden."

"He knows so much because he actually listens to me whenever I teach him the playbook," Tom said, sassily. He didn't want to blow Jonathan's cover. Dominic had warned Tom that Jonathan doesn't like to reminisce about his days as a football star before the accident.

"How about this, Elijah," Jonathan said. "I'll tell you how I know so much about football if you finish this year with more touchdowns and fewer interceptions than you did during your senior year of high school."

Elijah was intrigued. "Deal," he said. "Let's shake on it."

Jonathan and Elijah shook hands and the three continued working out. Tom and Elijah stopped bickering about play calling and decided they would take Jonathan's advice and incorporate a pistol formation and read options into the next scrimmage. "We'll see how it plays out," Tom told Elijah as he spotted him on the bench press. "Remember to exhale when you push up, and inhale when you bring it back down to your chest."

After about an hour, the three finished working out.

"You guys want to come over and play Madden?" Jonathan asked. "We could talk about how to incorporate the pistol and read options into your game, Elijah, and get you familiar with them."

"I'm down," said Tom.

"I can't, man, I'm sorry. I've got a party to go to. It's a football team party," Elijah replied. "You guys can come if you want."

"How would I get into a party?" Jonathan joked. "I can't even get through the door unless you guys pick my wheelchair up and carry me."

"Oh, true," Elijah said. "I'll pick you up!"

"I'm just joking, man. I don't really party."

"Me neither," said Tom. "We'll catch you later."

Elijah went to take a shower as Jonathan and Tom made their way back to Jonathan's apartment to hang out.

Jonathan was lost in thought, thinking back to the night before. Jonathan stared at himself in the mirror for at least ten minutes wondering how he had let himself get to the point where his hair went down to his shoulders, he had an unkempt beard, and dressed in sweatpants and T-shirts every day. He thought about the spiel Professor Hoffpower gave him about being handsome and smart but not looking the part. Now that Samantha was in the picture, Jonathan began to care about his appearance. He wanted to get a haircut and new clothes to impress her. He wanted her to think he was handsome.

His self-pity party was interrupted by his phone ringing. It was his mom. "I really like Samantha, Mom," he confided in her. "But I don't think she'll ever like me back if I don't clean myself up."

Rose was ecstatic to hear Jonathan wanted to clean himself up and dress better. Jonathan had been grungy for years. Hearing he not only wanted to clean himself up but was also romantically interested in Samantha meant the world to Rose. She was happy he was finally taking strides to get out of his rut and resume living a normal life.

"That's wonderful, Jonathan. I like Samantha, too. Get whatever clothes you need. I'll pay every dime. I think it's a great idea."

Jonathan envied Tom's fashionable clothes and clean haircut. He looked sharp and presentable while Jonathan was a mess.

"Yo, Tom," Jonathan said. "Where do you get your hair cut?"

Tom laughed. "You thinking of cutting off the mane, or just a trim?"

"I, uh, I guess I want to cut off the mane, jerk."

"What for? I've never seen you with short hair. And I've rarely seen you with no beard. You ditching both of those?" Tom stopped in his tracks and looked over at Jonathan. He had a sudden revelation. "It's that Samantha girl, isn't it?"

"No, man, I just want to get my hair cut short and shave my beard. It's getting really hot. It's much easier for working out, too."

"Dude, you and Dominic worked out for two years straight, and you never cut your hair short. Dominic literally tried every day to get you to cut your hair. I don't believe that. It's that new assistant of yours, isn't it? You're trying to impress her, aren't you?"

Jonathan sighed. "Yeah. I'm trying to impress her, jerk. But please don't make a big deal out of this. Please don't say anything. I'm sure she doesn't feel the same way, but I know she'll never be into me if I look like this."

Tom immediately realized how important it was for him to support Jonathan.

"Well, let's get you new clothes, too, then. Let's grab your van and head into Waco Center. I know where you can get your mane cut and buy some clothes to look real sharp."

"Alright. We'll need to stop by my apartment to grab my keys."

The two of them headed to Jonathan's apartment, grabbed his keys, and headed over to Jonathan's van.

"How do I get you in, man?" Tom asked as they approached the van.

Jonathan tossed him the keys. "Press that button on the bottom of the key fob. It'll lower a ramp for me."

Tom pressed the button, Jonathan got in the van, and Tom hopped in the driver's seat. Together they went to Waco Center to get Jonathan a haircut and some new clothes.

* * *

Waco Center was bustling with activity. It was a Friday night, after all. Most of the people roaming about were students from Central Texas University. The university was right outside Waco Center so, naturally, all of the college students flocked to the bars, restaurants, and live concert venues. It was the first time he had seen what the nightlife was like. He could feel energy in the air.

"A lot of students go into town at night, huh?" Jonathan asked as Tom drove slowly, careful not to hit one of the many students who were stumbling into the middle of the road without warning.

"Yeah, it's a real college town," Tom replied. "But they're all here for bars, restaurants, or concerts. The shops shouldn't be too packed, and I doubt many people are getting a haircut right now. We won't have any trouble. We'll be in and out before you know it."

"What shops are we going to?"

"We're gonna go to J Crew and Banana Republic. But let's hit the barbershop first and get that mane dealt with."

Tom drove over to a hole-in-the-wall barbershop with no sign. The only indication that it was a barbershop was a red neon "OPEN" sign and a spinning red, white, and blue barber pole next to the door.

"This is where I get my hair cut," Tom explained. "No one really knows about it, but I've been going here for years. It's cheap, and the guy who owns it cuts hair like a pro."

"Hey, Dan," Tom said as they entered the store. "Dan's the owner of the shop," Tom explained to Jonathan.

Dan was a tall, lanky man with a thick afro and chocolate skin. He was all alone in the shop sitting on a stool behind the counter. He smiled as Tom spoke his name.

"Hey there, Tom. Uh-oh," he joked. "Are you unhappy with the haircut I gave you last week?"

"Yeah. I want a refund," Tom joked back.

"No can do, sir." Dan walked up and gave Tom a half hug. "I'm guessing your buddy here wants me to clean up that mop on his head?"

"Yes sir," Tom replied. "He wants to look extra handsome for a special lady."

Dan had Jonathan wheel up to a mirror and started snipping off his long, blond, wavy locks in bunches. Jonathan's hair fell to the floor in clumps. When it was short enough, Dan began to buzz the back and the sides. He then stylized the top, making small snips here and there, worked some gel, and tousled it around until it was just right.

"Look at that handsome face," Tom jeered. "I never thought I'd see your forehead. Now, let's see what's under that beard, Dan!"

Dan took an electric razor and went over Jonathan's beard like he was mowing a lawn. He went up and down all across Jonathan's face. Once it was short enough to use a straight razor, Dan worked in some warm shaving cream and ran the razor across his stubble until Jonathan's beard was completely gone. Jonathan had a clean crew cut and a clean-shaven face. He looked like a different man. He itched with all of the hair that had fallen into his shirt.

Jonathan smiled at the sight of himself for the first time in years. He felt handsome. And hopeful.

"Let's get me some new clothes," Jonathan said as he petted his face and ran his fingers through his hair while looking in the mirror. "This shirt is itchy. Thanks, Dan. How much do I owe you?"

"Twenty bucks should do it," Dan replied.

Jonathan pulled a twenty-dollar bill and a five-dollar bill out of his wallet and handed them to Dan.

"Alright, then," Tom said. "Off to the stores. Thanks, Dan, I'll see you soon."

Dan waved as Tom and Jonathan left the shop. The drive to the mall wasn't long, only about five minutes. After parking, they headed in. The mall was a stark contrast to the barbershop. It was bustling. People of all sorts walked around, popped in and out of shops, and ate in the food court.

"Want to grab some dinner?" Jonathan asked as he eyed the food court.

"Yeah, but not here," Tom replied. "I know a spot in town that'll blow your mind. You'll love it. And it's a great place to take a date. That should come in handy once Samantha sees your new look," he said with a sly smile. "We'll be quick. J Crew and Banana Republic are around the corner, right next to each other."

The two made their way to the stores. They went into J Crew first. Jonathan enjoyed trying on new clothes in the changing room. Looking in the mirror with a fresh haircut, clean chin, and sharp clothes made Jonathan feel a whole lot better than he felt the night before when he was looking at himself in the mirror. He found a few outfits he liked. He brought them up to the counter and paid for them. They went into Banana Republic next and did the same. By the time they were done, Jonathan had nearly five-hundred dollars in clothes he could mix and match for the rest of the semester.

"Let's get some grub," Jonathan said as he wheeled along with a bunch of bags of clothes on his lap. "I'm starving. What's that place you mentioned like?"

"It's called Vitek's. They got something there called The Gut Pak. You'll love it."

Jonathan and Tom hopped in the van and drove over to Vitek's. As they pulled in, Jonathan noticed a white sign next with a red and black logo that read

"Vitek's BBQ." Under the name of the restaurant were the words "Family Owned and Operated Since 1915" stamped in black letters.

"Nice. Texas BBQ is my favorite," Jonathan said as they pulled into the only empty parking space left in the tiny parking lot in front of the restaurant.

"Then you're in for a treat," Tom replied.

They got out of the van and headed in. Jonathan grabbed a table while Tom went up to the counter and got two orders of The Gut Pak, an infamous and decadent pile of corn chips, cheddar cheese, hand-chopped brisket, sausage, beans, pickles, onions, jalapeños, and two slices of bread.

"Thanks for everything today, Tom," Jonathan said. "I appreciate you helping me out."

"Listen man," Tom joked. "I'm just happy you got that mane cut off. It's been too long. You looked like you belonged in a lion pride. Now you look almost classy! Samantha will be impressed. Make sure you don't stain your new shirt with BBQ sauce, though."

Jonathan chuckled. Silence passed between them for a few minutes as they both dug into their food.

"That was the bomb," Jonathan finally said as he scraped the remaining scraps off the bottom of the Styrofoam container The Gut Pak was served in. "I'm stuffed."

"Me too," Tom said. "Let's get back to your apartment."

Jonathan and Tom went back to campus and hung out in Jonathan's apartment for the rest of the night. Tom persuaded Jonathan to text Samantha asking if he could meet her after her study group the following day. She happily texted him back, saying she'd meet him outside the entrance of the library around noon.

After Tom left, Jonathan picked out an outfit to wear the next day and cleaned his room for the first time in months. He settled on wearing a crisp, plaid button-down shirt and a pair of nice blue jeans. He was going to look like a new man to Samantha. For the first time in years, he'd look like someone who was optimistic about the future and willing to work for a better life. But, most of all, Jonathan was going to do something he never expected to do in a million years. He was going to open up a side of his personality he had never before opened up to anyone. He never showed anyone this side of himself. Not Dominic, not Tom, and not even Rose. Only his dad had seen this side of him, and it had been years since they last talked.

Jonathan had wanted to open up to Samantha ever since they got dinner at the sushi restaurant. He couldn't wait anymore. He had already almost cried in front of her. He couldn't have been more vulnerable. And she didn't pity him. She was kind and accepting. He was sure she'd let him open up to her even more.

CHAPTER 17

— · · · ● ● ● ● · · · —

S amantha and Kylie were leaving the library after their study group meeting. Dean trailed behind them, seemingly trying to wedge himself in between them. But they purposely blocked that from happening by walking shoulder to shoulder. After the race, the two of them lost a lot of respect for Dean. They felt a lot of disdain for him after he treated Jonathan the way he did at the race.

"No," Samantha affirmed to Kylie. "No one knows what causes the phantom limb sensation." Kylie had asked Samantha whether Jonathan felt his legs as phantom limbs, a common experience of amputees where they continued to feel their limbs after amputation. Samantha didn't know if Jonathan had ever felt the sensation, but that wasn't the point. "It's a medical phenomenon," Samantha said. "There are only speculations."

"That doesn't mean that it doesn't happen," Kylie countered. "More than half of amputees report having felt the phantom limb sensation. I just read it in one of my textbooks an hour ago."

"That's not what I'm saying! I know that it happens. I'm just saying there's no explanation as to why it happens."

"They have speculations as to what causes it, though," Kylie said.

"I just said that! Aren't you listening?" The two continued to bicker as they walked out of the library. Samantha had completely forgotten she had agreed to meet Jonathan at the library entrance.

"Girls, girls," Dean said as he hustled up and stuck his hands in between their shoulders, again trying to wedge himself in between them. "Study time is over."

"Shut up, Dean!" They both said at the same time. Dean sighed and fell back in behind them as they walked out of the library.

"I'm just saying," Kylie continued. "There's a high probability that phantom limbs are the result of cortical remapping and—" She stopped dead in her tracks staring toward the stairs at the entrance of the library. She looked like she had just seen a ghost. "Wow!"

"What? What's wrong, Kylie?" Samantha followed her gaze and gasped. Waiting for her at the bottom of the stairs was Jonathan. He was wearing a brand-new plaid button-down shirt and a pair of nice blue jeans. Samantha was delighted to see him not wearing his usual sweatpants and T-shirt combo. She was also shocked that he had shaved his beard and cut his long, scraggly hair. He looked like an Abercrombie & Fitch model—a handsome, clean cut man with no facial hair. Butterflies fluttered in Samantha's chest. Her crush had gotten a whole lot bigger in just one moment. She was speechless.

"Is that you, Wheels?" Dean blurted out from behind the young women.

"Shut up, Dean!" Samantha and Kylie said at the same time, again.

The two girls stood there and stared at Jonathan for at least five seconds before Jonathan put his hand up and gave them a small wave. He had no idea why they were staring at him like he had two heads, and it made him uncomfortable. Samantha literally shook her head to snap out of her shock.

"I, uh," she said slowly, "I'll see you later, Kylie." She began to walk toward Jonathan. Kylie giggled as she watched her walk away. Dean shook his head in disbelief.

"Hi, Jon," Samantha said. She tilted her head down and pushed a wisp of hair behind her left ear. "You look . . . different."

Jonathan smiled. "Is that a good thing or a bad thing?"

"It's a good thing. You look . . ." She paused as the butterflies roared inside of her. She didn't want to come across too strongly, so she took her time and chose her words carefully. "You look sharp."

"Thanks, Sam," Jonathan replied. "I've got something else to show you."

"Ooh. What is it? I hate surprises."

"Too bad," Jonathan laughed. "It's a surprise. It's back at my apartment." He turned around and began to wheel away. He turned around to check if Samantha was following. She was still stuck in her tracks. "Come on!" He beckoned her to follow him. She tripped over herself a bit and walked after him, excited for whatever he had in store for her that afternoon.

* * *

"I can't take this," Samantha said as she and Jonathan traversed the hallway to his apartment. "I need to know what the surprise is!"

"We're almost there," Jonathan said.

Samantha broke into a jog and sped past Jonathan to open the door. She grabbed the handle and pushed, but it didn't budge.

"It's locked," Jonathan said with a chuckle. "You really want to see this surprise, huh? It seems to *me* that you *do* like surprises."

"I really don't, and the suspense is killing me!" Samantha stood by the door impatiently as Jonathan purposely took his time wheeling up to it. "You already surprised me enough for one day with that fresh haircut and sharp outfit."

"Hey, I'm more than just a pretty face," Jonathan joked. "I've got brains, too."

"Very funny. Now open the door!" Samantha stamped her foot eagerly. Jonathan wheeled up, put the key in the lock, and twisted the handle open. Samantha barged through the door and looked around the living room. Jonathan had obviously tidied the place up. "Is the surprise that you cleaned your living room?"

"No," Jonathan replied. "That'd be a lame surprise."

"Then what is it!?" Samantha was looking around the room as if she'd find a big box with gift wrapping and a ribbon on it.

"Follow me." Samantha followed Jonathan as he wheeled himself into his room and over to the cabinet in the corner, where he kept his books and notebooks. He unlocked the cabinet, opened it up, and pulled out a book. "This is it," he said. "I've read this book a few times, and after you told me what you told me about your sister, I thought you'd relate to the narrator of the book."

Samantha took the book and read the title of it aloud. *"Pride and Prejudice."* She inspected it for a few moments and rubbed the cover gently. "I haven't read an actual book—other than textbooks for classes—in years." She looked up at Jonathan, who was fidgeting with his hands nervously.

"I think you'd like it, but, uh," Jonathan stammered, "if you don't like to read, I totally understand. I just thought you'd relate to the narrator. No hard feelings if you don't want it."

"No, it's lovely, Jon." Samantha smiled at Jonathan and hugged the book tightly against her chest. "It's a very thoughtful gift. I didn't know you read books, though," she said. "I thought you were more into video games and going to the gym."

Jonathan chuckled. "Well . . . there is more to me than the gym and video games."

"Why do you keep your books locked up in that cabinet? Are you ashamed of being a reader?"

"I don't know," Jonathan said. "It's kind of complicated. I don't really know, to be honest."

"I think it's important to be proud of who you are. A lot of guys are too afraid to admit they are deep. Too many guys pride themselves on their machismo but, to me, they come across as arrogant and obnoxious. I like guys who aren't afraid to show their sensitivity and emotional capacity. I like the guys I can talk with."

"You can talk to me." Jonathan was happy to see he could open up to Samantha.

"I know I can. You clearly listened to me when I talked to you about my sister at the sushi restaurant."

"I've been thinking a lot about our conversation, actually," Jonathan admitted. "I've been thinking a lot about what you said about God's plan, too. You said God has a plan for everybody."

"He does."

"Well, uh," Jonathan hesitated, but he didn't know why. It was clear Samantha liked guys with sensitivity and emotional capacity. She had just said so. But Jonathan was still uncomfortable opening up about God. He had never opened up about God to anybody before. "I've been writing about this in my journal. Sometimes it's hard for me to believe God has a plan for everyone when those plans can turn out to be so cruel."

"What do you mean by cruel?"

"Well, like, what about Gabby? Why would God take her life like that?"

"Everything happens for a reason, Jon. God truly has a specific plan for each of us. And I know you will make an impact on this world and honor Gabby's memory."

Samantha wanted to hold Jonathan's hand like she had at the sushi restaurant, but she was too shy. "Do you mind sharing some of your journal entries?"

"Yeah, I guess so."

Jonathan was sad to think about Gabby, but it felt good to get his thoughts about God's plan off his chest. Talking to Samantha felt good, as if he was confronting his feelings in a healthy way for once. He wheeled back to the cabinet, opened his writing notebook to the most recent entry, and began to read it to Samantha.

"Every day I think about that night.
The night that took Gabby's life has taken sleep away from me every night that followed.
If God has a plan for everyone, why did He plan for that night?
What sort of trial is He testing me with?
What did I do to deserve this?
Gabby didn't deserve to die.
She was the most bubbly, sweet, and innocent person to ever roam this world.
Did God just want her all to Himself?"

"Wow," Samantha murmured. "I wish I had met Gabby. She means a lot to you, huh?"

"Yeah. She would light up any room. She was the sweetest, most innocent little girl I've ever met. I don't understand why God would want to take her from me."

"Maybe God needed her," she suggested.

"Wouldn't that be selfish?"

"She's still with you, Jon, in spirit. Maybe God wanted her to come up to heaven so she could become your guardian angel."

"I wish I had died in that car accident and Gabby had lived. It's just not fair. God must work in mysterious ways."

"No one knows why God does what He does, Jon," Samantha said. She mustered up the courage to put her hand on his. "But there's no doubt in my mind He does what He does because He loves each and every one of us."

Silence passed between them as they held hands. Samantha tried to make eye contact with Jonathan, but he was staring out the window, across the lake, with a sorrowful gaze. "I just wish I could make sense of His plan," Jonathan said. "I wish I could understand."

"I wish I could understand, too," Samantha agreed. "That's why I go to Bible study every week. We read the Bible and try to understand God's will and His teachings."

Holding hands with Samantha made tingles shoot up Jonathan's spine. It felt good to hold her hand. It felt good to connect with her. He really liked spending time with Samantha. He thought, if he went to Bible study, he'd be able to spend more time with her. He wasn't sure if it would help him understand God's ways, but spending time with Samantha would make it worthwhile either way.

"Maybe I can come with you next time?"

"Are you sure?"

"Yes. I'm sure."

"Awesome. We meet tomorrow night."

Samantha was excited Jonathan agreed to go to Bible study.

The pair spent the rest of the afternoon relaxing in Jonathan's living room. Samantha sat on the couch and read *Pride and Prejudice* while Jonathan sat in his wheelchair and went over reading assignments for class. He couldn't help but daydream about her as he watched her reading the book so peacefully.

Just like in the ride back from the race, Samantha was well aware that Jonathan was staring at her and pretended not to notice. She just let the giddy feelings she was feeling for him dance around in her, again.

She really wasn't reading the book, either. She couldn't focus. She was beginning to like Jonathan more and more. Just as she had wanted, she *was* helping him heal and get out of his shell. She had gotten him to come to the race, and she had gotten him to agree to go to Bible study with her. And while she didn't know it was because of her, he had gotten new clothes, a haircut, and cleaned his apartment because of her as well. Jonathan also knew he was changing for the better because of Samantha.

Maybe God's plan was for me to meet Samantha after all. I wouldn't have done that if not for the accident.

After a few hours, Samantha headed home. Jonathan and Samantha made a plan to meet at his apartment the next night and go to Bible study together. Jonathan didn't know what his expectations were when it came to understanding God through Bible study, but he was glad to spend as much time with Samantha as he could.

CHAPTER 18

‒‒‒‒‒‒‒‒‒ •••●●●••• ‒‒‒‒‒‒‒‒‒

Jonathan was buttoning the last button on one of the shirts he bought to impress Samantha when he heard her rapping at his door.

"Just a second!" Jonathan fixed the collar and gave himself one last look in the mirror, making sure to gussy up his hair, which was still wet from showering. He then rushed over to the door and opened it. Samantha was hugging a Bible the same way she had hugged *Pride and Prejudice* when he gave it to her. She looked beautiful, wearing a teal sweater, a black skirt that went just above her knees, and black boots that went to just below her knees. Her hair was tied in a ponytail, and her bangs fell in curls over her eyebrows. Jonathan liked it when she wore her hair up in a ponytail, but he thought she was beautiful regardless of how she wore her hair. She never wore makeup, either, and Jonathan respected her confidence. She didn't need it. She was naturally beautiful. He stared at her for a minute with his mouth open before he realized he looked dumbfounded. "Hi," Jonathan said, trying to recover from gawking at her.

"Hi," Samantha chirped. "Are you ready?"

"Yeah. Should I grab my keys? Do we need to drive there?"

"No, it's on campus. It isn't far from here."

"Okay." Jonathan wheeled out the door and locked it behind him as Samantha turned and began to walk down the hall ahead of him. Jonathan sped up and fell in beside her as they made their way down the corridor together to go to Bible study. "I don't have a Bible," Jonathan said as he wheeled beside Samantha.

"You don't need a Bible," Samantha said. "There are usually printed packets there that have excerpts for the section we are studying each week. But"—Samantha stopped walking, reached into her purse, and pulled out another Bible—"I brought you one." She handed it to Jonathan. It was an ancient-looking tome with a leather cover that had the words "Holy Bible" inscribed across it. "It's my old Bible, from when I was younger. I thought it would be a worthy way to reciprocate the book you gave me." She smiled as he took it, spun around with her ponytail waving behind her like a tail, and continued to make her way to the courtyard.

"Oh. Okay. I appreciate it," Jonathan replied as she walked away. He put the Bible in his lap and followed after her. Samantha opened the door to the courtyard and held it for Jonathan. "Thanks," Jonathan said as he rolled through the doorway. Usually he picked up speed going down the ramp—to get to the gym faster when he timed himself. But he didn't speed down the ramp that time. He was curious about Bible study and had a few questions for Samantha he wanted to ask before they got there. So, he matched her pace, and the pair walked down the ramp side by side. "How many people are gonna be there?"

"It differs every time. There's a core group of eight or nine people who show up every Thursday, including me. But there are always some new people."

"Have you ever brought someone to Bible study before?"

"No. I always just go by myself. Kylie isn't religious."

"Don't you have other friends?"

"Not really. I don't have many close friends—other than Kylie—who I spend time with outside of class. Remember," Samantha joked, "I'm a total nerd."

"What about me?" Jonathan was only half-joking, but Samantha took him seriously.

"You're the exception." She smiled at him, still hugging her Bible as she walked.

Jonathan smiled back. He still had one more question to ask. "Who runs the Bible study?"

"Pastor Ana Broussard. You'll like her. She's really nice."

For the rest of the walk, they didn't exchange any more words. As Samantha said, the Bible study wasn't far from Jonathan's apartment. It only took five minutes to reach the building. It was a tall, gray chapel of a gothic design with a large wooden door. The spires seemed to touch the clouds. Samantha swung open the large wooden door and held it for Jonathan. He had been at Central Texas University for two years but had never been to the chapel. Jonathan looked around curiously as he entered. Spectacular stained-glass windows lined the walls and reached almost all the way up to the ceiling where large wooden beams held the roof above. "This is beautiful," Jonathan murmured.

"This is the Central Texas University Chapel," Samantha explained. "I come here every Sunday for church service and every Thursday for Bible study. Bible study is held downstairs. There's an elevator over there." She turned to her left and started walking toward a staircase. As she got closer, she pointed to the elevator, which was to the right of the staircase. She pressed the button to summon the elevator without turning to see whether Jonathan had followed. Jonathan was still inspecting every detail of the interior chapel. He was so mesmerized by the beauty of the church that he didn't notice when the elevator doors opened. "Come on, Jon! We're gonna be late!" Samantha's voice snapped Jonathan out of his trance. He jumped at her voice, surprised, and proceeded to the elevator where she was waiting and holding her finger on the button to keep the doors open.

"Sorry," Jonathan said. "It's just so breathtaking."

"Haven't you been in a church before?" Samantha asked as the elevator doors closed and they began their descent.

"Yeah," Jonathan said. "But it's been awhile. I haven't gone since the accident."

Samantha didn't press him. She didn't know when the accident was. She wanted to know but didn't want to dampen his mood right before Bible study. He was already thinking that the chapel was beautiful. Maybe he would open up to attending church if he had a good experience at Bible study. She didn't want Jonathan to think about the accident and get sad.

"Well, you're right," she agreed. "This chapel is beautiful." Silence passed between them as the elevator lowered to the basement. The doors opened, and Jonathan let Samantha exit first in an attempt to be a gentleman. He followed after her into a room directly across from the elevator. When she opened the door, the scene in front of Jonathan was different than what he had expected. There was no pastor standing at an altar and preaching the word of the Bible. Instead, the room was broken into multiple groups of students gathered around small round tables with open Bibles in front of them. Some students were highlighting passages on printed packets of paper. Others were reading aloud. Everyone seemed engaged. They all looked like they knew what they were doing. Jonathan felt nervous.

What if I stand out because I'm not familiar with the Bible?

Jonathan tentatively followed after Samantha as she walked directly toward a tall, sleek woman with braided hair and mocha-colored skin. She looked to be in her early thirties. The woman was smiling, talking with one of the groups, and pointing at a passage on the top of one of the printed packets of paper.

That must be Pastor Ana Broussard.

Jonathan came in earshot as she finished what she was saying. "Just because you haven't seen Jesus with your own eyes or in your dreams doesn't mean He isn't watching over you. You must keep your faith. Blessed are those who have not seen Jesus and still believe. Look, right here, on the top of the third page." Ana tapped the top of the paper. "Look at that passage. 'Jesus said to him, have you believed because you have seen me? Blessed are those who have not seen and yet have believed.'" The students nodded along and murmured amongst one another.

Samantha waited patiently behind Ana, and Jonathan looked around nervously until Ana turned around and saw Samantha. A brilliant smile lit up Ana's face. "Hi, Sam!" Ana hugged Samantha affectionately and then pulled her body away while keeping her arms on Samantha's arms. "How are you? It's nice to see you."

"I'm great, Pastor Broussard," Samantha said. "I brought someone with me." Samantha pulled away from Ana's embrace and stepped aside to reveal Jonathan who had been hiding behind her. "This is Jonathan."

Jonathan's throat was dry from nerves. He swallowed and stuck out his hand for a handshake. "Hi, Pastor Broussard," Jonathan said. "It's nice to meet you."

"The pleasure is mine, Jonathan," she replied. She shook his hand with one hand and put the other hand on top of their handshake gently. "Is this your first time at a Bible study?"

Jonathan was relieved to hear that she didn't expect him to be a seasoned student of the Bible.

"Yeah. I haven't been to church in years, actually."

"Well, we are happy to have you back," she said warmly. She released his hand. "We're studying the book of John today."

The book of what?

"Oh, okay," Jonathan said. "I, uh, I'm not sure I'm familiar with the book of John."

"Well, then, I hope you enjoy it. Please, take a seat over there." Ana pointed at a table in the corner of the room. "I'm just about to start." She handed Samantha two of the printed packets. On the packets were verses from the Bible with a short synopsis under each verse.

Jonathan and Samantha went to the table Ana had pointed at. Samantha moved two chairs out of the way for Jonathan to wheel up with his chair and sat down next to him. After they had situated themselves, they looked to see Ana watching them from a pedestal by the back wall. She nodded at them and rang a bell. Everyone in the room turned to look at her.

"Hello, students," she began. "Today, as you know, we are studying the book of John. I'll let you continue your conversations in a moment, but I would greatly appreciate it if you could spare me some time and attention to talk about a very valuable lesson we learn from the book of John." The whole room went silent as Ana looked around it with a sincere smile on her face.

"All of us would take great measures to preserve the well-being of our loved ones. Some of us would give away every penny we have. Some of us would even give away our kidney. Jesus took the greatest measure to preserve the well-being of all of us, for we are loved by Jesus and by God. It's important to remember that." Her powerful voice echoed throughout the room as she spoke. There was no need for any microphone. "Jesus and God love us. If you all flip to the first page of your packets, you'll see the first quote tells us exactly this."

The first quote was from John 3:16 (ESV). Ana read it aloud. "For God so loved the world, that He gave His only begotten Son, that whoever believes in Him shall not perish, but have eternal life.'" A few people moaned in agreement as she read the verse. "If we are to feel God's love, we must believe in Him. If we believe in Him, we will feel the warmth of His love, and we will live in the Lord's grace. We will have everlasting life."

Ana kept talking for a few minutes, referencing several verses, and then dismissed the students to carry on with their round-table discussions. Samantha talked to Jonathan about the verses printed on the packet, and Jonathan listened intently. The teachings got Jonathan to think that everything in life had a purpose, even though he still couldn't accept Gabby's death as necessary. But he started believing God had a plan for everybody, even if he couldn't yet understand what God's plan for Gabby and him could be.

Since the accident, Jonathan had taken pity on himself and thought he had no purpose in life. He considered himself an amputee going nowhere in life. For the first time since the accident, though, Jonathan began to believe that maybe someone like him does have a place in this world. That God had a plan for him after all. It's straight from the Bible. He just hadn't stopped to think about it that way before.

ACT IV

CHAPTER 19

—————— ··•●•·· ——————

As the fall semester progressed into November, Jonathan and Samantha steadily grew closer and closer. They spent most days together. They studied together. Every Thursday, the two went to Bible study together. They even went to Elijah's scrimmages together. Sam had become close with Elijah and Tom, too, over several weeks. She was excited to be acquainted with people other than Kylie. Doing so while getting Jonathan out of his shell made her feel good about herself. In truth, however, Jonathan was getting Samantha out of her shell, too.

Before one of Elijah's scrimmages, Jonathan was studying at his apartment waiting for Samantha to come by and head to the scrimmage with him. She was supposed to show up at six o'clock. It was already ten minutes after six. Samantha was never late, and Jonathan was slightly concerned. He was debating whether he should call her when a knock sounded at the door. Jonathan opened the door and, sure enough, Samantha was behind it. She looked different. She was wearing makeup and had curled her hair. She looked like she was going on a date. Jonathan thought that must have been why she was late. She never did her makeup or hair, so she must have mistimed it.

Is she trying to look good for me?

"Hi, Jon," Samantha said sweetly. She was wearing a yellow sunflower-print sundress that went down to just above her knees and beige heels. She looked stunning. Perfect.

"Hi, Sam," Jonathan said. He felt embarrassed that she looked so good and he was just wearing a V-neck and jeans. If he had known she was going to dress up, put on makeup, and curl her hair, he would have put a little more effort into his appearance.

"Are you ready to go?" she asked him.

"Yeah, let's go."

The two headed over to Jonathan's van and hopped in. The scrimmages were a few miles off campus.

The scrimmage was just about to start when they got there. In the middle of the field was the full roster of second-string players from the Stallions football team. Tom was engaged in a conversation with Elijah—surely going over the plays—and Elijah was nodding his head impatiently. He clearly wanted to stop going over the playbook and just start the scrimmage.

As Tom talked and Elijah nodded his head, the offense and the defense took the makeshift field and lined up. Jonathan and Samantha situated themselves on the sideline a safe distance away and waited for the scrimmage to start. Elijah broke away from Tom and jogged over to the field.

"I guarantee you the first play is going to be a read option," Jonathan said to Samantha. "I know Tom too well. You can tell he told Elijah to run a read option by how the defense is lined up. They're really heavy on the right side, and the defensive end is lined up inside the tackle. Elijah is going to fake a handoff to the right and then run around to the left himself. The cornerbacks are on man-to-man coverage, so they're going to chase the receivers away from Elijah. That will give him enough open space to run for at least fifteen yards."

Sure enough, Jonathan was right. Elijah snapped the ball and pretended to hand the ball off to the running back who ran into the right side of the offensive line through the tackle and the guard. The linebackers and defensive linemen all fell for the fake and rushed toward the running back, tackling him even though he didn't have the ball.

By the time the defense realized the running back didn't actually have the ball, Elijah was already running past the line of scrimmage into a wide-open space on the left side. As Jonathan predicted, the cornerbacks were chasing their receivers in case the fake handoff led to a play-action pass. No one was around to tackle

Elijah except for the safety, who was fifteen yards downfield. If Elijah could get past him, he'd run all the way to the end zone for a touchdown.

All eyes were on Elijah as the safety sprinted toward him and dove to try to take out his legs. Elijah hurdled over the safety with ease and ran into the end zone. It was a perfectly executed play.

"Whoo! Touchdown!" Samantha said gleefully. "You called that play perfectly, Jon!"

Jonathan got a warm feeling inside. It made him happy seeing Samantha having such a great time at a football game. And, for a brief moment, he was able to enjoy football without the painful memory of his past.

"Yeah," Jonathan said. "Elijah has a lot of potential. We just need to get him to know the playbook better and be able to understand defensive alignments so he can call his own plays. Tom can't tell him what plays to call once the actual season starts next year. That's up to Coach Gustaffson. And Elijah will have to know when to change the play at the line of scrimmage when he sees the defensive alignment. He will, though, once he gets a better grip on things."

"You called that play before it even happened. I'm impressed. How do you know so much about football?"

"I don't know." Jonathan smirked. "Katy was a big football town. I grew up watching it. And I go over the playbook with Tom all the time. We play Madden together, too, so I guess I've just learned a lot since he started coaching Elijah."

"You'd probably get along with my brother," Samantha said. "He's really into football, too."

"I bet."

Jonathan's moment of enjoying football without the painful memory of his past didn't last long. As he sat there with Samantha, he couldn't help but think of Gabby. He could almost see her wearing her cheerleader outfit, her eyes eagerly glued to the players on the field.

Samantha looked over at Jonathan and noticed that his gaze was distant and sorrowful. "Are you okay?" She asked.

"I don't know," Jonathan replied. It was unusual for him to be honest about his feelings to anyone, but he had become comfortable talking with Samantha. "I'm thinking about Gabby, to be honest."

Samantha turned her attention from the players on the field and looked at Jonathan with an expression of concern. "What's making you think of her?"

"She used to love watching football," Jonathan said. "She'd dress up in this cheerleader outfit she made herself and would cheer at the top of her lungs whenever anything exciting happened. That play with Elijah just now would have made her day. She'd be jumping up and down right now if she were here."

"She sounds like a beautiful soul."

"She was. Gabby was the type of person who would walk into a room and light it up with her presence . . . the type of person who made you want to become a better person."

"You're a good person, Jon. You don't need to be a better person." Samantha was pained to see Jonathan so hard on himself. "Just because she died in the accident doesn't mean you're a bad person. You've always been a really good guy with me. You're not like other guys. You're deep and thoughtful. You've been through so much yourself. You don't have to beat yourself up over it." Samantha was starting to grasp the magnitude of Jonathan's love for his lost sister. He clearly had a special bond with Gabby. Samantha could only begin to imagine how painful it must have been to lose her let alone consider himself the reason he lost her.

"Before I met you, I wasn't deep and thoughtful. I was apathetic and crushed. You have that same gift Gabby had. You make me want to be a better person. I've been bitter and resentful these past five years. I didn't care about God. I thought He was cruel. I almost hated Him. You've made me see things in a new light. A better light. So, I'm not sure I can take much of the credit for the way I've been around you. You made that happen."

"That means a lot, Jon. But I think anyone would be bitter and resentful after going through so much. And, really, I appreciate you saying those things about me, but you did all those things. You didn't have to come to Bible study. You didn't have to open up. But you did."

"Yeah, but you've dealt with things, too, and aren't bitter or resentful. You said yourself that Scarlett is in her own world and your mom has you living in her shadow. It must be tough not to have support from your mom or any attention from your sister."

"I don't think I've gone through much with the family I've had. I think if I went through what you went through, I'd have been bitter and resentful, too. My mom might want me to be more like Scarlett, but she's not a bad person. She still cares about me and loves me even though it might not seem that way sometimes. And Scarlett, as much as she is in her own world, looks out for me, too. I'm blessed to have the family I have. Scarlett is *so* successful but doesn't gloat about her success. She doesn't look down on me or anyone else just because she's a beauty queen and an advertising executive. It takes a good soul to be able to handle the power that comes with those things and not abuse it. I respect her a lot."

Jonathan didn't respond. He just kept watching the players.

Samantha, on the other hand, couldn't focus on the scrimmage. She felt bad that Jonathan was in such a painful place. She stared at him for a few moments before continuing. "Hey, Jon," Samantha said in an attempt to change the subject. "Can I ask you a favor?"

"Sure thing, Sam."

"Well, Thanksgiving is coming up, and Kylie and I are both going home for Thanksgiving break. I don't know who else to ask." Samantha hesitated for a moment, afraid she was asking for too much. "Would you cover for us at Dr. Johanssen's zoology lab while we're away?"

"I'd love to," Jonathan said. "But I don't know anything about taking care of lab animals."

"I'll teach you!" Samantha chirped. "I'll show you the ropes. It's really quite simple."

"Okay," Jonathan agreed. Jonathan was more than willing to cover for both of them while they were away. He wasn't going home, anyway. The last thing he wanted was to see his dad and look into Gabby's room—unchanged since the accident. He'd go right back to feeling the guilt that had been haunting him since that night. For the first time, his days weren't full of towering waves of sadness and reflecting on the accident, what might have been with his football career, and losing Gabby. Years later, his memories of Gabby all led straight to the crash. He couldn't focus on all the positive things she brought to the world. Why couldn't he just think of Gabby and remember her for the beautiful soul that she was? Why was the thought of her nothing but a reminder that he got her killed? That she was dead because of him?

The guilt would feel even more overwhelming whenever he'd see his dad, who never missed an opportunity to remind Jon that he was the reason his princess wasn't alive anymore. Home was the last place on earth Jonathan wanted to be.

CHAPTER 20

———————— ·•◦●◦•· ————————

Jonathan felt anxious as he wheeled down the dimly lit corridor leading to Dr. Johanssen's lab. He wasn't sure what it would be like to help out in the lab, but he knew he was anxious about it. It had been a few days since the scrimmage, and Samantha was going to teach him how to feed the lab mice and the lab geckos and clean their cages before she left for Thanksgiving Break.

At the end of the corridor was a metal door that read "Authorized Personnel Only." Samantha told him earlier this was the door to the lab. She said she would be waiting for him inside with a pass he could use to enter when she was away. He opened the door to see Samantha waiting for him. She looked like a doctor with all the gear she had on.

"Hi, Jon!"

"Hi, Sam," Jonathan said, smiling. "Let's do this."

"Thank you so much for covering for us," Samantha said. "It means a lot."

"No problem at all."

"We've got to get you dressed up in your PPE gear before we go in." She reached into her pocket and pulled out a card attached to a lanyard. "This is for you." The card read "Jonathan McCalister, Volunteer, Central Texas University Zoology Laboratory."

"How'd you get this? What's PPE gear?"

"I told Dr. Johanssen you'd be filling in for me and Kylie, and she had it printed. It's really easy to make. It's just a piece of paper in a plastic container. Nothing too official. PPE gear stands for Personal Protective Equipment. It's what I'm wearing. It just makes sure you don't spread any diseases to the lab animals and vice versa. Here." She handed Jonathan a bag. "This is your PPE gear."

"Oh, okay. Where do I put it on?"

Samantha pointed to the back wall. There were two doors. One read "Women" and the other read "Men." Jonathan quickly put two and two together and figured those were the locker rooms.

"Oh," Jonathan said. "I'll be right back then." Jonathan wheeled over to the men's locker room and let himself in. It was a small room with only about twenty lockers lining the walls. In the bag there was a pair of nitrile gloves, a lab coat, a mask, and a hair net. Jonathan laughed as he put on the hair net and looked in a mirror hanging on the back of the door.

I look like a lunch lady.

With the mask and lab coat, he thought he looked more like a doctor, too. He felt professional seeing himself all dressed up in the PPE gear. He stopped looking at himself and opened the door to go back out to the room Samantha was waiting in.

"Alrighty then," Samantha said, smiling as Jonathan wheeled over to her all dressed up in his PPE gear. "Let's get you educated on taking care of lab mice and lab geckos!" She turned around and walked through another door that read "Authorized Personnel Only." Jonathan followed. The corridor on the other side of that door was much brighter than the one that led to the laboratory. Bright luminescent lights hung from the ceiling, and doors lined both walls. At the end of the corridor was a door with a big sign that read "Dr. Johanssen's Office." Samantha turned into one of the first doors in the hallway, one with a little sign that read "Lab Animals."

Inside the lab animals room were three glass enclosures, each with one small, white mouse inside, and two glass enclosures, each with one gecko inside. One gecko was yellow with black spots, and one was red with black spots. All five cages were in the center of the room on a large table with a cabinet and garbage can underneath it. The rest of the room was empty except for a table in the corner, which had a sink, a bag of mouse pellets, a bag of wood shavings, and a few small empty plastic cages on it plus two boxes labeled "Water Containers" and a mini fridge underneath it.

Samantha pointed at one of the white mice. "This is Tom." She pointed at another. "This is Jerry." And she pointed at the last one, smiling by now. "And this is Mickey."

"How can you tell which one is which? They all look the same."

"Jon," Samantha said with a sarcastic tone. "That's rude. They're all unique in their own way."

"I can't tell the difference. Does that matter? Do I have to know which one is which?"

"No," Samantha replied. "They all get fed the same and all of their cages are cleaned the same." She then pointed to the yellow gecko with black spots. "This is Sandra," she said. And then pointed to the red gecko with black spots. "And this is Larry."

"You really have a name for each of them?" Jonathan was amused. "What type of gecko's are they?"

"They're leopard geckos."

"Okay, so how do I clean the cage and feed them?"

"I'll show you how to clean Tom's cage and then you can do Jerry's and Mickey's cages." Samantha grabbed one of the empty plastic cages from the table in the corner and the bag of wood shavings. She picked up Tom by the loose skin at the back of his neck and held him for a moment as he squirmed in her grasp. "This is how you pick them up," she instructed, "and what you're going to do first is place him in one of the temporary cages while you change his bedding." She placed Tom gently down in the temporary, plastic cage and proceeded to take what looked like a garden hoe to scoop out the wood shavings from his enclosure. She dumped the wood shavings into the garbage can under the table until all the shavings were gone. "You just clean the enclosure by scooping out the old wood shavings and replacing them with new ones." She dumped some wood shavings from the bag of wood shavings into the enclosure until about an eighth of it was filled up. "We only change the bedding once a week so you'll only have to do this once. The next step is to replace the water container." Samantha reached into one of the boxes under the table in the corner, pulled out a water container, and filled it. "You need to refill the water containers twice a week. Make sure you always grab a fresh bottle."

"Why can't you just refill the bottle that's already in there?" Jonathan asked.

"Bottles shouldn't be refilled because any contamination accumulated in the bottle will be retained," Samantha explained as she took the old bottle out and put the new one in. "When you install a clean bottle you have to check them to make sure the stopper is firmly fastened and water has entered the water-delivery tube. You can check if the water has entered the water-delivery tube by holding the bottle downward and shaking it gently until air bubbles come out of the tube. If air bubbles come out of the tube, that means the water-delivery tube has been filled with water." Samantha held the bottle downward and shook it gently. Bubbles came out of the tube. "See? That means the water has entered the water-delivery tube."

Jonathan listened attentively. "Okay, I think I've got it."

"The last thing you've got to do—before putting the mouse back in—is refill their food bowl. Don't touch the food yourself. You've got to use this metal scooper." Samantha reached into the cabinet under the table and pulled out a metal scooper. "I'm not going to use it, though, because Tom still has food. But if they run out, you know where to find this. The pellets are on the table in the corner, right over there, next to the sink."

Jonathan began to change Jerry and Mickey's cages to show Samantha he understood. As he worked, Jonathan asked Samantha how she felt about going home for Thanksgiving break. He knew very little about her family other than what she told him at the sushi restaurant before the race. "How do you feel about going back home?" Jonathan asked as he shoveled out the old bedding in Jerry's cage.

"Honestly, I'm dreading it," she replied. "I miss my brother and dad, but I'm not looking forward to seeing my mom and sister. They expect me to be someone I'm not. They want me to be all girly and charming, like them, but I'm no beauty queen. It's just not who I am."

"I think you could be a beauty queen," Jonathan interrupted.

"Thanks, but no thanks. That's not my way. I don't need looks and charm to get ahead. I'm smart. That's what matters to me."

"I think you've got beauty *and* brains."

Samantha always got embarrassed when people called her beautiful. She quickly changed the subject. "Your mom is really nice and easy to talk to. She's really sweet."

"Yeah, she is."

"She told me she wants you to go back to physical therapy with Dr. Bui."

Jonathan felt betrayed. He thought his physical therapy with Dr. Bui was between him, Dominic, and his mom. He didn't like that Rose had told Samantha about it.

How often does Samantha talk to my mom, anyway?

"I don't know," he responded. "I don't really see a point in it. I go to the gym a lot. I'm still in good shape. I don't see myself ever getting out of this wheelchair."

"Why not?" Samantha asked. "I think you should try getting prosthetics and do physical therapy with Dr. Bui to get used to them. It'll change your whole world."

"I don't know. Look, it's whatever." Jonathan didn't want to talk about Dr. Bui or getting prosthetics with Samantha. He was mad that Rose had told Samantha about that whole situation in the first place. "I'll think about it." Jonathan finished cleaning up the bedding in both cages and then took the bag of wood shavings and emptied them into each cage until they were both filled about an eighth with fresh wood shavings. He then grabbed two water containers as Samantha watched in silence. Samantha was disappointed that Jonathan didn't have any interest in getting prosthetics. She realized she still had a lot more to do if she wanted to get him fully out of his shell. Jonathan didn't think prosthetics would help him get out of his rut, but Samantha was confident that they would.

"Remember to check if the water has entered the water delivery tube," she advised. "Just—"

"—just turn it downward and shake gently until air bubbles appear," Jonathan interrupted, finishing her sentence. "I know. I was listening." Air bubbles appeared as he turned the first container downward and shook it gently.

Samantha was impressed with how well Jonathan had listened to her instructions. He didn't need help from her whatsoever on his first attempt to clean the cages. Time again, Jonathan impressed her with his intelligence. She loved that he listened well, read books, wrote beautiful poetry, and even how well he under-stood football. Intelligence and thoughtfulness were top qualities she looked for in a romantic interest. Her crush on Jonathan was only growing stronger.

"So what makes you think your mom and sister want you to be a beauty queen?" Jonathan asked as he secured the water bottle on the other enclosure, turned it downward, and shook gently. "I'm sure they love you for who you are." Air bubbles appeared as Jonathan backed away from the enclosures and looked into Samantha's eyes.

"Hey!" Samantha sassed. "We were talking about your family. If you share something about your family I'll share something about my family. How about that?"

Jonathan was reluctant but also curious about Samantha's relationship with her mother and sister, so he obliged. "Okay," he agreed. "Well, how about this: my dad hasn't spoken to me in five years."

Samantha was shocked. "What?"

"Yeah. Ever since the accident he's basically disowned me. I'm the reason his little princess died, so I guess it's only fair."

"That's not fair at all," Samantha argued. "He shouldn't blame you for that. An accident is an accident. He should be grateful you survived and that he still has you."

"I wish he saw it the way you do. But I *am* the reason why Gabby is dead. If I hadn't reached for my phone—" Jonathan sighed. "That's enough about that. Your turn."

"Well, to answer your question, I know that my mom wants me to be more like Scarlett because she said so. She told me 'stop being so stubborn and be more like Scarlett.'"

"Ouch," Jonathan said. "I'm sure she didn't mean that. What prompted her to say it?"

"I refused to sign up for the whole beauty pageant thing. I guess that's what prompted her to say it. She just doesn't understand that I care more about books than looks."

"Well, if you did sign up for that beauty pageant—and I'm not saying you should have—you would have been a winner just like her and Scarlett. I think it's awesome you don't care about those types of things, though. I think it's awesome that you have goals and ambitions that aren't as shallow as that."

"Thanks," Samantha said. Silence passed between them as they looked in each other's eyes, sympathizing with one another's struggles. They both wanted to know so much more, but the urge to stop talking about such painful topics was mutual.

"Alright, whatever, let's just move on to the geckos. I'll show you how to feed Larry and then you can feed Sandra." Samantha opened up the cabinet again and pulled out a can that read "EZ Wormz." She then opened the mini fridge and pulled out a can that read "Can O' Crickets." She put them both on the table and reached back into the cabinet to pull out a container that read "Calcium and Vitamin D3 Powder."

"This part is gross," she said. "We have to feed them dead crickets and live mealworms." Samantha opened up the cap of the powder container, placed it down on the table, and poured some powder into the cap. "First thing's first, though. We have to roll them around in this powder." She opened up the can of mealworms and dumped a few into the powder on the cap.

"Those things are *nasty*," Jonathan said. "And how do we open the crickets container? Won't they jump out?"

"I said they're dead, silly," Samantha giggled. "But that's why we don't get live crickets. Yes, they jump. We learned that the hard way. These ones are dead and they get kept in the fridge for about a week. Dr. Johanssen just put a new supply in today so these should last until Kylie and I get back."

After stirring the live mealworms in the powder she picked them up with her gloved fingers and dropped them into Larry's cage. He immediately raced over to them and gobbled them up. She then opened the Can O' Crickets, put some crickets in the powder, and dropped them in Larry's cage as well. He gobbled those up just as fast.

"You've got to feed them every other day. So come back here the day after tomorrow and feed them. When you come to feed them, make sure you also check on the mice and make sure they have food and water. If they don't, you know what to do."

"Sure thing," Jonathan replied. He followed Samantha's example and dumped some crickets and mealworms into the powder, stirred them around, and dropped them into Sandra's cage.

CHAPTER 21

Thanksgiving break passed slowly for Jonathan. He was lonely now that Samantha was home and he wasn't in touch with Dominic anymore. Final exams were just around the corner, so when he wasn't taking care of the lab animals, he spent his time studying. At home, Samantha also spent much of her time locked in her room studying, avoiding her mother. Before she left to head back to Central Texas University, her mother scolded her for spending all her time isolated in her room. She wanted her to be more of a socialite, a southern belle. She told Samantha she was too obsessed with her studies for her own good. Whereas most parents would be proud of Samantha's work ethic and bookish nature, her mother was distressed by it. Samantha simply wasn't well rounded enough in the eyes of Sara Reid. But Samantha was used to this criticism and paid no mind to it.

The moment she got back to campus she went with Jonathan to the library to continue her studies. "Quick," Samantha asked Jonathan. "Can you help me study these flashcards, please? Just say the name term and I'll tell you the definition. Then tell me if I'm right."

Jonathan and Samantha were sitting at a table studying together, yet separately. They had been in there for three hours. Their plan was to study for three and a half hours—from two o'clock to five-thirty—and then meet Tom and Elijah for dinner.

"This stack of flashcards is thicker than a textbook! What do you mean by 'quick?'" Jonathan joked. "Alright, quick, what's Neuroplasticity?"

Samantha furrowed her eyebrows and thought for a brief moment. "Neuroplasticity refers to the physiological changes in the brain that happen as the result of our interactions with our experiences and environment."

"Correct," Jonathan said as he flipped to the next flashcard. "What are the three major anatomical planes?"

"Oh, easy," Samantha said. "The sagittal plane, the coronal plane, and the transverse plane."

They went back and forth for the next thirty minutes. Jonathan read out a term, Samantha gave the definition, and then Jonathan would move to the next flashcard. Samantha didn't get a single one wrong. They had only got through a little over half of the stack by the time it was five-thirty.

"Alright, we ought to go meet up with Tom and Elijah," Jonathan said when it reached five-thirty. "You know these cards better than the back of your hand at this point, anyhow. Any more studying and you'll know more than your professor. I think it'd be healthy for you to take a break from studying."

"Okay," Samantha said. "I'm hungry anyway."

Jonathan and Samantha packed up and made their way out of the library. As they made their way out of the main entrance, they were intercepted by Dean Pilling. Dean positioned himself in front of Jonathan with his arms crossed, stopping Jonathan in his tracks. He stared at Jonathan as if he was better than him, and Jonathan had to fight the urge to take his backpack off his wheelchair and swing it at him.

"Yes, Dean?" Samantha asked.

"I haven't seen you around, Sam," Dean said. He still had his arms crossed as he moved from being an obstacle to Jonathan to being uncomfortably close to Samantha. She reared back as she caught an overwhelming whiff of cheap cologne.

"Yeah, I've been busy I guess," she replied.

"You don't come to study group anymore. What's up with that? It's just me, Kylie, and those other losers. I've missed you."

Samantha almost threw up in her mouth. *He barely knows me,* she thought. *How does he miss me?* "I've been hanging out with Jon," she replied. "Jon and I study together now."

Dean scoffed at her. "Well, suit yourself."

Dean glared at the pair as they made their way to the grass in front of the library, where Tom and Elijah were playing catch and waiting for them. Elijah spotted them making their way over and tossed the football at Jonathan. "Heads up!" He called out. Jonathan put one hand up and caught the football nonchalantly. He wrapped his fingers around the laces of the football, patted it with his free hand, and then rifled it back to Elijah. It was a perfect spiral. Elijah was so surprised at the velocity of Jonathan's pass that he nearly dropped it.

"Whoa," he exclaimed. "How do you know how to throw a football like that? I need to know your secret now!"

Jonathan just laughed. "I told you. I'll tell you my secret if you finish with more touchdowns and fewer interceptions than you did last season. You're already looking good at the scrimmages, man. You'll know my secret in no time if you keep it up."

"But I want to know now!" Elijah whined jokingly. Jonathan waited at the edge of the grass, next to Samantha, as Tom and Elijah walked over. "Let's get some food," Elijah said. "Tom said there's a really good place in Waco Center I want to check out. You guys like Tex-Mex?"

"I could eat anything right now," Samantha said. "I'm starving. Tex-Mex sounds good to me."

"Agreed," Jonathan said.

The four followed the sidewalk to the student parking lot and all got into Jonathan's van, while Dean glared on. "I need to know your secret too," Dean said under his breath. In Dean's eyes, Jonathan had stolen away the girl of his dreams. He wasn't going to let him take her away from him easily. He'd find out the real story behind Jonathan McCalister and prove to Samantha that Jonathan wasn't the sweetheart she thought he was. He was determined to dig up some dirt on Jonathan.

CHAPTER 22

••••••••

While Samantha spent most of her time studying with Jonathan, she started studying with her old study group again every once in a while. Kylie often complained to Samantha about how she left her all alone with Dean and how Dean would constantly ask about Samantha in a creepy fashion, so Samantha felt bad. To make up for it, she joined them to study from time to time.

After an intense study session with Kylie and Dean, Samantha walked out of the library to meet Jonathan, who was waiting outside with Tom and Elijah. This was the perfect opportunity, Dean thought, to move forward with his plot to expose Jonathan's true story.

As the three walked out of the library into the chilly October air, Jonathan rolled into sight. Samantha waved to Jonathan while Dean smirked from behind her. He was eager to tell everyone Jonathan's secret. He had done his research. He knew that Jonathan was once a star quarterback, which explained his ability to throw a perfect spiral. But he didn't want to expose that part of Jonathan's story because it would make Jonathan look good. If Samantha knew he was once a five-star prospect she'd probably just be impressed. No, Dean wanted to expose the less glorified part of Jonathan's past. He wanted to tell everyone how Jonathan got in a horrific car accident that killed his sister because he was responding to a suggestive text from his girlfriend. He wanted to tell everyone that Jonathan's legs were amputated and his ten-year-old sister was dead because he couldn't help himself from looking at a suggestive picture.

He wasn't sure how Kylie and Samantha would react—and he didn't know Samantha already knew that Gabby died in a freak accident with Jonathan behind the wheel—but he was desperate to paint Jonathan in a bad light any way he could.

"Hi, Jon," Samantha said as the group approached Jonathan.

"Hey Sam. Hey Kylie."

"Hi," Kylie said.

"Jonathan," Dean said as he clapped his hands together triumphantly, wedging himself between the girls to stand over Jonathan. "I learned some interesting things about our Mr. Perfect here. Apparently, he has a deep dark secret he's been keeping from you girls."

"What are you talking about, man?" Jonathan despised Dean more every time he saw him. He couldn't stand even looking at his face. Once Dean opened his mouth, however, his personality took over and really irked Jonathan.

"What are you doing, Dean?" Kylie asked.

"I'm exposing the truth, that's what I'm doing," Dean replied. "Do you know why Jonathan has no legs? Do you know what happened?"

Samantha was furious. She couldn't believe Dean was being so cruel to Jonathan. She hated bullies more than anything in the world. Her disdain for Dean had festered into utter contempt at this point.

"Well," Dean continued. "I hate to break it to you ladies, but after a little research I found a newspaper article in the *Katy Times* that said Jonathan was driving recklessly when he killed his sister. He wasn't looking at the road because he was too busy texting his girlfriend about the racy picture she had just sent him and he wrapped his car around a tree. Even worse, his little sister was only ten years old and he let her sit in the front seat. He didn't even make sure she had buckled up. What a guy, right?" Dean sneered at Jonathan and his smirk grew wider. "Well guess what? He crashed the car, his sister died, and they had to amputate his legs. He killed his little sister because he couldn't wait to reply to a suggestive text from his girlfriend until he stopped."

Dean's words stung. They hurt Jonathan more than he thought words could. Dean's words did more damage in ten seconds than four years' worth of his father disowning him had. Jonathan was speechless. Dean had struck him where he was most vulnerable. Samantha and Kylie were speechless too. Slowly, Jonathan backed away, turned around, and started to head down the ramp to leave. He didn't know what else to do. Dean's words made him want to hide away under his shell again, to get back in his rut and disappear for good.

"Don't ever talk to me again. I don't ever want to see you again," Samantha retorted at Dean with a furious expression across her face. "I don't want someone like you in my life. Period."

"You jerk," Kylie added. "Don't talk to me again, either. I can't believe you."

"The heck is your problem, man?" Tom asked.

"Boy . . . you better back up before I hurt you . . ." Elijah added, shaking his head.

Dean's smirk faded into a frown as both girls reacted with such contempt. He expected Samantha to think less of Jonathan, but it backfired big time. He thought she'd react by confronting Jonathan, asking if it's true or becoming upset he hadn't told her what happened. Instead, she was chasing after Jonathan as he sped down the ramp, with Kylie, Tom, and Elijah following.

Jonathan picked up more and more speed as he went down the decline. He wanted to disappear. He wanted to get away from everyone. Samantha was sprinting as fast as she could to catch up to him.

"Jon!" She cried out as she ran.

Jonathan didn't hear her, he just sped forward down the long ramp. She finally caught up to him and jumped into his lap, nearly crashing the wheelchair. They continued to speed up narrowly missing a student who screamed and jumped into some bushes at the last second. Other students started jumping out of the way and screaming to others to watch out. A couple of students raised their arms in anger and cussed at the pair as they rolled past. The wheelchair was completely out of control at this point and heading directly for a curb leading to a grassy area. Jonathan tried to stop it, but their combined weight and the velocity he had picked up before Samantha leapt into his lap made the brakes pointless. They hit the curb and both of them launched off of the wheelchair and into the grass, with Samantha landing on top of him.

Jonathan was angry at Dean but didn't want to take his anger out on Samantha like he had on the ride to The Competition Corner. He felt embarrassed, unsure how he would get back in his chair, but it was nice to have Samantha lying on top of him. The two just stared at each other with a look of awkward shock for a few moments until Jonathan broke the silence with a bellowing laugh. Samantha joined in.

Kylie had caught up and was looking on with a relieved smile. Dean was looking on, too, with shock. The shock soon turned into rage when Jonathan wrapped one hand around the back of Samantha's neck and pulled her in for a kiss. Their lips met and their noses pushed into each other's faces in the most impassioned kiss either of them had ever experienced. It only lasted a few seconds, but time slowed down as they each savored every passing moment.

When they pulled away from each other they both smiled and stared deeply into each other's eyes before connecting their lips again for a second kiss.

Dean couldn't watch and stormed back into the library with jealousy consuming him. Kylie approached Jonathan and Samantha and looked on with a different kind of jealousy. While Dean was jealous that Samantha and Jonathan were kissing, Kylie was jealous they had found such genuine romance. She could only hope that someday she would find romance as powerful as the romance she had just witnessed. Tom and Elijah gave each other a high-five and looked on approvingly as they approached Jonathan and Samantha. They were equally excited for Jonathan and Samantha and happy Dean's attempt to expose Jonathan backfired.

CHAPTER 23

······•●●•●••······

When Kylie, Tom, and Elijah crowded around Jonathan and Samantha on the grass, Jonathan thought they would be wondering about what Dean had said. What Dean said was true. Jonathan wasn't sure if they would be disappointed in him, pity him, or what. To his relief, they were all smiling.

Samantha was looking so deeply into Jonathan's eyes she didn't notice their friends staring at them. But she realized Jonathan had moved his gaze away from her and followed his gaze until she noticed. She quickly became embarrassed, hopped off Jonathan, and sheepishly tried to fix her hair and clothes, which had become ruffled by the tumble onto the grass.

"Are you two alright?" Kylie asked. She didn't know what else to say.

"Uh, yeah," Samantha said. "We're okay." She looked down at Jonathan and smiled. "More than okay." She grabbed Jonathans' wheelchair and wheeled it over to him.

Jonathan slowly lifted himself into his wheelchair as an awkward silence passed between the five of them. He then cleared his throat. "Well, I can't deny what Dean said. It's all true. I have no legs because I got in a car crash that killed my little sister. I was looking at a suggestive text message from my girlfriend, ran a red light, and wrapped my car around a tree. I live with the guilt every day, and I'm sorry that—"

135

"Jonathan," Kylie interrupted. "None of us would have expected you to tell us something so deeply personal. It's really none of our business. There's nothing to be sorry about."

"I'm still sorry that it happened, Kylie," Jonathan replied, choking back tears. "I'm sorry it put an end to my sister's life and ended my football career."

"Football career?" Elijah asked. "What do you mean?"

Jonathan sighed. "I know I said I wouldn't tell you unless you finished with more touchdowns and fewer interceptions than last year, but at this point, I might as well. Actually, why don't you all come over to my apartment? We can order some pizza and I'll tell you my whole story."

* * *

Samantha, Kylie, Tom, and Elijah all gathered in Jonathan's living room. Samantha and Kylie were sitting on the couch while Tom and Elijah sat in chairs they dragged over from the dining table. Jonathan sat in his wheelchair with his back to the window. They all looked at Jonathan with undivided attention.

"Five years ago," Jonathan began, "I was the quarterback of the Katy Tigers, my high school football team. I wasn't just any quarterback, either. I was a five-star prospect with a full scholarship lined up to play Division One football at Texas University."

The reason why Jonathan was able to call plays before they even happened at Elijah's scrimmage became clear to Samantha. It wasn't because he played a ton of Madden or learned a lot from Tom. It was because he himself had once been a star quarterback. She was understanding more about the trauma Jonathan had experienced, the trauma that Rose had warned her about.

While Tom already knew this, Elijah was confounded by this news. This was Jonathan's secret. This was how he threw such a tight spiral and why he was so helpful when teaching him the playbook.

"On the night of the accident," Jonathan continued, "I had just won the Texas 6A State Championship Game. I was the MVP and had won the game with an exhilarating play. We were down by four with ten seconds left and I dodged two defenders and flipped over a third to score the winning touchdown. Everything was surreal for me that night. To celebrate, I was going to meet my family for dinner. My little sister, Gabby, wanted to ride with me. She was always so excited to talk with me about football . . ." Jonathan trailed off with tears forming in his eyes as he thought of Gabby. The memory was obviously painful for him. He wiped his eyes and continued. "She was so excited to talk about football that she didn't put on her seatbelt. She just bounced up and down in her seat and asked me all about the game. I told her to put her seatbelt on, I swear, I—" His voice was becoming hysterical. "I . . . I told her to put on her seatbelt . . . but I guess she didn't and I didn't notice. I don't know . . . I . . ."

"I believe you, Jon," Samantha said. "It's not your fault."

Jonathan looked at Samantha and gathered strength from the supportive expression on her face. "So, I was driving and . . . got distracted by a text from my girlfriend. She sent me a suggestive picture and I couldn't wait to look at it until I got to the restaurant. So, I picked up my phone and started to text her back. Gabby kept telling me not to text and drive, but I didn't listen."

Jonathan wasn't weeping, but there were tears falling down his cheeks as he spoke. He didn't want to cry in front of everyone, but he couldn't help it. He tried to wipe them away, but they just kept coming. "I didn't see the red light. I can still hear the sound of her screaming when she saw a truck coming right at us. I swerved out of the way of the truck but crashed head-on into a large oak tree. I still know the address of the accident. I still know where that oak tree is... 2612 Cherryhill Lane."

Samantha and Kylie both had tears in their eyes as they listened to the story. Tom and Elijah looked on sympathetically.

"They had to amputate my legs and put me in a medically induced coma to prevent a severe brain injury. I lost my scholarship to Texas University. The worst part of it all, though, is Gabby lost her life that night. I'll never forgive myself for texting and driving. I'll never forgive myself for being the reason Gabby is dead."

Samantha got up from the couch, walked over to Jonathan, and hugged him. Kylie wiped the tears from her eyes and sniffled. Elijah and Tom were too choked with emotion to say anything. After Samantha pulled away from their embrace, the room remained silent while everyone registered what Jonathan just said.

"I hope this doesn't change anything," Jonathan said, "but I understand if it does. I don't want you guys to feel sorry for me or anything. I'm glad to have you all as friends and I appreciate you being my friends despite my disabilities."

"It's an honor to know you, Jon," Elijah said. "I only respect you more for telling us your story."

"Truly," Tom added. "I know Elijah and I both feel fortunate to have someone with your football knowledge in our lives. And you're a good dude, too. We love hanging out with you."

The five friends hung out for the rest of the evening, eating pizza, watching TV, and laughing. Eventually, Kylie, Elijah, and Tom had to leave and Jonathan and Samantha had some time alone.

"It was really brave of you to tell your story to everyone," Samantha said as the two of them sat on the couch.

"Thanks," Jonathan replied. "I just thought everyone deserved to know it from my perspective."

"Dean's a jerk. I can't believe what he did today."

"Yeah, he is a jerk. I think he just really likes you and feels threatened by me."

"Ew. I don't think so."

"Why wouldn't he?"

"I don't know," Samantha said. "I just don't think I'm that desirable."

"What!? C'mon now . . ." Jonathan said, "I've had the hugest crush on you since the day we met."

"Really?" Samantha blushed. "I feel the same way about you, Jon."

Affection welled up inside Jonathan. "I know you're just supposed to be my assistant, but you feel like you've been so much more than that to me. You've been a great friend and I feel like we could be even more than friends."

Samantha didn't reply. She just leaned in and kissed Jonathan. When she pulled her lips away, she brought them next to his ear and, in a hushed whisper, said, "so... are you asking me to be your girlfriend, Jonathan McCalister?"

Jonathan turned to look her in the eyes. "Yes... I guess I am."

Samantha smiled. "Hmm... then it's settled."

Jonathan smiled back, and the two shared another kiss.

CHAPTER 24

$\bullet\cdot\bullet\bullet\bullet\bullet\cdot\bullet$

amantha listened to Jonathan's heartbeat as her head rested on his chest. They were on the couch watching the sunset over the pond out Jonathan's living room window. Snowflakes slowly descended from the December sky and seemed to vanish when they landed on the frozen pond. It had been a little over a month since Jonathan and Samantha started dating. Now that their feelings were out in the open, both of them couldn't be happier with their relationship. They had been in relationships before and both knew all about the honeymoon phase, but what they had seemed different. It felt like they were meant to be together.

"It's so beautiful," Samantha murmured.

"Yeah," Jonathan agreed. "I'm so glad you're here to see it with me. You make this moment twice as beautiful. I never really noticed these things until you came into the picture."

"Seriously . . ." Samantha joked. "Is this some line you use with all the ladies?"

"No, I'm serious, you're more beautiful than any girl who wins a beauty pageant or who models for a magazine. You're the most beautiful girl I've ever seen in my life. I'm the luckiest guy in the world."

"You wouldn't want to tell my mom that," Samantha said with a lighthearted giggle. "She'd sign me up for a beauty pageant so I could be more like my sister. Too bad I'm too stubborn. She just adores my stubbornness."

"Why do you think she wants you to be a beauty queen? You're so much more than that."

"I don't know, but I'm sick of always being compared to her and Scarlett. I never wanted to be a beauty queen. I've always wanted to be a doctor. I feel like beauty queens aren't strong women. You know what I mean?"

"Nah. What do you mean?"

"Well, I feel like beauty queens just pose to satisfy the expectations of femininity. They paint their nails, put on makeup, and fix their hair to look pretty and feminine. They look like what guys want a girl to look like. They aren't being themselves; they're being puppets to male-dominated society. As a feminist, I really have a problem with that." Samantha had lifted her head off Jonathan's chest while she spoke and was looking at him with fervor. This was a subject she was clearly passionate about.

"I see what you're saying." Jonathan nodded and smiled at her. "It makes total sense. You sound like a strong woman talking about it," he joked.

"I want to be a strong woman. I want to be independent. I don't care about looking beautiful."

"But you are beautiful."

"Stop," Samantha blushed. Even if they were dating, being called beautiful always embarrassed Samantha.

"You should be really proud of yourself. I mean it. You're a smart, beautiful young lady with an amazing goal. You're going to make a difference in this world and your mom will know it one day."

"You'll make a difference in this world one day, too, and your dad will know it," Samantha countered. "What was your relationship with your dad like before the accident?"

"I mean, Gabby was his world. It was always clear that I was his second favorite, but he still loved me. We bonded mostly around football and books. We used to always exchange books. He's an avid reader too. Well, he was before the accident. Now he just seems miserable. He doesn't read anymore. I miss talking about books with him."

"Have you tried to talk to him?"

"No, not really. I think he wants me to atone for the accident somehow, but I don't know how to. I've already told him I'm sorry a million times. I wish I could atone for the accident myself so I didn't always feel so guilty about it. Just thinking about it now upsets me, to be honest."

"The accident really changed your life. I'm so sorry."

"Yeah. The accident is by far the worst thing that's ever happened to me. That's why I wonder about God's plan. I don't see why He would have wanted such a cruel fate for me or Gabby. In one swift motion, He took everything away from me and took life from her." Jonathan felt guilt creeping up his spine once again. "Maybe it wasn't in God's plan. Maybe I just screwed everything up because I was a selfish person. Maybe I've sinned so badly God doesn't even want to forgive me. Maybe I'm not a part of God's plan. Maybe He's forsaken me."

"You can't blame yourself, Jon," Samantha said. "You have to forgive yourself before anything else can get better. You have to realize there's a reason for everything, even if really bad things happen like this. God is good. God is kind. Maybe His plan is to show you how to forgive yourself." Silence passed between them as they watched the colors of the sky dwindle like a slowly extinguishing candle. "You should come to church with me. Not just Bible study. You'll learn how to forgive yourself once you listen to the words of the Bible. You'll learn how God forgives those who believe in Him. He would never forsake you. You are constantly in God's grace."

"I guess I can try," Jonathan replied. "Nothing else has worked."

Jonathan hadn't been to church in years. He would do whatever he could, though, to learn to forgive himself. He knew he had to forgive himself someday. Maybe church was the answer. If going to church meant he could learn what it took to forgive himself, he was willing to go. If going to church meant he could be assured God hadn't forsaken him, and indeed had a plan for his life, he was willing to go.

"I think it will really help you to atone for your mistakes. You've got to embrace the accident and forgive yourself to move on. Once you move on and believe in the mercy of God and His plan for you, you'll lead a happier life. I promise you that. We should go tomorrow morning to the ten o'clock mass."

"Alright," Jonathan agreed, "let's do it."

* * *

The church bells rang as Jonathan and Samantha made their way toward the steepled spires. It was Sunday morning, ten o'clock sharp, and they were dressed in their finest Sunday clothes. Under her winter coat, Samantha was wearing a lilac-colored dress and her wavy hair fell over her shoulders with a purple bow to accent it. Under his winter coat, freshly-shaven Jonathan was wearing a collared shirt and khakis, basic but practical.

The entrance of the church was bustling with students. It was the same church that housed the Bible studies, but Jonathan had never been into this part of the church. It was even more breathtaking than the other areas.

"Jon," Samantha said. "Let's go to the left, in the back. I see a space to sit."

Jonathan looked over and saw a pew with an empty space at the end of it. It was perfect. Samantha could sit on the pew and Jonathan could sit next to her in the side aisle. "Okay," Jonathan replied, and the two took a left and went to the back wall to sit there. They were lucky to find a seat. Most of the pews were filled and many students were standing. "It's quite crowded," Jonathan commented.

"Yeah, it always is."

As people sat down the view cleared. Samantha and Jonathan could now see the pulpit and, lo and behold, Pastor Ana Broussard standing and looking around with her signature sincere smile. Jonathan was used to seeing her at the weekly Bible studies, but it felt different now that she was in the pulpit, about to address a church full of people. She wasn't wearing her normal outfit of jeans and a T-shirt. She was wearing professional business attire.

The sermon began and Jonathan started to zone out, admiring the beauty of the building. The stained-glass windows were a myriad of colors and the beams of light that shot through them looked like heavenly rays descending straight from the heavens. One particularly beautiful window was located above a balcony at the other end of the church, where an organist played. Jonathan found himself frequently lost in the music that interluded each session of preaching.

Jonathan zoned out for the most part and only really listened to the music. Samantha paid close attention the entire time, tapping Jonathan on his arm whenever Pastor Broussard brought up the concept of forgiveness in the Bible.

Samantha would point the passage out in her Bible and Jonathan would read. One passage made him think about what Dean said and how God would want Jonathan to forgive Dean for his offensive behavior.

"For if you forgive others their trespasses, your heavenly Father will also forgive you, but if you do not forgive others their trespasses, neither will your Father forgive your trespasses" (Matthew 6:14–15 ESV).

If Jonathan didn't forgive Dean, God wouldn't forgive him for his mistakes, he realized. So Jonathan had to forgive Dean. Forgiving Dean would seem ludicrous to Jonathan, normally, if he wasn't sitting in a serene church with such tranquil compositions flooding through his ears. They mollified him to the point where he was actually willing to forgive Dean. After all, Dean was probably just insecure and desperate to win Samantha over. He probably felt similar feelings about Samantha as Jonathan did. As he thought about Dean's misgivings, he began to zone out again. Samantha roped him back into reality with another nudge. Her finger was on another verse in her Bible.

"To Him all the prophets bear witness that everyone who believes in Him receives forgiveness of sins through His name" (Acts 10:43 ESV).

The verse she pointed to augmented what she had said the night before. If Jonathan believed in God, God would forgive him. Maybe, he wondered, the reason the accident was in God's plan for Jonathan was to test his faith. Jonathan lost his belief in God after the accident and felt guilty for doing so. But he doubted God would be "cruel enough" to ruin his life and take Gabby's life. He realized now that he had tried everything else and nothing worked. He must have been wrong the whole time. Maybe forgiveness and faith—the only two things he hadn't tried—were the answers.

God with a plan that required Jonathan to forgive himself was the only thing that made sense at that point. If he didn't believe that Gabby was in God's Kingdom now, and if he didn't believe God had a plan for him after all, the accident was meaningless and life was hell. Jonathan refused to believe that. Sitting in that church, there and then, was proof enough that life wasn't hell at all. Life was beautiful and there was a higher purpose. The accident may have ended one part of Jonathan's story, but it opened a new chapter to another one he was experiencing with Samantha—someone who loved and accepted him and wanted the best for him.

CHAPTER 25

· •●●●●· ·

Months passed in harmony between Jonathan and Samantha as they grew more and more fond of each other. They attended Bible study every Thursday, church service every Sunday, and spent their time studying together, going on dates in Waco Center, and relaxing together at Jonathan's apartment.

It was the middle of March, the Friday before Spring Break, and Rose was visiting Jonathan, hopeful she could convince him to spend Spring Break with her at home in Katy. She had been trying to get Jonathan and Jeff to reconcile for years, and a week together in the same house might be what they needed to finally mend fences.

Jonathan was already expecting Rose to ask him to come home. When Samantha asked him a week before what he was doing for Spring Break, Jonathan told her he was planning on staying at his apartment but was afraid his mother would make him come home. Samantha invited him to come home with her instead, to meet her family, but he politely declined. "Although I would love to spend time with you," Jonathan said, "I don't want to be a burden." The truth was, Jonathan was nervous about meeting Samantha's family. He feared what they would think of him.

Jonathan had brought Samantha to Katy during one or two of his sporadic visits home. Rose was delighted whenever he brought her there, but his dad always had an excuse to not be home. He'd always go on "business trips" and wouldn't be around. Jonathan knew his dad wasn't really going on business trips. He was just avoiding Jonathan. It pained him that his dad was still so cold to him and didn't seem to love him, but at that point, he was used to it. It had been that way for more than five years.

Rose was in Jonathan's living room vacuuming. She had just restocked his fridge with lots of healthy fruit and vegetables she had picked up on the way over. Jonathan was getting frustrated with her performing all of these motherly tasks.

"Stop cleaning up after me, Mom," he urged. "I'm fine. I'm an adult now. I can take care of myself."

"I'm just helping, honey," Rose said.

"Is there anything I can do?" Samantha asked as she sat next to Jonathan on the couch.

"No, I'm going to finish vacuuming in just a minute, and then I'll be done. Thanks, though."

Samantha smiled. She was happy to see Jonathan had at least one parent who still treated him with love. When Rose finished vacuuming, she asked Jonathan the question he had been waiting for.

"When are you going to come home, Jon?"

"I came home not even a month ago, Mom." Jonathan didn't like coming home often. If him coming home meant that his father had to go on one of his "business trips," it clearly meant he was disrupting family life. He didn't want that.

Samantha picked up on Jonathan's reluctance and quickly came to his rescue. "He's actually coming home with me, Mrs. McCalister," Samantha said.

Rose was surprised yet delighted. "Oh, okay, I didn't know that. You've got to tell me these things, Jon."

"Sorry, Mom," Jonathan said. He didn't want to be a burden on Samantha's family by visiting her house, but since Sam said that, he had no choice. He felt bad lying to his mother to get out of going home. At least it would be better to go to Sam's than his own home, he figured.

"Where do you live, Samantha?" Rose asked.

"I live in Southlake. It's a suburb right outside of Dallas. It's about a two-hour drive from here."

"Well, I hope you two enjoy your trip," Rose said. "When do you leave?"

"Tomorrow," Samantha said as she slyly smirked at Jonathan, knowing full well she had just dragged him into coming home with her. "We leave at eight o'clock sharp. Right, Jonathan?"

Jonathan smirked back. "Right."

The three went out to get lunch at a bistro on campus, and then Rose headed back home to Katy. She was delighted Jonathan would be meeting Samantha's family and that the couple had gotten to that point in their relationship. But she was also sad he didn't want to come home. The accident had torn the family apart, and things didn't seem to be improving. Jeff was constantly in mourning and didn't even talk to their only surviving child. And Jonathan seemed to give up on having a relationship with his father, too.

Rose just wished things could go back to normal. She knew they couldn't, but she wanted to at least try to help Jeff and Jonathan find peace. She wanted Jeff to be at peace with Gabby's death. She wanted Jeff and Jonathan to be at peace with one another. All she wanted was peace, but it seemed so far away.

After lunch, Jonathan told Samantha he was going to go back to his apartment to pack for their visit to her home in Southlake. Samantha insisted she would help Jonathan pack, but Jonathan said he needed to do it alone. "No offense," he said, "but I need to do this alone."

While Rose and Samantha were talking to each other at lunch, he decided he would get creative and romantic with the journey to Southlake. He was going to make the drive into a memorable, mini road trip. It would only take an hour or so to pack, so he decided to spend the rest of the night creating a playlist and planning stops along the way. He also wanted to make a good first impression on the Reids by showing up at their house with gifts. More than anything, though, he wanted to impress Samantha with some thoughtfulness.

After some research, Jonathan decided he would have them stop at the Czech Stop, a gas station that served a popular Czech pastry called Kolaches, to pick up some treats for the Reids. Jonathan also decided they would make a detour to Ennis, Texas, where bluebonnets—the state flower of Texas—would be in full bloom. It would be a romantic spot to sit and picnic and enjoy the warm weather. By the time Jonathan had made the playlist and researched all he needed to research, it was late in the night. He went to sleep, eager to initiate the road trip but nervous about meeting Samantha's family.

* * *

Jonathan laughed as Samantha belted out lyrics to her favorite country song, "Chicken Fried" by Zac Brown Band. She couldn't have been happier.

Jonathan joined in, and the two enjoyed the lighthearted ride.

Samantha pointed at Jonathan and nodded her head as they both began singing as loud as they could.

Jonathan laughed but pointed at the road, reminding Samantha, "Look at the road, Sam!"

Samantha kept singing as she turned away from Jonathan to look at the road. She knew every word. Jonathan was happy she was enjoying the playlist. She was singing along to every song. That was just her playful nature. But she seemed to especially like "Chicken Fried." It was obviously an old favorite, judging by the enthusiasm with which she belted out every single word.

When the song ended, Samantha turned the dial on the dashboard to lower the volume. "Where are we going?"

Jonathan had told her they were going to make some stops along the way, but he didn't tell her where. He had set the GPS to the address of the Czech Stop. It was only fifteen miles away from Central Texas University. They had been in the car for twenty minutes, and now they had only a minute before they'd get there. "It's a surprise."

"You know how I feel about surprises, Jon," Samantha said.

"Yeah. You love them."

Samantha playfully faked a scowl at Jonathan. "They're my favorite," she said sarcastically.

"We're going to an iconic establishment."

"An iconic establishment? Here?" Samantha had been observing their surroundings as they drove through West, Texas, the town where the Czech Stop was located. "This is a really small town. I've only seen like five stores. What could possibly be here?"

"Well, you're about to see a sixth," Jonathan said as they approached the brown building that was the Czech Stop. He had seen pictures of it when he was doing research on the night before.

Samantha read the bright yellow letters imprinted on the front of the brown, wooden building. "Czech Stop," she murmured. "Is this where you're taking me?"

"Sure is. Tom told me about this place a while ago, but I've never been. He told me their Kolaches are to die for."

"What's a Kolache?"

"I'm not really sure. It's a pastry filled with stuff."

"Very helpful, Jon," Samantha half sassed.

The two of them pulled into a handicap space and entered the store. Jonathan wheeled up to the front counter, where there was an assortment of pastries neatly displayed behind a glass window.

"Hello there," said a teenage boy behind the counter. He had a thin black vest on with a red lining and the logo of the Czech Stop on the front of it. "How may I help you?"

Jonathan had done the research. He knew what to get. "I'd like two boxes of sausage Kolaches and two boxes of fruit Kolaches."

"Certainly, sir," the boy replied. "What type of fruit would you like in your fruit Kolaches?"

"Mix it up," Jonathan said. "Give me a variety of flavors."

The boy nodded before he began grabbing Kolaches and putting them into a box.

"That's so many Kolaches," Samantha said. "We'll never eat that many!"

"They're not all for us," Jonathan assured her. "I'm getting extra to bring home to your family."

"Aw. Thanks, Jon. You're so sweet."

Jonathan paid for the Kolaches, and the pair got back to the van. Before they left the store, Samantha looked at Jonathan expectantly.

"Well? Aren't we going to eat some?"

"We are. Not yet, though. We're going to eat them somewhere special."

"Let me guess. Another surprise?"

"You got it." Jonathan plugged the address of the Bluebonnet Trails in Ennis, Texas, into the GPS. They were then on their way with more country music blasting and plenty more singing to go along with it.

The drive to Ennis took triple the amount of time the drive from Central Texas University to the Czech Stop took. Singing along to the music distracted Samantha from wondering where they were going. She liked that Jonathan was being spontaneous and romantic. As much as she hated surprises, she liked that Jonathan was surprising her with stops along the way home to Southlake. She thought it was romantic, creative, and thoughtful. She felt special.

As they got closer to the Bluebonnet Trails, it became impossible to miss the beauty of the azure fields rolling by. Samantha knew what bluebonnets were—she grew up in Texas, and they were all over the place—but she had never seen so many at once. There seemed to be hundreds of thousands of them.

"Why are there so many bluebonnets here?" Samantha asked. "It's beautiful."

"Welcome to Ennis," Jonathan said. "This place is considered the official bluebonnet city of Texas."

Once they arrived at the parking lot for the Bluebonnet Trails, Jonathan wheeled around to the back and pulled out a checkered red and white picnic blanket. "Let's go have a picnic in the flowers," he said.

Samantha was blown away. He had put so much thought and care into making the drive to Southlake romantic. She had no idea it would be that way when she woke up that morning.

The two started down a dirt path with bluebonnets surrounding them on both sides. A few minutes in, a sea of blue flowers appeared as far as their eyes could see, stretching all the way to the horizon.

"You could get lost in here," Samantha exclaimed.

Jonathan chuckled. "Let's hope we don't."

They followed the dirt path farther into the field and then set up for a picnic. Samantha laid the picnic blanket down, and Jonathan took out some Kolaches for them to munch on. The sun, high and bright in the clear blue sky, warmed their skin as they bit into the flaky pastries.

"These are delicious," Samantha said with her mouth still full. "And this is beautiful. I can't believe you, Jon. I thought we'd just be sitting in the van all morning. I never expected this. This is so thoughtful. Thank you."

"That's what I hoped for," Jonathan said with a smile as he reached for Samantha's hand. He looked into her eyes. "I can't imagine doing this with anyone else."

"Me neither."

The two of them finished eating their Kolaches and cuddled on the blanket for another hour before Samantha jumped up.

"I totally forgot," she said. "My family is expecting us."

"We have time," Jonathan said, "Southlake is only an hour from here. We should get going, though."

The two headed back to the van and started the drive to Southlake after a serene time together in the bluebonnet fields of Ennis.

CHAPTER 26

———————————— ••●•●•●•• ————————————

"Wow," Jonathan said. "Those are some big houses."

They were minutes from Samantha's house in Southlake. Jonathan was gawking at the size of the houses they were passing. The one he was looking at in that moment looked like a castle. It was at least three stories tall, with at least 10,000 square feet of living space, and multiple spires towering over the roof. Judging by the size of the roof, Jonathan estimated the attic was large enough to be a house on its own.

"Yeah. We like big homes in Southlake."

As they meandered up the long driveway leading to Samantha's house, Jonathan remarked that it was just as impressive as the other houses they had driven by. It was only two stories, but it stretched wide, across a large yard. It looked like an old house that had been maintained impeccably over many years. It was of ranch-style architecture with a large front porch. Jonathan thought it had a guest house next to it, at first, but when they got closer, he realized it was a five-car garage. It was clear that the Reids were very much a part of the affluent community of Southlake.

"Well," Samantha said. "Here we are."

Jonathan noticed a wooden ramp leading up the steps to the front porch and realized the Reids had installed a ramp in preparation for his arrival. His anxiety subsided slightly when he saw that gesture, but he was still nervous. He worried about what they would think of him, and his nerves had been dancing in the pit of his belly since he and Samantha left the Bluebonnet Trails.

Jonathan grabbed the Kolaches as they took their luggage out of the back and went to the front door—Jonathan wheeled up the ramp and Samantha walked the stairs. Samantha tried to turn the doorknob, but it was locked, so she knocked on the door three times. Jonathan could hear footsteps approaching the door. He could tell the floor was wood. He gulped as the door creaked open. As the door opened, a tall, beautiful young woman appeared with blonde hair brushed over her right shoulder. She wore black mascara, red lipstick, a red sundress, and red-toed flats.

This must be Scarlett.

"Well, hello there," she said in a sweet, pleasant voice. "Welcome home." She hugged Samantha and then extended her hand to Jonathan. He shook her hand, and they smiled at each other. "You must be Jonathan."

"Yes ma'am, I'm Jonathan. Pleasure to meet you. I'm guessing you're Scarlett?"

"That's me," she said. She held on to the handshake and studied Jonathan for a few moments. "Yeah, Sam. You're right. He *is* cute."

Samantha's cheeks flushed red. She immediately tried to change the subject, utterly embarrassed. "Well, it's been a long drive over here," she said. "It's great to be home. Let's head in."

Jonathan felt flattered by Scarlett's compliment.

The door was on the same level as the porch, so it was easy for Jonathan to wheel right in after Samantha. Standing there, behind the door, was the rest of Samantha's family. On the ride over, Samantha told Jonathan the names of everyone in the family. She said it would be okay for him to call everyone by their first name, but Jonathan only felt comfortable calling Scarlett and Sam's brother Steven by their first names. For Sara and Dan Reid, Samantha's parents, he'd stick with Mrs. and Mr. Reid.

Sara greeted and hugged both Jonathan and Samantha as soon as they entered. When she pulled away from her hug with Jonathan, she smiled at him. "You must be Jonathan," she said. "It's so nice to meet you."

Dan and Steven weren't as warm as Scarlett and Sara. They hung back and eyed Jonathan with skepticism. They were both burly and intimidating. Steven looked quite large for a junior in high school, and Jonathan could see how he started for the Southlake High School football team as a wide receiver. Jonathan gulped as they stared at him with cold expressions. Dan was the first to speak.

"Steven, let's take Jonathan to the back and see what kind of intentions he has with your sister."

"Sure thing, Dad. Do I need to bring towels and bleach? Last time we brought a guy back there, it got really messy."

Jonathan's eyes widened as the nerves he was feeling escalated to outright terror. But the smiles on their faces betrayed their words as they both broke into a fit of laughter. Sara hit Dan on the arm scoldingly.

"That wasn't funny," Samantha said. "You guys need to grow up."

Jonathan breathed a sigh of relief.

Phew.

"Jonathan brought you presents, but I guess you two don't deserve any," Samantha continued.

"Aw, c'mon, we were just kidding, Sam," Steven said. "What'd he bring?"

"I brought some Kolaches," Jonathan said as his heartbeat began returning to a normal pace. "You two had me pretty good there."

"They're delicious," Samantha added as Jonathan handed the boxes to Sara.

"How thoughtful," Sara remarked as Dan looked on nodding his head approvingly. "I just finished preparing dinner. It'd be lovely for you to join us, Jonathan."

"Of course," Jonathan replied. He exchanged pleasantries with Steven and Dan, introducing himself formally, and then wheeled after the Reids as they walked into the kitchen. Jonathan looked around as he followed them, admiring the antique furniture decorating the house and a magnificent crystal chandelier that hung above a grand staircase.

When he entered the kitchen, he was impressed by the elaborate meal set up on the counter. It looked like Martha Stewart was catering the dinner. Plates and utensils were neatly organized on an impressive dining room table. The table looked like it was made of mahogany or some other type of premium wood.

The dining room area and the kitchen shared one large room. The dining room side had a marble fireplace, a large liquor cabinet that matched the dining room table, and the dining room table itself. The kitchen side had a large fridge that was at least eight feet tall and twice the width of a traditional fridge. Surrounding the fridge was a stove and a multitude of other appliances plus a large kitchen island. The food was arranged on the kitchen island in a buffet style.

"We're having fajitas tonight," Sara explained as she opened the top of several stainless-steel chafers. One chafer had diced chicken, another had diced steak, and a few others had sides, including black beans, caramelized peppers and onions, and Spanish rice. Tortillas were steaming, placed carefully in tortilla warmers next to the toppings. As if that wasn't enough, there was a slow cooker with chicken tortilla soup next to the toppings and two pitchers of beverages next to the crock. One of the pitchers had strawberry lemonade in it, but Jonathan didn't recognize what was in the other. It was a dark red drink with what appeared to be diced fruit inside. Sara noticed him trying to figure out what was in the second pitcher. "That's sangria. It's a Spanish drink of red wine mixed with lemonade, fruit, and spices. Would you like a cup?"

"Yes please, Mrs. Reid. I've never had it before."

"There's a first time for everything," Sara said quaintly. She poured Jonathan a cup and handed it to him as Dan, Steven, Scarlett, and Samantha all made their way through the buffet, filling their plates. Samantha got Jonathan a plate since he wouldn't be able to reach the chafers easily. She then moved a chair out of the way for him at the table, and the Reids sat down.

Jonathan was trying to figure out how to tackle his fajita without making a mess until Dan interrupted. "So, Jonathan, what are you going to school for? What do you want to do for a living?"

"I'm studying Political Science, Mr. Reid. My goal is to become a lawyer."

"Oh, interesting," Dan said. "What made you want to become a lawyer?"

"My dad's a lawyer." Jonathan cringed internally, realizing he didn't have a very inspiring reason to become a lawyer. He wasn't doing it to save the environment, to fight for justice, or for any other inspiring reason. He was reminded of the night at the sushi restaurant when Samantha suggested him becoming a lawyer instead of a football player might be part of God's plan for him. "I guess I just feel it might be God's plan for me to become a lawyer. I think it's how I can best serve this world."

Samantha smiled. She remembered that conversation. "Jonathan has been going to Bible study with me every Thursday and church service every Sunday."

2612 CHERRYHILL LANE | 155

"That's good to hear," Dan said. "I'm glad he's a man of the Lord."

"I hope you show up to church service in a better outfit than what you have on right now," Sara said to Samantha. "You should take note from your sister." Samantha was wearing a pair of jeans and a lilac blouse and had her hair in a bun. Sara was wearing an extravagant emerald jumpsuit, green high heels, and her dark auburn hair was curled. Scarlett looked camera ready in her red sundress, red toe flats, and perfectly styled hair around the nape of her neck, dangling over her right collarbone. They were much more dressed up than Samantha. Usually when Sara critiqued Samantha's appearance, it stung, but she had Jonathan by her side this time.

"She dresses up in beautiful outfits every Sunday," Jonathan said. "But she looks perfect no matter what she wears."

Samantha felt butterflies in her stomach as Jonathan leapt to her defense. She ignored Sara's words, happy to know Jonathan thought she looked perfect regardless of how much makeup she put on, how intricately she did her hair, or how fashionably she dressed.

"It's nice to see you two are so happy to have one another," Scarlett said. "I've never seen Samantha so happy before, Jonathan. You really make her shine."

"Jonathan," Steven said before Jonathan could reply to Scarlett, "what happened to your legs?"

Everyone at the table stopped chewing their food and looked over at him. Samantha was horrified.

"Steven! I—" Dan began.

"No, it's okay, Mr. Reid," Jonathan said. "I'm sure you're all wondering why I have no legs. Well, Steven, it's a long story. I'll try to make it quick, but long story short, I got into a car accident. A terrible car accident. I was texting and driving, like an idiot, and ran a red light."

Jonathan had told the story a few times by then. While it made him emotional, he was able to keep his emotions in check better as he told the story more. "As I sped through the intersection, an eighteen-wheeler was coming through the other way. I swerved out of the way but lost control and hit a large oak tree head-on. They had to amputate my legs. As bad as that sounds, that's not the worst part."

Everyone was silent. Steven was so engrossed in the story that he wasn't even chewing the bite of fajita that he still had in his mouth.

"The worst part is my little sister was in the car with me and didn't make it." Everyone but Samantha gasped as he said this. "She was ten years old. Her name was Gabby. I'll never forgive myself for texting and driving. But I'm learning to forgive myself thanks to Samantha."

Jonathan grabbed Samantha's hand and held it as she looked at him with an encouraging expression. "Sam has helped me open up and heal. She's leading me on a path to self-forgiveness. Pastor Broussard, the pastor who runs the Bible study and conducts the masses at school, is helping me cope with the tragedy a little better as well. Learning what the Bible says about forgiveness has really helped."

Samantha couldn't have felt prouder of Jonathan. It took a lot of courage to open up to her family like that and a lot of maturity to not get upset with Steven for asking him such a personal question. The rest of the family forgot about Steven's lack of a filter; their hearts were won over by Jonathan's response.

After dinner, Jonathan helped Sara clean the table. With that gesture, he was only impressing the family more. For the Reids, it was a family tradition for everyone to play an after-dinner board game to end the night. The Reids invited Jonathan to partake in this family tradition, and he gladly obliged. That night, they decided, they would play Trivial Pursuit.

With Jonathan playing, the Reids were excited to have even teams. Usually one person had to play alone, because they were five in total. With Jonathan, they could split into three teams of two: Dan with Sara, Steven with Scarlett, and Jonathan with Samantha. Dan and Sara rolled first and landed on a yellow space.

"History? Let's go, baby!" Dan said gleefully. It wasn't the yellow pie space, but the yellow pie space was at the end of the spoke they were moving down. Dan and Sara went that direction because they both were great at history.

Samantha took a card from the top of the deck. "The Statue of Liberty," she read, "was given to the US by which country?"

"Easy," Dan said. "France."

"Correct."

Sara rolled again, and they were able to move to the yellow pie square. Samantha read the next History question. "Following the death of Gianni in

1997, his sister Donatella took over as creative director of his fashion business. What is their shared surname, which is also the name by which the business is known?"

"I got this," Sara said. "I wear Versace all the time. The answer is Versace."

"Bingo," Samantha said, trying to ignore Sara's incessant bragging about her fashionability.

Sara put a yellow slice of pie in her game piece. They rolled again and landed on a blue square. Geography.

Samantha asked the question. "What is earth's largest continent?"

Dan and Sara looked at each other, leaned in, and whispered into each other's ears. After a hushed debate, they pulled away from each other. Dan took a crack at it. "Africa."

"Wrong," Samantha said. "It's Asia."

A few turns later, it was finally Jonathan and Samantha's turn. They rolled the die and landed on an orange square. Sports & Leisure. This time Scarlett took the card off the top of the deck. "Which NFL team appeared in four consecutive Super Bowls from 1991–1994 and lost them all?"

Jonathan knew this question right away. Back when he played with the Katy Tigers, they went to every championship from his freshman to senior year and lost all except for the championship he won on the night of the crash. His coach had joked to him before the game that they'd be like the '94 Buffalo Bills if they were to lose for the fourth time in a row. Jonathan helped them avoid that fate, which was the only redeeming quality about that night. "The Buffalo Bills," Jonathan said immediately. Everyone looked at him in surprise.

"Correct," Scarlett said after a skeptical hesitation. "Well done."

"Wow. Even I didn't know that," Steven said. "I'm impressed. You must know a lot about football."

Jonathan just laughed. Samantha had no idea how he knew the answer to that question, but she went along with it and just rolled the dice nonchalantly. They moved their game piece to a green square. Science & Nature.

Scarlett picked up a card and asked the question. "Who discovered Penicillin?"

Jonathan wasn't surprised when Samantha said the answer just as fast as he answered the previous question. "Alexander Fleming."

The game went on for another hour. It was close, but Jonathan and Samantha took the lead toward the end. Their bond was powerful, and everyone noticed that something special was starting between them. The connection they had was palpable.

When they got to the center of the board, they had to answer one last question to win the game. The others agreed to choose Arts & Literature for the final question, expecting neither Jonathan nor Samantha to be well-versed in that category.

Scarlett read the question. "Who wrote *The Alchemist*?"

Jonathan clapped his hands and jumped in his wheelchair triumphantly. "Paulo Coelho." He had read the book at least twice. Samantha and Jonathan high-fived while Steven playfully slammed his fist on the table, pretending to be upset.

Jonathan had made a good impression on the Reids with the Kolaches, opening up about his accident, helping Sara clean up, and then demonstrating broad knowledge during Trivial Pursuit. He no longer felt nervous. He felt at home with the Reids, unconditionally accepted for the first time since the accident. The Reids were glad to have him as a guest, too, especially Samantha.

CHAPTER 27

· • • ● ● ● • • ·

Over the next few days, Jonathan learned a lot about Samantha's family. One day, Steven and Dan were playing catch in the backyard. Samantha, Scarlett, and Sara were all watching from the back porch while sipping on iced tea. Jonathan had the choice to either play catch with Steven and Dan or have a conversation with the girls. He had all his life to play catch, he figured, so he decided he would stay on the back porch and get to know Scarlett and Sara.

"Why don't you play catch with them, Jonathan?" Samantha asked.

"I'm okay. I can play catch whenever I want. I'm fine right here."

"Jonathan has an incredible arm," Samantha bragged to her mother and sister. "He used to play quarterback before the accident."

Jonathan didn't want to talk about that. He changed the subject. "I heard you two were once beauty pageant winners," he said to Scarlett and Sara. "Do you still do beauty pageants?"

"Beauty pageant winners would be an understatement," Sara replied. "Scarlett won Ms. Texas two years ago. She's won several beauty pageants. She was the recurrent champion for four years running from ages 18 to 22."

Scarlett didn't revel in Sara's boasting. "I'm so done with beauty pageants, to answer your question, Jonathan. You have to stick to a strict diet, and exercise all the time. It's just so stressful. Work is too busy for me, and I'm getting married in a little over a year. Life is too hectic to worry about beauty pageants."

"What do you do for work?"

"I'm an advertising executive at a public relations firm in Dallas."

"You're an executive? Already? That's really impressive."

"Thanks. It took a lot of hustling over the past few years. It's never really slowed down. The work has gotten harder, and the hours have gotten longer, but it pays my rent."

"Where do you live?"

"I live with my fiancé William right around here, near Southlake, in the Dallas and Fort Worth area. I come here to visit my family quite often, since I live so close."

Jonathan nodded along as Scarlett spoke. "What does William do?"

"He works for an investment firm in Fort Worth."

Jonathan and Scarlett went back and forth for the next twenty minutes or so. As they spoke, Jonathan watched Steven and Dan playing catch in the backyard. Steven was making some impressive catches, and Jonathan was quick to realize he had a lot of athletic ability. After twenty minutes, Steven and Dan joined Jonathan, Samantha, Scarlett, and Sara on the porch.

"You were looking pretty good out there," Jonathan said as Steven walked up the steps to the back porch.

"Thanks, man," Steven said. "I've got to practice for next season. It'll be my senior year. I've got to impress the colleges."

"What colleges are you looking at?"

"I really want to be a part of South Texas A&M. The coach contacted me last September."

"They just got a new coach, right? Bob Williams or something like that?"

"Yeah, that's right," Steven said, clearly impressed with Jonathan's football knowledge. "Coach Williams is running things now."

"Well, boys, you can talk about football all you want," Sara said. "But the girls and I are going to run to the market to pick up some groceries."

"Alright," Dan said. "I've got some work to do, so I'll be in my office."

Everyone dispersed. Scarlett and Samantha went with Sara to the market while Dan went to do some work in his home office. It was just Jonathan and Steven on the porch.

"Do you play Halo?" Steven asked.

"Yeah, man. I love Halo."

Jonathan followed Steven to a room with a large leather couch, a flat-screen TV mounted on a wall, and an Xbox under it. "Welcome to the man cave," Steven said as they entered the room. Pictures of legendary Dallas Cowboys players lined the walls. All the greatest players were represented, including Troy Aikman, Tony Romo, Emmit Smith, Deion Sanders, and more. All of the pictures were autographed, too. To the right of the couch, there was a pool table. To the left, a foosball table.

"So do you play for the Carroll Dragons?" Jonathan asked Steven, as he set up Halo on the TV.

"Yeah. I do. How'd you know? You know a lot about football, man."

"Well I know the Carroll Dragons are the football team for the secondary school here in Southlake. I played them in the 6A championship game like five years ago."

"So that's how you know so much about football," Steven said as he tossed Jonathan a controller and sat down on the couch. "You used to play?"

"Yeah. I was a quarterback."

"Were you a starter?"

"I was."

"So you led your team to a championship?" Steven extended his fist for a fist bump. Jonathan fist bumped him. "What team was it?"

"Yeah. The Katy Tigers."

"Congratulations, man."

"Thanks. We barely won. We were down by four points with ten seconds left in the fourth. Not to brag, I did a pretty absurd play to score a game-winning touchdown."

"How absurd?"

"I flipped over a guy."

"No way." Steven took out his phone. "What's your name?"

"Jonathan McCalister. Why?"

"I'm gonna see if it's on YouTube." Steven typed into his phone. "You've got a highlight reel with 200,000 views!? That's crazy."

Jonathan knew he had a highlight reel, but had no idea it garnered so much attention. Steven watched in awe as he saw Jonathan running with long legs and incredible athleticism. Play after play, Jonathan ran back and forth horizontally across the field, evading countless defensive players who broke through the Tigers' offensive line. Whereas most quarterbacks would go down and take a sack, Jonathan scrambled across the field and found open receivers time after time. He would throw tight spirals into triple coverage and somehow come away with a completion. If no receiver was open, he'd run it himself. It was as if the whole team depended on Jonathan's skills. When the final play on the highlight reel came, the absurd play Jonathan mentioned played, and Steven couldn't help but holler.

"What!? Are you even human!? You just broke two tackles and flipped over a third guy! You definitely would have made the pros if—" Steven broke off as Jonathan's gaze went from warm to distant. "I'm sorry, man, I didn't mean it like that. You were really good is all I'm saying."

"Nah, it's okay." Jonathan thought about what Dr. Bui had said to him at the end of the summer, that he'd had a "career-ending injury." Maybe Dr. Bui was right. There was no way Jonathan would ever be able to play football again. That didn't mean he couldn't compete in other sports, though. Gerry Bertier, the football player from *Remember the Titans* whose poster Jonathan hung on his wall, went on to win gold medals in the Paralympics for discus throw and shot put. His football career ended, but he was still able to leave a legacy in sports.

Jonathan wondered to himself what legacy he could leave as he and Steven played Halo for the next few hours.

* * *

Two days later, Jonathan woke up to a loud buzzing sound coming from somewhere in the house. He wheeled around, trying to find it, getting closer and closer until he found an open door to a room from where the buzzing sound was coming. He wheeled over and looked into the room. Dan was using a power sander on a beautiful car Jonathan immediately recognized as the same type as the one they drove in the television series *The Dukes of Hazard*. The one Dan was working on was black, not orange like they had in the show, but it was stunning.

Jonathan quietly admired the beauty of the car for a few moments until Dan saw him in his peripheral vision. He turned to look at Jonathan and smiled. "You like the car?"

"I *really* like it. It's a beauty. Isn't that the same type they drove in *The Dukes of Hazard*?"

"That's right," Dan said, delighted that Jonathan recognized it. "It's a 1978 Dodge Charger. Fourth generation B-body car. Last of its kind. Only 2,735 of these were produced."

"Wow! How'd *you* get one?"

"My dad got it when they first came out. He gave it to me as a graduation present when I finished college. I drove it for quite a few years until it finally kicked the dust. I never got rid of it, though. I've always hoped I could restore it. It's been sitting in the garage for a while now, and I'm just starting to restore it."

"You must know a lot about cars to be able to do that," Jonathan said.

"Well, to be honest with you, I don't actually know much about restoring cars. It's a learning process for me at the moment."

"It looks great, though."

"Yeah. I've done a lot of work on the external components of it, but it's the internal components that have me in a tizzy. It's hard to repair it on the inside."

"Are you going to sell it once you've finished restoring it?"

"Oh no," Dan laughed. "This is my pride and joy. I love this thing almost as much as my children. I've had some real memories with this beaut. Some of the best years of my life. I'll be cruising around in this thing when I'm retired, hopefully listening to that V8 engine purr." He slapped the hood of the car and took a sigh of satisfaction. "*If* I can get that V8 engine to purr, that is."

Jonathan and Dan talked a little while longer and bonded over Dan's 1978 Dodge Charger. Jonathan had successfully bonded with every member of Samantha's family.

The next day, Jonathan and Samantha had to head back to Central Texas University, and everyone was sad to see Jonathan go.

"Thank you all for having me," Jonathan said as he and Samantha stood with their bags next to the door. "I'm grateful for your hospitality."

"It was great to have you here, Jonathan," Sara said with a warm smile.

"Samantha is lucky to have met you."

Jonathan didn't have anything planned for the ride back; he was all out of surprises. There was one place he thought could give them a nice break, though. The place was Granbury. It was a small Texas town south of Fort Worth that was a popular romantic getaway for Texans. When he was researching surprises for the trip out to Samantha's house, he stumbled across Granbury. It was known as a charming town with many bed and breakfast establishments, a beautiful lake, and a quaint and iconic town square. He decided not to stop there on the way to Southlake because there was so much to do. It was a much better place to spend a night or two.

During the ride home, Jonathan concluded he would surprise Samantha with a trip to Granbury Memorial Day weekend to celebrate finishing their final exams for the spring semester. It was only two months away and would make the perfect romantic getaway for the pair.

hink that's a good way to think of it."

nce passed between them for a bit as Samantha watched water lap on the
y the bed and breakfast and Jonathan watched the sun illuminate Saman-
skin and reflect off of her cerulean eyes.

turned her gaze to Jonathan.

n having a really good time here," she said. "I appreciate having this time
r."

do, too," Jonathan replied. "I've got something even more special planned
tonight."

u and your surprises, Jonathan McCalister."

* * *

ha clutched Jonathan's arm and buried her face into it, trying to hide
e horrors on the big screen in front of them. They were at Brazos theater,
in movie theater that paid homage to classic drive-in theaters. Jonathan
ure what he and Samantha were watching. It was some cheesy zombie flick
ked like it was made in the 1970s. He and Samantha were lying on the
ith blankets, pillows, movie nachos, and hot dogs. They were up on a hill
king the cars pulled up to the screen.

don't know where I'd be without you to protect me from these zombies,"
tha joked as she pulled away from Jonathan's arms, grabbed a chip, and
it into the nacho cheese. She smiled as she bit off half the chip and fed
an the other half. In Samantha's eyes, the food could not have been more
for such a date. She looked at all the cars parked in front of the screen.
ever been to a drive-in theater before. This is really cool."

m glad you like it," Jonathan said as he chewed the chip Samantha put in
uth. "I didn't mean to terrify you. Maybe I should have looked up what
was playing first."

Oh, please, this movie doesn't terrify me. Look at all those kids watching
roofs of their parents' cars down there. They aren't scared at all. I just used
excuse to snuggle with you." She buried her face back into Jonathan's
ramatically.

nathan laughed, put his finger under Samantha's chin, and lifted her chin
meet his. He slowly brought it closer and closer until their lips touched.

CHAPTER 28

$\bullet\bullet\bullet\bullet\bullet\bullet$

For the next two months, Samantha and Jonathan focused mostly on their studies. They still went to Bible study every Thursday and church service every Sunday, but they went on fewer dates. Jonathan hoped the surprise trip to Granbury on Memorial Day weekend would make up for the lack of dates. Plus, he didn't want Samantha's grades to suffer because of him.

After Samantha finished her exams, she went over to Jonathan's apartment. When Jonathan opened the door to let her in, she walked right past him and collapsed onto his couch. "I'm so happy all that stress is over with," Samantha said, her voice muffled as her face was buried in a pillow. "Now I can finally relax."

Jonathan smirked. "I'm looking forward to relaxing, too. In Granbury. With you."

Samantha lifted her head off of Jonathan's pillow and looked at him curiously. "What do you mean?"

"I've booked us a stay at the Admiral's House on the Lake for Memorial Day weekend. It's a bed and breakfast in Granbury. It's right on the lake and a short walk from Granbury square."

"Jon," Samantha said, "are you serious?" She put her hand over her heart. "That's so sweet."

Jonathan smiled. "I thought a romantic getaway would be nice. We haven't been going on many dates because we've been so busy with finals. But now we can finally relax."

"I've heard of Granbury. I've always wanted to go." Samantha got up off the couch and hugged Jonathan. "You're the best Jonathan. Thank you."

* * *

"That's a beautiful old building," Samantha murmured as she looked at the Hood Country Courthouse in the middle of Granbury square. They had been walking around the square all day, browsing the many shops, eating ice cream and people-watching.

"It looks like it's been here for at least a hundred years," Jonathan said as he craned his neck to look up at the enormous clocktower protruding from the middle of the courthouse.

"Who's that guy?" Samantha pointed at a statue next to the courthouse. The statue was a man with a mustache, a hat, and a buttoned-up trench coat.

"I don't know. Let's go see."

Jonathan and Samantha approached the statue. Samantha read the inscription upon it out loud.

ERECTED BY THE U.D.C.
GENERAL GRANBURY
CHAPTER NO. 663
IN MEMORY OF
BRIGADIER GENERAL
H.B. GRANBURY
AND HIS
VALIANT FOLLOWERS

"He must be who the town was named after," Jonathan mused. He observed that under the inscription were the years 1861–1865. He realized by the outfit the man was wearing, the fact that he was a general, and the dates listed below the inscription, that he must have been a Confederate general during the American Civil War. "Looks like he was a Confederate general. I wonder if it'll get taken down with all of the Confederate monuments being taken down these days."

"Yeah. I don't know," Samantha said.

Jonathan and Samantha walked around Granbur[y] so and then headed to the Admiral's House on the L[ake] blown away by the view of the lake from their room.

"Let's go out on that pier," Samantha said as she e[yed] onto the lake.

"Alright," Jonathan replied, and off they went.

They held hands as they strolled along the pier loo[k]ing them. "Some things give life meaning," Jonatha[n] Samantha with a warm smile. "It's hard to believe there[ ] you're looking at a sight as beautiful as what I'm looki[ng]

"Are you talking about me or the lake?"

"Both."

Samantha giggled and let go of Jonathan's hand, pu[t] the railing of the pier and gazing out to the water. Jona[than] and did the same, his eyes looking right under the raili[ng] For the first time in a long time, he thought about pros[thetics]

"If I had prosthetics," he said softly, "I'd be able to[ ]

"Do you ever think about getting them?" Samanth[a]

"No. Both times I tried, I got upset with my physi[cal]

"What made you upset?"

"Well, my first one, Dr. Austin, was just a jerk. I[ ] upset with the second one. His name was Dr. Bui. He[ ] good guy. I just thought he was taking pity on me, I[ ] because he referred to my condition as a 'career-ending[ ] ing of it that way."

Samantha knew about Dr. Bui. Rose had told her, a[nd] tha had talked about him once before. But she didn't wa[nt] bad mood by pressing him to consider going back to Dr.[ ] go back when he was ready.

"How *do* you like to think of it?"

Jonathan thought for a moment. "I think of it as a[ ] drive. That's pretty much it. If I hadn't texted, I'd have m[ ] I did, so I don't. If I think of it as career-ending, that make[s]

The sounds of the zombies began to quiet as Jon and Sam shared a passionate kiss under the stars. They were no longer interested in the movie and ignored it the rest of the night. Their minds were absorbed by one another. They spent the next hour snuggling and kissing until the credits began to roll. It was time to go back to their room at the Admiral's House on the Lake.

* * *

When they arrived back at their room, they both reluctantly climbed into separate beds. Jonathan had been respectful enough to request to have a room with two beds knowing Samantha may not feel comfortable sleeping in the same bed. Both of them secretly wanted to sleep in the same bed, but Jonathan didn't want to pressure Samantha, and Samantha wasn't sure if Jonathan wanted to sleep in the same bed because he had requested two beds.

"Well . . . Goodnight, Jon," Samantha said as she faced Jonathan with her head on her pillow. "This was the best Memorial Day weekend I could have ever asked for."

"It really was special. Goodnight, Sam."

Jonathan turned off the lights, and the room became pitch black. Both of them tossed and turned as they tried to go to sleep. Jonathan debated if he should make a move. Samantha wondered if he was going to make a move, too. It took at least thirty minutes for Jonathan to start to fall asleep. Samantha was still wide awake, though, and decided to get into Jonathan's bed. When she got into the bed, she didn't say anything. She just kissed him on the cheek.

Jonathan, surprised, turned and smelled the sweet scent of Samantha's hair as it brushed against his face. He made out her lips in the blackness and passionately kissed them.

"Thanks for such a wonderful day, Jon," Samantha said as she pulled away. "Is it okay if I stay in your bed?"

"Of course, Sam."

"Just keep things innocent, please. I'm not quite ready for things to go further. But I don't want this day to end."

"I totally understand." Jonathan couldn't deny that he felt slightly disappointed. But he was happy to be spending time with Samantha and feel her warmth beside him in his bed.

Samantha climbed under his sheets and pressed her face into his chest. He wrapped his arms around her. There was no more tossing and turning as they quickly fell asleep.

CHAPTER 29

As summer began, Jonathan was desperate to find a reason to not go home. He didn't want to force his dad on another "business trip" and because Samantha was going to be taking summer classes, he wanted to stay at Central Texas University to spend time with her. He told his mother he was taking classes, which he was, and had to stay at his apartment for the summer. It upset her, but she understood.

Jonathan was sitting in his room writing in his journal when his phone began to ring. Expecting it to be Samantha calling to hang out, he excitedly reached to answer it. His excitement was fettered into curiosity when he saw that the call was coming from an unknown number. Hesitantly, he answered.

"Hello?"

"Hi, I'm calling for Jonathan McCalister. Is this the right number?"

"Uh, yeah," Jonathan replied. "Who is this? What are you calling about?"

"This is Meghna Angadi. I'm not sure if you remember me, but I met you at the Race for the Kids 5K, very briefly."

"Oh, hi, Meghna. I do remember you."

"Great! As you know, I host a number of charity events. I know I already invited you to speak at one event celebrating unlikely heroes, but I'm not calling you about that. I'm calling you about a different event."

Jonathan wondered why she had such a keen interest in him and how she got his number.

"What event? What do you want me to do?"

"I'd like you to speak at an event about the perils of texting and driving. It's a rampant issue in our world today, and I've caught wind of your story. I think you'd be an excellent choice for one of our main speakers. The event is called "The Celebration of Life," and it's sponsored by the Waco Children's Hospital. It's an event to celebrate children who have made recoveries from long-term illnesses, donors who help support the hospital, and an array of inspirational speakers. An anti-texting message from you would go along with the hospital's goal in helping children live healthier and more fulfilling lives."

Jonathan began feeling paranoid and furious at the same time. Did his mom put her up to this? Few people knew his full story *and* had his number. It couldn't be Rose. She didn't know Meghna Angadi. Feelings of betrayal brewed inside of Jonathan as he realized who must have called Meghna and recommended that he speak about texting and driving.

Sam.

Jonathan took a deep breath to calm himself down before replying. "I'm sorry, Meghna, but I'm not interested."

Meghna's disappointment was palpable, even over the phone. She cleared her throat before speaking. "Okay, well, if you change your mind, feel free to call me back. The event is this weekend, so you have a few days to sleep on it. It'd mean a lot to me and our community if you decide to share your story with people so they can realize why texting and driving is such a bad idea. Your story would be instrumental in spreading the anti-texting and driving message. It could save a lot of lives."

"Thanks, Meghna. We'll see." Jonathan had absolutely no interest in calling Meghna back. As soon as he hung up the phone, he called Samantha. He was fuming.

After a few rings, Samantha answered in a delicate voice. "Hi, Jon."

"Sam, did you tell Meghna Angadi about my story with texting and driving?"

"Um, no," she replied innocently.

"How does she know my story, then? She just called me about speaking at some event about the perils of texting and driving."

"I don't know how she knows about your story. But that's awesome, Jon! You've got to do it."

"Absolutely not. I'm a horrible speaker and have no interest in talking about my accident in front of a bunch of strangers."

"But we talked about how you need to move on from the accident. We talked about how you want to atone for your mistakes. This is a great opportunity to do just that! Texting and driving is something you really care about. I know that because I've seen how much you care about it. I saw you when you got angry at me for texting at the stoplight on the way to The Competition Corner. I saw how you almost cried at the sushi restaurant when you talked about how you thought Gabby's death was your fault because you couldn't refrain from texting while driving. I saw you cry when you told your story to Kylie, Tom, and Elijah. It's something you clearly care a lot about. And, Jon,"—Samantha's voice cracked with emotion—"I care a lot about you. This will help you move on. This will help you deal with your guilt. This will help a lot of people."

"I do care a lot about it, Sam," Jonathan replied. "But I don't feel comfortable sharing my story with so many strangers. I've only told my closest friends about my story. The only people I've told my story to are you, Kylie, Tom, Elijah, and your family."

Silence passed between them for a few moments. Finally, Samantha spoke.

"I really think you should do it. I don't know anyone as passionate about texting and driving as you. Your story will change lives. You may even save lives. People will remember what happened to you, and that will remind them that they shouldn't text and drive."

"That's a stretch," Jonathan muttered.

"It's not! I don't text and drive or even text at stoplights ever since you told me your story. But changing people's lives is just a bonus. Even if the only benefit you get from speaking at this event is atoning for your mistakes and moving on from the past, it's *still* worth it. Don't just do it for yourself; do it for Gabby."

That last line echoed through Jonathan's head.

Do it for Gabby . . .

Jonathan had been living in constant guilt since the accident. He hadn't done anything to atone for his mistakes. He just suffered in his rut and never cared about anything. He had been bitter and closed off. Samantha had helped him get out of his rut, but he knew that he was far from being completely himself again. Maybe speaking at the event would help him cope with his guilt. And maybe he would hear stories from others that were similar to his and learn from people who were able to forgive themselves. Maybe this speaking engagement was the big leap Jonathan needed.

"Fine," he said. "I'll do it for Gabby."

After Jonathan got off the phone with Samantha, he called Meghna back to tell her he would do the event. She was ecstatic. "You won't regret it," she promised. "Nothing is more powerful than using your story to change the lives of others." Jonathan still wasn't sure how Meghna knew about his story or how he would change lives by telling people not to text and drive. The event wasn't about texting and driving. It was about celebrating life. How would a story about a girl *dying* because of texting and driving fit into an event about celebrating *life*?

But he was doing it for Gabby, Samantha, and, partially, for himself. Samantha was sure it would help him move on from the accident, and her confidence instilled hope in Jonathan.

CHAPTER 30

•●●●●●●•

"**M**y dear Cindy—my one and only daughter—passed away a little over a year ago."

Standing on the stage was a middle-aged man—probably in his mid to late fifties—sporting a ponytail, a grizzled beard, a Harley Davidson T-shirt, and ripped jeans. Meghna had introduced the topic of texting and driving before the man took the stage, and Jonathan and this man were the two speakers on that topic. There had been several speakers before them. Some were people who overcame a terminal illness thanks to donors. Some were people who donated hundreds of thousands to Waco Children's Hospital and wanted to talk about why they did it. Jonathan was still unsure how talking about the perils of texting and driving fit into the event. But if it helped children live healthier and more fulfilling lives, as Meghna suggested it would, he was willing to share his story.

Jonathan was nervous. It wasn't the crowd that bothered him. He was used to being in the spotlight from his football days. He was nervous to revisit the darkest depths of his mind. He was nervous to talk about the accident and share his feelings about Gabby to a room full of strangers. There were at least five hundred people stuffed into the small auditorium the event was being held in. And although Jonathan didn't know it, his parents were sitting in the back, hidden from Jonathan's sight. Samantha had invited them. Rose was proud that Jonathan had the courage to talk about his story. She had forced Jeff to come along with her,

175

much to his dismay, but he was interested in seeing whether Jonathan would take responsibility for killing Gabby. He still harbored resentment and anger toward Jonathan and wanted to see whether Jonathan was in as much pain as he was in because of the accident at 2612 Cherryhill Lane.

"She passed away one week before what would have been her twenty-fifth birthday," the man on stage continued. "But she never got to see it. When I talk with people about what happened to my daughter, they assume she was killed because *she* was texting and driving. But, the truth is, my daughter *wasn't* texting and driving. She was driving responsibly. She had both eyes on the road and was driving the speed limit when another driver—who *was* texting and driving— veered his car across the road and collided with my baby's car head-on. By the time she got to the hospital, she was dead. The other driver—the one who was texting and driving—the one who took my baby's life—was undamaged."

Sympathetic murmurs erupted from the audience. "She was driving a Honda Civic, and he was driving a Ford F-150 pickup truck. The size of his car compared to my baby's likely protected him from any injury. He went to prison, where he is serving ten years for vehicular manslaughter. As soon as he got to prison, he sent my wife and me a letter apologizing that his reckless driving took my daughter's life. His words were sincere. He seemed to be genuinely sorry. He was nineteen years old when he crashed into my daughter's car and will be twenty-nine when he gets out of prison. His entire twenties have been ripped away from him just because he couldn't wait to reply to a text. But you know what? His apology didn't impact his prison sentence. But I forgave him. I miss my baby more than words can express. But this young man realizes he made a mistake and was sincere in his apology, and I accepted it."

Jonathan was surprised to hear this man say he forgave the man that killed his daughter. His own father, Jeff, surely would never relate to this man, he thought. Meanwhile, Jeff was sitting in the back of the auditorium wondering whether he had been too harsh with Jonathan. He hadn't spoken to Jonathan since the accident and hadn't forgiven him, yet this man forgave the man who killed his daughter after reading one letter of apology.

"I visit him every month in prison," the man continued. "I want him to know he is forgiven. His punishment is severe enough. He will lose an entire decade of his life—some would say the *best* decade of his life—over a single, stupid text message. He feels remorse about it and takes responsibility for my daughter's death. And that's more of a punishment than any prison could provide. So, I guess my message for you all is to forgive your loved ones. If they texted and drove and paid the ultimate price for it, forgive them. Don't hold a grudge against them. Mistakes happen. Accidents happen. We must be grateful for the people we still have in our lives. Thank you." The audience applauded the man as he made his way off the stage.

Jonathan gulped. He was up next. He was behind the curtain on the side of the stage, next to Samantha. He was trying to go over what he would say in his mind but had no speech prepared. "I can't do this," he said to Samantha. "I don't know what I'm going to say."

"You can do it, Jon. I believe in you," Samantha reassured him. "Do it for Gabby."

Meghna's voice filled the auditorium. "Thanks, Peter. I'm sure everyone can learn something about your willingness to forgive. We can all use more forgiveness in our lives. Our next speaker, Jonathan McCalister, has another powerful story about texting and driving to share that will just tug at your heartstrings."

The audience clapped their hands as Meghna stepped away from the microphone and beckoned Jonathan to come over. He wheeled over with a knot in his gut and his mouth as dry as a desert. He slowly lowered the microphone and took a deep breath as he prepared to speak.

"Hey, everyone," he began. "My name is Jonathan McCalister. As you can see, I have no legs. I used to have them, but I had to have them amputated after I crashed my car into a tree. I still remember the address where the crash happened, 2612 Cherryhill Lane. I wasn't looking at the road because, as you probably have guessed, I was texting and driving. I woke up after a two-week coma to discover that my legs were gone and I had killed my sister."

The room was completely silent. You could have heard a pin drop. The spotlight blinded Jonathan from seeing the audience beyond the first few rows of people who were all looking at him expectantly. Everyone else was hidden behind the bright glare of the light.

"Every day, I beat myself up about why I reached for my phone. I think about how differently life could have turned out if I hadn't. There was nothing important to look at, either. It was a stupid text message from my girlfriend at the time that any teenage boy would dream of seeing. I could have looked when I got home. In fact, I could have not looked at it at all and nothing in my life would have changed. But I chose to look at it, everything in my life changed for the worse, and I killed my little sister."

Jonathan cleared his throat and thought about the next words to say. It wasn't as hard as he thought it was going to be. He didn't enjoy feeling like an example of "what not to do," though. In football, he had been an example of how to do things right. Now, he was an example of how one bad decision could destroy lives.

He also didn't like that everyone was looking at him as though he was teaching them a lesson on how to not mess up your entire life. But he thought that might have been God's plan for his future. Maybe God was calling him to lead by example and show others that texting and driving was a bad idea. Maybe he could be the reason someone else didn't crash.

"Let's just back up a bit to before the accident. On the night the accident happened, I had just won the state championship game for my high school football team, the Katy Tigers. I was the star quarterback who led them to the state championship every year. But we never won until that night. I was so happy to have finally won. My world was perfect. I had a full scholarship to play Division One football at my father's alma mater, Texas University, and I had a good chance to make it to the NFL.

"My little sister, Gabby, was even happier than I was. She was my biggest fan.

"My family and I were going to a celebratory dinner at my favorite restaurant. Gabby was so eager to talk with me about the game she asked to ride with me to the restaurant. As I started the car, she was hopping up and down in her seat, asking me all about the game, why I called the audible that led to the winning score, whether I meant to run or pass the ball on the play, and so on."

It was painful for Jonathan to remember the last conversation he had with Gabby. His mind went back to that night, and he could visualize her in his mind. It was painful to see her face again in his memory, so bright and exuberant.

"I told her to put on her seatbelt and everything, but—" Jonathan's inflection was filled with emotion. He was struggling as he relived the accident. "But I guess she didn't."

Jonathan wasn't able to compose himself like he had when he told his story to the Reids. Tears streamed down his cheeks in front of everyone in the audience. Samantha looked on from the side of the stage, fighting the urge to run over to hug him and wipe away his tears.

"When Gabby saw me look toward my phone, she shouted at me to stop. She *told* me not to text and drive. If I had listened to her, she'd still be alive, and I would have been playing football at Texas University, living my dreams. The seconds I took to text my girlfriend has caused me a lifetime of regret and agony. I lost my family that day. Every single day, I think about why I was spared and Gabby wasn't. Every single day, I think about how unfair it was that she died and I lived. Every day, I wish I could trade places with Gabby. I'm so sorry. I broke up my entire family."

Jeff and Rose both watched on with tears in their eyes. Jeff had no idea the accident weighed on Jonathan so much. He thought Jonathan regretted losing his legs and lamented that his dreams of playing football were thwarted. He had never imagined that Jonathan wished he could trade places with Gabby.

"Oftentimes, I dream of her and don't want to wake up because I know when I wake up she'll no longer be there." Jonathan took a deep breath, trying to stifle his tears.

"I hope my story will inspire all of you to never text and drive. I believe it's my mission to spread the word about texting and driving, to honor my sister, and to do something good with my second chance at life. I believe that's what God's plan is for my life. I believe that's why God spared my life."

Jonathan tried to say more but was too choked by emotion. The tears were still pouring down his face. He had to end it before he began to sob.

"Thank you."

The audience got up from their seats and gave Jonathan a standing ovation. He put his hand up in a gesture of gratitude and wheeled over to Samantha, who was watching with an expression of commiseration. Tears were welling up in her eyes, too. Meghna was beside her with a look of equal commiseration.

"You did great, Jon," Samantha said. "I agree with what you said about God's plan. He spared you for a reason. There's a reason you aren't with Gabby. He needs you here."

"I hope so," he replied. "I'm just glad that speech is over."

"I hope it brought some closure," Meghna said. "It was a very touching story. You told it brilliantly."

"Thanks," Jonathan said. "It sort of brought me some closure, I guess. Mid-speech, I really started to believe God's plan for me is to spread the word about texting and driving. I think that's the reason He spared me. Realizing that definitely brought me a bit of closure about the accident." Meghna nodded along as Jonathan spoke. He paused and eyed Meghna quizzically. "How did you catch wind about my story, anyway?"

"It was all over the news when it happened. I saw you at the Race for the Kids 5K and recognized you immediately even under all that scruff you had on your face. I didn't want to bring it up then, but I made a mental note of it. When this event was getting close, I thought of you. I remembered your story and knew it was powerful enough to change lives for the better. That's why I invited you to speak."

"I see." Jonathan felt guilty for initially assuming Samantha had gone behind his back.

"Have you been back to the scene of the accident since then? I've connected with a lot of people who had their lives changed from car accidents. Many of them say it brings them even more closure to visit the scenes where their accidents happened," Meghna added. "It's a way to turn the site from a site of despair to a place to be reborn. Maybe visiting the site of your accident could help you, too."

"I think that's a good idea." Rose's voice surprised Jonathan as she stepped out of the shadows behind Samantha and Meghna.

"Mom? What are you doing here?"

"I invited your mom, Jon," Samantha explained. "I thought she should see you give your speech."

At first, Jonathan wasn't sure how he felt about his mom coming. It only took him a brief moment to decide he didn't care too much. He was close with his mom. There was nothing wrong with her hearing him talk about how he felt about the accident. He had never opened up to her about it before.

"I think it's a good idea, too." Jonathan did a double take after hearing his father's voice. Seconds later, Jeff stepped from out of the same shadows Rose had just stepped out of. His dad hadn't spoken to him in years. This was confounding. Jeff walked over to Jonathan and opened his arms in a gesture as though he wanted to hug him.

"I'm sorry, Jon. I've been so pent up with rage over these years because Gabby passed away. When I heard that guy with a ponytail talk about how he forgave the person who killed his daughter, I realized it was neither fair nor mature of me to hold a grudge against you. I've got to move on. I think we should visit Gabby's grave together. It'll help us both receive the closure we need."

"It's okay, Dad," Jonathan responded as he embraced him. The two shared a hug as Rose and Samantha welled up with tears of joy. After Jeff and Jonathan finished their hug, Rose hugged Jonathan.

"I'm so proud of you. Gabby would be, too." Tears began to pour down Jonathan's face again as she said this. Everyone, including Jeff, had tears streaming down their face.

"Jonathan . . ." The voice that spoke his name surprised Jonathan. It came from behind him.

Dean.

Jonathan immediately started to wipe the tears from his face. He didn't want Dean to see him like this.

Won't he just leave me alone?

"What do you want, Dean?" Jonathan said as he whirled around to face Dean. To Jonathan's surprise, Dean wore a look of equal parts sympathy and guilt.

"Look, man, I'm really sorry. What I said to you was totally uncalled for and, after watching you speak, I know I was being an absolute jerk for making you into the bad guy. You're a good dude. An amazing guy. I had no idea you blamed yourself for Gabby's death, and I made it even worse for you with what I did."

Tears were forming in Dean's eyes too. "I'm . . . I'm really sorry, man. I guess I was just jealous of you and the connection you and Sam have together. Samantha and you seem to belong with each other. You two are so perfect together." He turned to Samantha and then looked down at the floor, shaking his head regretfully.

Jonathan couldn't hide his surprise over Dean's apology. He thought about the first time Samantha brought him to church. She had pointed out a passage to him about forgiveness over trespasses.

"For if you forgive others their trespasses, your heavenly Father will also forgive you, but if you do not forgive others their trespasses, neither will your Father forgive your trespasses" Matthew 6:14–15 (ESV).

God would only forgive Jonathan if he was willing to forgive Dean. It made total sense to Jonathan. What good Christian wouldn't be willing to forgive? Why would they deserve forgiveness if they weren't capable of it themselves?

"Thank you for that, Dean," Jonathan said. "I know it took a lot for you to say all of that, and I truly appreciate it and accept your apology."

Dean smiled and nodded to Jonathan and Sam.

Jonathan nodded back before Dean turned around and walked away. Suddenly Samantha's arms wrapped around Jonathan from behind. Jonathan turned around and embraced Samantha. Her fragrant perfume wafted pleasantly into Jonathan's nose, and the smell of her hair comforted him as they hugged each other tightly. "I love you, Jonathan McCalister," she whispered into his ear. Jonathan clutched her even tighter.

"I love you too, Sam."

CHAPTER 31

· · ● ● ● ● · ·

A few weeks later, Jonathan and Samantha visited Gabby's grave. He had been planning to go with his father so they could both get closure, but he couldn't visit right away. Summer classes started a few days after the speech, and Jonathan and Samantha both wanted to get acquainted with their schedule to see if they wanted to drop any classes before making a trip to Jonathan's hometown. That extra time helped Jonathan prepare emotionally for the visit, too. A few short weeks later, the day of the visit had come.

There was a slight drizzle and an ominous fog over the Magnolia Cemetery as Jonathan, Samantha, Jeff, and Rose, all looked upon Gabby's grave. Jonathan was in a coma when the funeral had happened, and he had never been to the grave. As he looked at it, he realized why. It was sad to look at the headstone. Gabby's death was literally etched in stone. He couldn't help but think that Gabby was just six short feet underneath them lying in the dirt, cold and alone. He couldn't shift back to the reality that she was up in the warmth of God's grace looking down on him. Beneath that headstone, in the physical form, Gabby was lifeless and decomposing. Depression settled in Jonathan's chest once again as he thought about this, but it subsided as he redirected his attention to the first Bible study he attended with Samantha and the quote Pastor Ana Broussard had read aloud to the students.

"For God so loved the world, that He gave His only begotten Son, that whoever believes in Him shall not perish, but have eternal life" John 3:16 (ESV).

Gabby may have perished and be decomposing in the physical form—like any other deceased person would—but she was up in heaven now. Her life was everlasting. Only her body was lifeless. Her soul was up in heaven living an everlasting life.

Jonathan wheeled forward, approached the grave, and bowed his head. "Hey, Gabby," Jonathan said quietly. "I know I've never visited, but I think about you every day. I can feel you constantly with me, like my guardian angel. Life has been going really great for me lately. I met a girl named Samantha, and we've fallen in love. You'd really like her. I'm sure you've been watching over us as our romance has blossomed."

He held out a bluebonnet he had picked earlier that day and placed it on the grave. "When we sat in the fields of bluebonnets, I felt like I was in heaven. I know that's the type of place you're in right now. It's where you belong. I promise you, Gabby, I will honor your memory down here on earth. I will make you proud. I will make anti-texting your legacy, and I will devote my life to spreading that message."

Jonathan backed away from the grave and wheeled over to Samantha, Jeff, and Rose. They were all looking at him lovingly. Samantha brushed her fingers through Jonathan's hair and smiled as Jeff and Rose both took turns paying their respects.

"Hi, princess," Jeff said. "It's me again. I know I come here a lot, but this time it's extra special. This is the first time I've come here with Jon. It's been a long time since I've spoken to him, and it took me a while to forgive him. I'm sorry for that. I know you'd have wanted me to forgive him a long time ago. Well, I have. It just took me so long because I love you so dearly and wish you were down on earth with us instead of up in heaven. I miss you so much. I realize that's selfish of me. Like Jon said, you belong in heaven."

It was Rose's turn. "Hey, sweetie," Rose said. "I know you're in a better place, but you made earth a better place when you were here, and we all miss you terribly. So many people miss your shining smile and compassionate soul. Heaven got you way too soon."

After Jeff and Rose paid their respects, Samantha placed another bluebonnet on Gabby's grave. As she did, she closed her eyes and recited a short prayer in her head.

After a few minutes, the four said goodbye to Gabby. They had gone separately to the cemetery. Jonathan wanted to go to 2612 Cherryhill Lane to visit the scene of the accident—Meghna suggested he do so—but only with Samantha. He thought going with his parents would be too emotional. The point of visiting the scene was to forgive himself, leave the accident in the past, and begin a new phase of his life spreading an anti-texting-and-driving message to preserve Gabby's legacy. After Jonathan, Jeff, and Rose had paid their respects, Jonathan and Samantha got in Jonathan's van and drove to the large oak tree that took Jonathan's legs and Gabby's life.

* * *

Jonathan never got a good look at the oak tree he crashed into at 2612 Cherryhill Lane. He only saw the thick trunk of the tree for a split second as his car rammed into it. Looking at it, he thought of how old the tree must have been. It was tall and wide, with many large branches. It must have been growing for hundreds of years.

"Well, here we are," Jonathan said as he and Samantha looked at the tree from the sidewalk.

"Here we are." Samantha handed Jonathan a cross Pastor Ana Broussard had given her.

Jonathan rolled up to the tree and placed the cross beneath it. He sat there for a moment, looking at the tree and the intersection in front of it. It was a three-way intersection in the shape of a T with a stoplight on each road going into the intersection. Jonathan figured out he had run a red light on the road perpendicular to the intersection and had gone forward and to the left in order to hit the tree. There were no skid marks. There were no car parts. All that was left of the collision was the large oak tree standing tall in front of 2612 Cherryhill Lane.

As Jonathan sat there looking at the road and rebuilding the accident in his mind, Samantha whispered a prayer. "Please, Lord, I ask you for your strength and wisdom as Jon embarks on his mission to help others. Amen."

Jonathan heard her whisper the prayer but didn't turn around. He placed his hand on the tree. "Years ago, 2612 Cherryhill Lane was the place where I crashed my car, lost my legs, killed my sister, and robbed myself of my scholarship and football career. Today, it becomes the place I commit to spending the rest of my life building Gabby's legacy. It's where I launch into my true calling, to spread the word about texting and driving and honor Gabby's memory. May she rest in peace."

Samantha smiled proudly. "May she rest in peace."

ACT V

CHAPTER 32

· · · ● ● ● ● ● · ·

A chilly October gust breezed by and leaves scattered in the wind as the Central Texas University marching band played in the bleachers overlooking the field. It was the fall semester, and the campus was in full football mode. Jonathan and Samantha sat in the front row. They had preferential seating both because of Jonathan's disability and their relationship with Tom and Elijah. Tom had been recently named the assistant quarterback coach, which was unprecedented for someone who had been a graduate assistant the year before. Elijah was the starting quarterback. He won the position over a senior and a junior during summer practices.

The band was playing the chorus of "Build Me Up Buttercup," their go-to song after a play went in the favor of the Stallions. The clock was winding down—it was the fourth quarter—and the Stallions were up by six. Elijah had just solidified the lead and put the Stallions up by twelve by correctly reading the defensive end with a read option. Jonathan and Tom had taught him a million times over that if the defensive end was lined up inside of the tackle and the play was a read option, Elijah needed to fake the handoff and run it himself. He had done just that and ran the ball all the way into the end zone. It wasn't a special run by any means; the Stallions' offense only had three yards to go to score a touchdown, but it was still a good job reading the defense by Elijah. Jonathan was happy to see all the hard work over the previous year paying off.

"Let's go, Elijah!" Samantha called out. She was wearing a Stallions jersey over a sweatshirt with Elijah's number, 18, on the back.

"His number-one fan," Jonathan joked.

"Hey, I'm allowed to have a little fun. This is probably the last game I can go to."

"Why?" Jonathan and Samantha had gone to every game so far. He was surprised to hear Samantha wouldn't be continuing their tradition. Over the previous month and a half, Samantha had become a huge football fan, and Jonathan had fallen in love with the game again.

"Med school interviews are coming up. I'm gonna be a busy girl."

"Oh, I completely forgot about that."

"Yeah. They start in late October and early November. When do you take your LSAT?"

"I'm going to wait until the summer," Jonathan answered as the kicker kicked the extra point. "After school's done. I'm going to focus on graduating first, and then I'll focus on the exam."

"You should still study for it whenever you have time."

"I've been studying a bunch. Are you graduating early?"

"If all goes according to plan, yeah. I should graduate after this semester."

Jonathan felt a bit of anxiety when he heard that. He knew Samantha had been working hard to graduate early, but he didn't like that it meant she would be done with school so soon. He wasn't sure if that meant she'd have to go back home. For the time being, he didn't want to think about it. He let his worries dissipate and focused on the game.

* * *

"You see how that linebacker immediately blitzed?" Tom asked Elijah.

"Yeah," Elijah said. Tom had brought his computer and some game tapes with him to Jonathan's apartment. He and Elijah joined Jonathan to go over Elijah's performance.

"You know the play was a 32 slant. That means your number-two receiver is going to be running right down the middle where that linebacker should be," Tom explained. "That's the receiver you should pass to. He'll be wide open after the linebacker starts running at you." Tom rewound the play and played it again. "See? He's wide open."

"If you had thrown it to him, you would have avoided the sack," Jonathan added. "While it wouldn't have been a huge gain, a gain is better than a loss. I'd take a few yards rather than lose a few yards any day."

"Not to mention it hurts to get sacked," Elijah said. "All right, we've been going over the game tapes for like an hour now. Let's have some fun. C'mon. We're six and two. We're doing great. There's no need to act like we're in a crisis or anything."

"We're in no crisis, true," Tom replied. "But you've got to keep your head in the game at all times. What if you never learn who to throw to and get sacked in the championship game? We can never watch too many game tapes."

"I know. I have no idea where I'd be without you two helping me out. You've both brought me a long way from where I was last year. But let's grab some BBQ or something. I'm starving."

"Alright," Tom agreed.

CHAPTER 33

—————— ·•◦•●•◦•· ——————

Samantha fidgeted with her hands nervously under the table as she smiled at the panel sitting across from her. The panel was composed of medical school admissions officers. It was her first medical school interview. She was quite anxious.

"Thank you for being here, Ms. Reid. We've reviewed your application and, we must say, we're very impressed with your GPA and your extracurricular activities."

There were three admissions officers across the table, two men and one woman. The woman was the first to speak. "We have no doubt you meet our expectations for undergraduate performance, but we'd like to get to know you better before we make a final decision."

Relief washed over Samantha. She wasn't too surprised they were impressed with her grade point average—she had a perfect 4.0—but it was good to hear them say it. It made her a lot less nervous to know she had started out on the right foot. She was still nervous, though. She had no idea what they were going to ask her to "get to know her better."

"Ms. Reid," one of the men started. "How do you envision using your medical education?"

"I'd like to become a pediatrician," Samantha quickly answered. "So, in that regard, I envision using my medical education to manage the health of children."

"I see," the man said as he looked at his clipboard and wrote something down. Samantha wondered what he was writing.

"Why is being a pediatrician important to you?" the other man asked while the first man continued to write.

"I care a lot about children," Samantha explained. "I want to be able to help as many children as I can. With the exception of the elderly, they are more vulnerable to diseases and sickness than any other group of people. If I can make a difference in their lives by vaccinating them or keeping tabs on their health, that's what I want to do. I want to make sure every child who comes to my practice gets the best medical attention and treatment they can."

"Mhm. Right," the man responded.

The two men asked Samantha more questions for another twenty minutes. Some questions were about her ambitions as a doctor. Others were about her character. And others were about her opinions on things like euthanasia or medically assisted suicide. The questions ranged from topic to topic, and the panel kept her on her toes. Samantha didn't know what to expect. She carefully listened to each question, considered her answer, and replied as honestly as she could.

The last question really caught her by surprise. It wasn't something she expected to be asked during a medical school interview.

"One last question, Ms. Reid," the woman said. "If you could invite three people from the past to dinner, who would they be, and why would you invite them? What would you talk about?"

"Um," Samantha nearly fumbled over her words as she answered. "That's a good question." She stalled for a moment as she dug into the depths of her brain and thought of people she admired who she wanted to meet. "I suppose I'd invite Eleanor Roosevelt. I really respect how she fought so hard for human rights and did what she thought was right no matter what people thought. She was outspoken for a First Lady and is a great example of a strong woman. I would talk to her about how she fought for civil rights and where she found the courage and inspiration to do so when very few people who had power would do the same at the time."

"Okay," the woman responded, showing no emotion or reaction. "And who else?"

"I would invite Clara Barton because I respect how she pursued her dreams to become a nurse at a time when most women didn't work outside of the home. I would ask her about how she taught herself to be a nurse without any formal education and what motivated her to become a nurse when a profession like that wasn't seen as appropriate for a woman until many years later."

"Okay," the woman said, again showing no emotion or reaction. "And third?"

Samantha thought for a moment. She opened her mouth to say Susan B. Anthony because she admired her as a feminist, but as her lips separated, another name came out. "Gabby McCalister. My boyfriend's little sister. She passed away at a young age, and I never got to meet her. The way my boyfriend talks about her makes it clear she was one of the sweetest people to ever walk this earth. She meant so much to him. He talks about how she'd light up any room she went into. She'd be great company at any dinner."

"Interesting," the woman replied, that time showing a slight glimpse of emotion. "Well, thank you for coming. That concludes the interview." All three of the admission officers stood up. Samantha shook each of their hands. "We'll be in touch," the woman said as Samantha shook her hand.

"Thank you," Samantha replied. She was happy with how the interview went. It was the first of many, and Samantha was stressed out over the prospect of messing up her interviews. She figured if she was able to do okay on her first one, she'd be able to do okay on the rest of them. She now knew what to expect.

* * *

While Samantha was at her first medical school interview, Jonathan was in his apartment studying for the LSAT. Earlier that day, he met with the prelaw advisor at Central Texas University and discussed following in his father's footsteps to become a lawyer.

Tom was over, too, playing Madden while Jonathan looked at a copy of a previously administered LSAT he found online. He was trying to familiarize himself with the different types of questions he would see on the test. He was flying through question after question and gaining confidence as he looked to the answer key and saw he was correct.

"C'mon man, quit studying for that stupid test," Tom said. "You have all year to study. Come play some Madden."

"It's not a stupid test, Tom. It's really important if I want to get into a good law school. It's the most important component of my application. It's more important than my GPA."

"Where are you applying to law school?"

"I don't know yet. I've got to figure out what I get on my LSAT before I decide what schools I can apply to."

"You should apply to law school here and become a graduate assistant," Tom said. "Now that I'm the receivers coach, I'm sure I can get you a coaching gig for the Stallions."

"How would I coach from a wheelchair?"

"I don't know, man, but you coached Elijah from a wheelchair, and he's doing great. I think you could really make a career out of coaching. Seriously, there's a great ESPN documentary called *Who Says I Can't*. It's about a guy with no arms and no legs who became a head coach for a high school football team and brought them all the way to the championship. Coaching from a wheelchair isn't impossible."

Tom's offer was tempting. Jonathan was thinking of becoming a lawyer because he didn't know what else to do. He thought becoming a lawyer was his best option for a career path because he saw the success his dad had as a lawyer. Jonathan definitely preferred coaching but wasn't sure he could do it and knew it wouldn't be as lucrative as the latter.

Tom's idea that he could become a graduate assistant would help him pay his way through law school, which would help, although if he decided to coach after law school, he'd make chump change as a coach and wouldn't be using his law degree. Then again, having a law degree would give him options if coaching didn't work out. He didn't want to say this to Tom, though, because Tom was a coach and might take offense to Jonathan pointing out how little money he made. If Jonathan coached part-time and worked full-time as a lawyer, though, he could seriously picture himself taking up Tom on his offer.

"I'll think about it," Jonathan said. "Let's play some Madden."

The two played for an hour until Samantha came knocking at Jonathan's door.

"How'd the interview go?" Jonathan asked, as he let Samantha in.

"It went well," Samantha replied. "They asked me some questions I didn't expect them to ask, though."

"Like what?"

"Well, they asked me if I could have three people from the past over for dinner, who would I choose and why."

"That's strange. They were probably just trying to get a grip on your personality and see how fast you could think on your feet," Jonathan said. "I don't know why else they'd ask a question like that."

"Yeah," Samantha said. "I don't know, either. It had nothing to do with medical school."

Tom got up from his seat on the couch and put on his coat. "I'll see you lovebirds later. I'm gonna go to the gym."

"Alright," Jonathan said. "Later, Tom."

"Bye, Tom," Samantha said.

Tom walked out of the room, and Samantha sat on the couch as Jonathan turned off the TV.

"So, what have you been up to today?" she asked.

"I was preparing for the LSAT until Tom distracted me with a game of Madden," Jonathan replied. "I met with the prelaw advisor and talked with him a little bit, requested some transcripts, and stuff like that. Tom said if I applied here, I could become a graduate assistant and he'd land me a coaching gig. It sounds kind of tempting. I don't know if being a coach would sustain me, though. They don't get paid too much compared to lawyers."

"I think you should do what your heart tells you to do. I wouldn't chase money. Money can't buy happiness."

"Easy for you to say," Jonathan joked. "You're gonna be a doctor. Doctors make bank."

"Maybe. That's not why I want to be a doctor, though."

"I know. I'm only kidding."

"Anyways, I've got some good news for you."

"Yeah?" Jonathan said, "What's that?"

"You're going to meet the rest of my family."

"The rest of your family? Do you have forsaken siblings hiding up in your attic or something? What do you mean?"

Samantha laughed. "No, silly, like my extended family."

"Really?" Jonathan was happy to hear that Samantha was willing to introduce him to her extended family. It showed him she was just as serious about their relationship as he was. "When do I meet them?"

"This summer. You know how Scarlett's getting married? Well, Scarlett invited you and—" Samantha's phone began to ring. She took it out of her pocket to see who was calling. "Perfect timing," she said. "Scarlett's calling me right now." She put the phone on speaker. "Hi, Scarlett."

"Hi, Sam!"

"I'm with Jonathan right now. I was just telling him about the wedding."

"Oh, hi, Jonathan," Scarlett said with her sweet, bubbly voice. "I'm looking forward to seeing you again. Samantha just doesn't shut up about you," Scarlett continued, laughing. "You'd think she's the one getting married by the way she talks about you."

Samantha turned red in the cheeks.

Jonathan felt warm inside to hear about Samantha gushing over him. He didn't gush about her to anyone—because he didn't have many friends or anyone in his family with whom he had the type of relationship Sam had with Scarlett. But he constantly wanted to tell the world how lucky he was to have her and how much he loved her.

"Hi, Scarlett. I'm looking forward to seeing you again, too," Jonathan replied. "Thanks for inviting me to the wedding."

"Of course! Listen, Samantha. I called because I want you to be my maid of honor."

Samantha gasped. Scarlett was popular and had a bunch of friends. Samantha had assumed she would choose one of them. Scarlett and Samantha were close, but Samantha didn't think they were *that* close. "I—" Samantha stammered. "I'd be honored, Scarlett." She put her hand over her mouth and looked at Jonathan wide-eyed as she began to bounce up and down giddily.

"Great! Thank you so much. It'll mean a lot to have my sister at my side when I tie the knot. I gotta go now. I'll call you later. Love you! Bye!"

Scarlett hung up the phone, and Samantha began to squeal with delight. "I can't believe she wants me to be her maid of honor!" She was bouncing up and down on the couch so hard that Jonathan thought she might break it.

"Congratulations," Jonathan said. "I can see that it means a lot to you."

"It does!" Samantha was exhilarated.

"You seem surprised," Jonathan observed.

"I am! I didn't think she'd choose me. I mean, we're close and all, but I thought she'd want to choose one of her southern belle friends. I'm just her nerdy sister. I'm nobody."

"You let your mom get into your head too much, Sam." Jonathan took Samantha's hand. "Just because you didn't sign up for any beauty pageants doesn't mean you're nobody. That's a really slanted way of looking at things, and your mom should know better than to say you should be more like your sister or that you're stubborn because you're not skin deep."

"Thanks, Jon," Samantha said, smiling. She was still thrilled at the news from Scarlett. She rubbed Jonathan's hand affectionately. "So, Jon, I've got a lot of med school interviews coming up over the next few weeks. I've also got a lot of studying to do for the MCAT and a bunch of classes to take if I want to graduate early. I'm gonna be really busy. It's going to be a hectic few weeks. Is it okay if Kylie takes over for me every now and then?"

Jonathan had been anticipating that for a while. He knew preparing for medical school was hectic. He didn't want to spend less time with Samantha, but he also didn't want to get in her way. He wanted her to succeed. If it meant he had to sacrifice some time with her for her to have the best chance of getting into medical school, he was willing to do it.

"Yeah," he said. "That's fine. Just don't abandon me altogether. I still want to spend time with you. I can manage on my own, and Kylie can definitely come take over your duties if she wants to, but I treasure every moment with you." He kissed her hand and smiled as he pulled his lips away. "I want to spend as much time with you as I can. Don't forget about me."

"I won't, Jon," Samantha murmured. "I promise."

CHAPTER 34

· · • • ● ● ● • • ·

Jonathan had felt very lonely the previous two weeks. Samantha had been driving from place to place for medical school interviews weaving her way through what seemed like every county of Texas. Jonathan couldn't help but feel as if he had been left in the dust. He didn't feel abandoned, but he did feel as though he wasn't a priority for Sam anymore. She wasn't just his assistant; she was his girlfriend, but they had only seen each other once in those two weeks. It was like they were in a long-distance relationship.

Jonathan tried reading to pass the time, but he couldn't focus. He and his dad were finally on speaking terms again and started recommending books to one another, again, too. Jeff recommended the book *The Kite Runner*, by Khaled Hosseini, to Jonathan. He was trying to read it but just *couldn't* focus on anything. He couldn't get motivated to go to the gym, either. Everything felt empty to him because he couldn't shake the feeling that Samantha was forgetting about him.

Samantha wasn't forgetting about Jonathan, though. She was thinking about him whenever she had a break from class or interviews. She felt guilty that she had only hung out with him once over the previous two weeks after she promised she wouldn't forget about him. She texted whenever she could, but she was rarely able to even look at her phone. Her texts were infrequent, and Jonathan was always ready to reply right away. The fact that she usually didn't text him back until hours later upset him even more. He didn't know she wasn't doing it on purpose. He didn't know that she was trying her hardest. Things were just hectic for her.

Kylie had been visiting him every few days to go on grocery store runs. That day, Kylie was going to drive Jonathan out to Waco Center to get a haircut from Dan. Jonathan's hair was getting long again. It wasn't nearly as long as it had been when he met Samantha, but his curly blond bangs were approaching his eyebrows. Every few months, he had gotten a haircut from Dan, and they had developed a friendship. They never hung out outside of the barbershop or anything, but they enjoyed chatting with each other whenever Jonathan visited his shop. Jonathan would share what was going on in his life, and Dan would talk about what had been going on in Waco.

Jonathan put *The Kite Runner* down only a few pages in after staring at it for more than an hour, frustrated at his inability to focus. He couldn't stop worrying about why Samantha was disappearing from his life.

She promised me she wouldn't forget about me.

Suddenly, a knock sounded at his door. "Coming," Jonathan called out. He opened the door to see Kylie, dressed up in a dark green turtleneck, a beige vest, khakis, and dark green high heels.

"Hi, Jon," she cheerfully said with a smile. "Are you ready to go?"

"Yeah," Jonathan replied glumly. He felt empty inside. Lately, it felt like his heart was void of any excitement or energy, like he was just going through his actions without any feelings. He'd reverted to wearing sweatpants and a T-shirt, too. He didn't feel any need to impress Kylie. As much as he liked her, he wished it were Samantha who had showed up at his door to take him to Dan's barbershop. He didn't want to let Kylie into his apartment. She would see how much of a mess everything was. He had clothes strewn across the floor, empty takeout containers all over the place, and dishes with food encrusted on them piled in the sink. So, he wheeled out to her in the hallway and closed the door behind him. "Here, you'll need these," he said as he handed her the keys to his van. She nodded, took the keys, and followed him to the student parking lot to get into the van and head to Waco Center.

Kylie had driven the van twice before when she took him grocery shopping, so she knew the drill. She clicked the button to lower the ramp and got into the driver's seat. Jonathan wheeled himself up the ramp and positioned himself in the passenger side. They didn't talk at all on the ride over. Kylie could sense that Jonathan seemed down, but she didn't know it was because of Samantha. If she had known, she would have explained that Samantha's schedule had been so hectic that even she hadn't spoken or spent time with her. She assumed Jonathan was upset for another reason, and she politely decided not to investigate.

Jonathan was depressed again, and that's mostly why he wasn't talking. But the song on the radio didn't help. It was "The Dance" by Garth Brooks. The lyrics told a story about a couple who shared a dance together under the stars, but they didn't know they wouldn't end up together. It made Jonathan think of Samantha because they had also spent magical moments together and Jonathan was afraid they wouldn't end up together. He was afraid Samantha had forgotten about him and would go on to med school to never see Jonathan again. Jonathan turned off the radio and spent the rest of the ride in silence with the exception of the directions sounding from the map app on his phone.

When they got to the barbershop, they pulled into one of the empty spaces in front. When he wheeled out, he realized Kylie would have to get him over the curb. He usually went to Dan's barbershop with Tom, who was muscular, so it was easy for Tom to lift Jonathan. Kylie was petite, and Jonathan doubted she'd be able to lift him up to get over the curb.

Kylie immediately voiced Jonathan's fears. "How do we get you over that curb?"

"I don't know," Jonathan said. "Usually Tom lifts me over it."

"Chair and everything?" Kylie looked flustered.

"Yeah. Maybe there will be an indent on the sidewalk further down the road."

"This shouldn't be an issue. I thought there were laws in place for this type of stuff."

"Yeah," Jonathan agreed as he demonstrated his lawyer knowledge. "There *are* laws in place. The Americans with Disabilities Act requires that *some* businesses make reasonable accommodations for people with qualified disabilities, but not *all* businesses need to. I guess Dan's shop doesn't have to. To be fair, it's basically a hole in the wall with one employee—Dan himself—so I doubt he's big enough to trigger the laws. It's fine. Don't worry about it. It's not the first time I've had a problem like this."

"I mean I can try to lift you over the curb," Kylie insisted.

"No, it's fine, let's just look for an indent in the sidewalk." Jonathan began to wheel down the sidewalk and around a corner as Kylie followed. Around the corner there was, indeed, a curb cut. Jonathan wheeled himself through the indentation and onto the sidewalk, and the two of them headed back to Dan's barbershop.

"Hey, Dan," Jonathan said as he wheeled into his shop. Dan was sitting in the only barber chair in the shop and looking at his phone. He peeled his eyes off of it as Jonathan wheeled in and smiled wide.

"Yo, Jon," Dan said enthusiastically as he walked up to him and gave him a half hug. "How've you been?"

"I've been alright," Jonathan said. He didn't want to tell Dan he had been lonely, especially not with Kylie there. Kylie was behind Jonathan, shyly shuffling her feet. "This is Kylie," Jonathan explained. "She's helping me out today."

"Nice to meet you, Kylie," Dan said. He stuck out his hand, shook hers, and then grabbed his afro pick and started running it through his hair. "What happened to Samantha? I thought she was the one helping you out normally." Dan had never actually met Samantha, but Jonathan had talked about her when he had come in for a haircut in the past.

"She's been busy," Jonathan said dejectedly. He could hear the gloom in his own voice and could feel a knot in his throat almost choking him up as he said the words. "She's been swamped with medical school interviews and stuff. Kylie's taking her place for a little while. She's her roommate."

"Oh, word. I wouldn't know the med school struggle," Dan joked. "I didn't even go to college."

"It's tough," Kylie jumped in, "I'm in premed, too. You've got to make sure you're taking the right classes to graduate early. You have to visit the schools you apply to for interviews. And you have to study for and pass the MCAT exam."

Why does Kylie have time to spend with me, but Samantha doesn't?

"Sounds crazy," Dan said. He inspected Jonathan's overgrown crew cut. "Alrighty," he walked a circle around Jonathan and studied his hair, "let's cut that hair, Jonny boy."

Jonathan wheeled over to the mirror. Dan put a haircut cape on him and started to snip away, restoring his hair to the shape it had been a few months before.

2612 CHERRYHILL LANE | 203

"So, what's new?" Dan asked as hair fell on Jonathan's shoulders and then to the floor.

"Not much. I've been studying for the LSATs mostly."

"What are LSATs?"

"LSAT stands for Law School Admission Test. It's basically the test you need to take to get into law school."

"The classes you take in college aren't enough?"

"Nope."

The sound of Dan's scissors snipping off Jonathan's hair filled the air for a few moments.

"See," Dan broke the silence. "I thought you had to go to college after high school for two years. I thought you just had to get your associate's degree. And then my buddy told me he was in college for four years to get his bachelor's degree, and I thought that was wack. Now I'm hearing you can go to law school or medical school, and that means you have to go to college for more than four years. That sounds even *more* whack. How long do you spend in law school?"

"Three years," Jonathan replied with a laugh. Dan was making him feel a bit better.

"What!? And medical school?"

Jonathan laughed more heartily. "You don't want to know, man."

"How long?" Dan stopped cutting his hair and was looking at Jonathan with a comical expression. He looked at Kylie with the same comical expression. "And what's that you mentioned about taking the 'MCAT' or whatever? Is that like the LSAT for doctors?"

"Yeah," Kylie said, "It stands for Medical College Admission Test. Med school is four years for the degree and then another three to seven years for residency. A lot of people do a fellowship after their residency, too, so there could be another year or two. It's different for me, though, because I'm becoming a veterinarian instead of a doctor. After my four years of veterinary school, I'll do a residency for only two to five years."

"MCAT, LSAT, I'm getting confused." Dan shook his head jokingly, as if he couldn't believe his ears. "So, to become a doctor, you could spend another ten years after you get your bachelor's degree? That's crazy! You'll be like thirty by the time you become a doctor!"

Jonathan laughed, but he couldn't help but feel a tinge of sadness settling back in after Dan pointed that out. He felt overwhelmed by the thoughts whirling through his head. If he and Samantha were going to be together, that would be an obstacle they'd have to face. She wouldn't become a doctor until long after he became a lawyer. It was too much to think about right then. He could hear Kylie laughing as she watched Dan's reaction to the tedious process of becoming a medical doctor.

"Did you have to go to barber school?" Kylie asked amidst her bout of laughter.

"Yeah, but it only took me like a year. Fifteen-hundred hours, to be exact. Not a decade."

The three joked around for another few minutes while Dan finished cutting Jonathan's hair. It was good to think about something other than Samantha for a change. Jonathan had been cooped up in his room for two weeks worrying about what was becoming of them. He feared the worst, but the fear was subsiding momentarily as the three laughed together. After Dan finished cutting his hair, Jonathan paid, and Jonathan and Kylie made their way to Vitek's to get the infamous Gut Pak Tom had introduced Jonathan to a year ago. Jonathan thought he was hungry, but his appetite faded as he sat in the van thinking again about Samantha abandoning him. He had been abandoned by his dad before. He had been abandoned by Lacey. The worst feeling Jonathan had ever felt was that of abandonment. He didn't want to feel it again.

The Vitek's BBQ sign came into sight as Kylie turned Jonathan's van into the restaurant's parking lot. The little red brick building had become a staple in Jonathan's memory. He and Tom would stop by whenever they went to Dan's together for a haircut. Tom would have taken Jonathan that day, too, but he had to go over football tapes with Coach Gustaffson. Jonathan would finally see Samantha tomorrow, or so she said, and he wanted to have his hair cut. He couldn't wait for Tom to be free.

"They've got something here called The Gut Pak. I don't know if you can stomach it—very few can finish it 'cause it's so massive—but you should give it a try. I promise it won't disappoint. I come here with my friend Tom all the time. He introduced me to it like a year ago, and I've never looked back."

"I'll give it a try," Kylie replied. "You'd be surprised at how much I can eat. I may be small, but I'm actually a bottomless pit."

"Suuure," Jonathan joked to Kylie, who was waiting next to the ramp as it lowered from the side of the van. "We'll see if your bark has any bite." He wheeled down the ramp once it touched the ground. "I'll pay for the Gut Paks. My treat. Just grab us a table."

"Okay," Kylie replied. "Thanks."

Thankfully, there was no curb to find a way over that time. Jonathan wheeled through the front door, which was at ground level, as Kylie grabbed a table. Jonathan paid for the Gut Paks, waited for a few minutes for them to be ready, and brought them to the table. He still wasn't very hungry. As he was waiting, though, he decided he would use the opportunity to ask Kylie about Samantha. He figured she'd know how Samantha was doing, since they lived together.

Jonathan watched Kylie dig into her Gut Pak as he picked away at his own without much of an appetite. She was eating carefully, careful not to let each bite fall on her clothes. She took each mouthful over the Styrofoam container it was served in, and chewed thoughtfully.

Jonathan took a deep breath and built up the nerve to ask Kylie about Samantha.

"So, Kylie, how has Samantha been?"

Kylie covered her mouth with her hand, chewed her mouthful, and then spoke.

"What do you mean?"

"Well, I don't know," Jonathan said. "I mean, I haven't really talked to her for the past two weeks."

"Oh," Kylie replied. "She's been really busy with med school interviews and taking classes. I think it's gonna be that way for a little while longer. We're both in a big rush to get our applications in. I haven't really seen her, either. She's so exhausted when she gets home that she goes straight to bed."

"So you think she'll be too busy to hang out with me for a while?" Jonathan was crestfallen.

"I don't know, Jon. I'm sorry."

Kylie seemed to sympathize with him.

"Why don't you ask her?"

"I can't really ask her." Jonathan stabbed at his Gut Pak, playing with his food. "Every time I text her, it takes forever for her to respond. I don't want to call her 'cause I could be interrupting an interview or calling her during class or while she's studying. She just seems to have left me in the dust, honestly, and it's really frustrating."

"She hasn't left you in the dust, Jon," Kylie replied. "Don't worry. She loves you. She wouldn't just forget about you."

"It just feels like it sometimes. She said in a text she can come over tomorrow. It's gonna be only the second time in two weeks that I've seen her."

"Med school interviews won't last forever. You two will be hanging out as much as you used to in no time."

Jonathan wasn't so sure. Samantha would be working to get into medical school until the summer. Maybe she would have no choice but to leave Jonathan in the dust. Maybe they had shared their last dance. Was she as committed to him as he was to her?

CHAPTER 35

———————————— •••●●●••• ————————————

Jonathan sat in his room, writing in his journal, as he waited for Samantha to arrive. She had texted him early that morning to remind him she'd be coming over that afternoon, and Jonathan was excited. It felt like a year had passed since he had seen her, although it had really only been two weeks.

He had started the journal entry after he got back from Vitek's BBQ the night before, in an attempt to cope with the loneliness he had been feeling. Sam would be out of classes at five forty-five, and it would take roughly fifteen minutes for her to get to his apartment. It was now five fifty-eight.

The truth hurts.

And sometimes we don't want to see the truth because it's so much easier to turn a blind eye. It's so much easier to make excuses. So, we try to justify things. We try to convince ourselves the truth of the situation is just something we overreacted to. But did we? We let doubt creep into our thoughts. And, in the end, we dismiss the truth because it's something we're not ready to accept.

Sam is saying the right things. She says I'm important to her. She says that she loves me. But her actions say something else. Am I making excuses for her? I hope not. What if—

Jonathan was writing another line when a knock sounded at his door. It was a little after six o'clock. He locked up his journal in the cabinet in the corner of his room, wheeled over to the door, and opened it. He smiled from ear to ear when he saw it was Samantha waiting for him behind the door.

"Hi, Jon," she said sweetly. She was wearing a white crocheted crop top with a quilted faux leather jacket over it, jean shorts, and brown Birkenstock sandals. Jonathan didn't feel underdressed this time like he had the day before when Kylie came to take him to Dan's barbershop. He was wearing a gray long-sleeved shirt and navy blue jeans. His hair was freshly cut, and he was clean shaven. He looked just as good as the day he impressed Samantha the day they met in front of the library, along with Dean and Kylie.

"Hi, Sam," Jonathan said, still smiling. "Come on in." He had cleaned up his room and spent most of the day sitting in his room hoping Samantha wouldn't cancel. He grew impatient just sitting around so he cleaned the apartment, shaved his stubble, and picked out his outfit. He studied a little bit for the LSATs, too, while simultaneously musing over Tom's offer to become a graduate assistant and coach for the Stallions.

Samantha entered the room, sat on Jonathan's couch, and lay on her back. "It's been quite the day," she said with an exhausted tone as she lay down. "I had a med school interview at eight o'clock in the morning, all the way in San Antonio, which was almost a three-hour drive. Then I had to drive all the way back for my three o'clock class."

"Wow," Jonathan said sympathetically. "Is every day like that?"

"No," Samantha said. "Today was especially busy."

"What are most days like?"

Jonathan wanted to know how busy Samantha really was. He wanted to know whether he was a priority of hers. If Kylie was able to come visit him from time to time, why wasn't Samantha able to as well?

"Most days, I don't have a med school interview. Those only happen like twice a week, at most. Usually, I'm in the library studying for my classes or the MCAT in case I need to retake it."

"We should study together," Jonathan said in an attempt to spend more time with her. "I barely see you. I miss spending time with you."

"No offense, but I think you'd be too much of a distraction. I've really got to focus on my classes if I want to graduate early and get into a good med school.

It's not like it used to be. I've been walling myself off in the silent study areas and going at a different pace than before. I don't even study with Kylie."

Jonathan was offended. "But we've studied all the time together, and you still did great in your classes. Why is it any different now?"

"It's just different, Jon."

Samantha sighed. "I can't have any distractions. It's great studying with you and all, but I often get distracted by just looking at you study. It's hard to explain."

"It seems like you don't want to spend time with me at all. It seems like med school is your priority over me. It seems like you aren't as committed as I am about this relationship." Their conversation was heating up. Jonathan didn't intend to get in a fight with her, but the emotions he had been feeling for the previous two weeks were getting out of control.

Samantha shot up from her position on the couch. "What do you mean?"

"I mean that you don't seem to be committed to hanging out with me. I've seen you *once* over the past two weeks. I've seen Kylie three times. How is it that she's going through the same process as you—applying to med school and every-thing—and she's able to visit me more?"

"I told you it would be like this! I warned you!"

"You said you wouldn't blow me off, and it seems like you're so obsessed with getting into med school that you don't have time for me anymore. It seems like you've moved on."

"My world doesn't revolve around you, Jon!" Samantha's voice was raising into a shout. She was already stressed out enough, and that confrontation just put her over the edge.

"Well, my world revolves around you, Sam," Jonathan said. "You mean the world to me. I don't see how we're going to stay together in the future if you're going to be so obsessed about med school that you don't have any time to be with me. If you can't even study next to me, we're going to have problems in the future. How can we make this work if you have that attitude?"

"I'm not going to be like my mother. I'm not going to become a housewife whose world revolves around my husband and prioritizes him over my own inde-pendence. That's not who I am."

"That's not what I'm saying, Sam."

"That *is* what you're saying, Jon. You're saying you'd rather I prioritize *you* and our relationship, and tend to *your* needs, than prioritize med school or *my* dreams and goals."

"You're taking what I said out of context, Sam. I—" Jonathan let out an exasperated sigh. Anger flared up in him. He couldn't hold back. His voice, too, escalated to a shout.

"I'm not your charity case, Sam! I'm not saying you need to give up pursuing your dreams just to make sure you 'tend to my needs!' I've been supportive. I let you pursue your dreams, and I was fine with you spending less time with me because things were getting hectic with applying to med school. I'm just saying that it feels like you aren't committed to me, that you don't prioritize me at all, and that you only prioritize getting into med school. It feels like you're just abandoning me like everybody else in my life."

"Jon, I'm not abandoning you. I'm—"

"—No, Sam, you *are* abandoning me. You're leaving me behind in the pursuit of bigger and better things. But you know what? That's fine. You can go study. There's no need to spend time with me. You don't need to 'tend to my needs.'"

"Jon, please—" Samantha began to cry. Tears poured down her cheeks as she pleaded for Jonathan to stop yelling. "Don't get so angry with me. You've got to understand that things have just been hectic."

"I don't need you. Just leave. Get out of here. I just used you like I used everyone else in my life."

"Jon . . ." Samantha tried to wipe the tears away with the cuff of her jacket, but they just kept coming. "Please . . . What do you mean you just 'used' me?"

"Get out, Sam. Leave me be. I'll tend to my own needs."

"You can't be serious—"

"LEAVE!"

Jonathan wheeled over to the door and opened it. "Get out! We're over!"

Samantha got up off the couch and walked out the apartment door, crying hysterically. She looked back at Jonathan as if he would change his mind, but he just slammed the door shut in her face.

CHAPTER 36

···●●●●···

Weeks passed by with a mixture of anger and stubbornness being felt by both Samantha and Jonathan.

Jonathan thought Samantha should have known better than to leave him feeling abandoned because she knew how his father abandoned him and how that impacted him. He felt that if he had shown her anything, it was that they could work through any issue if they cared enough about each other. He believed he had made Samantha a priority in his life, but she had not made him a priority in hers; her quest to become a pediatrician ruled over everything there was between them.

Jonathan was scared. He had already loved someone more than himself—Gabby—and had lost her. Going through that again with Samantha would be devastating. He was scared he'd lose her forever, too.

Samantha felt strongly that making medical school her priority for a short period of time was the right decision. Her self-worth had always been tied to achievement, and her ultimate goal was to become a pediatrician. She thought Jonathan should have known that by then and that she was the type of person to not let anything stand in the way of achieving her goal, including him. She had seen her mother take a backseat with her father and become a homemaker instead of pursuing her dreams. She didn't want to end up like that.

If Jonathan truly loved her, she reasoned, he would be patient and not try to stop her from achieving her goals. He would have found a way to fit into her life instead of insisting on being her entire life.

Samantha and Kylie had graduated but still lived together until their lease expired in March. Samantha often confided in Kylie about the breakup, and Kylie would support Samantha. "I like Jon a lot," Kylie would say. "But if he's 'the one,' he would support your goal to become a doctor. He wouldn't have ended things."

November was almost over. Jonathan could feel himself falling back into his rut. He was wheeling down a sidewalk in the courtyard outside his apartment building on the way back from his morning class. His head was down, and his eyes were focused on the pavement flying by underneath him as he sped along. Suddenly, he heard Pastor Ana Broussard call out his name.

"Jonathan!"

He had passed her without even noticing. She was behind him. He turned around and saw her standing in the same outfit she wore to the Bible study, jeans and a T-shirt. He hadn't seen her since he and Samantha broke up. For a moment, he wished he hadn't turned around when she called out his name. But it was too late, so he wheeled over and forced a smile.

"Hi, Pastor Broussard," he said. "Long time no see."

"It's been weeks! Where have you been, Jon?! We've missed you at Bible study."

"I *would* go," Jonathan explained, "but I don't want to see Samantha. We broke up, and it'd just be too much for me to bear."

"Sam doesn't go every Thursday anymore, so you might not see her. She's been busy with getting into medical school."

"Really? Well, still, I don't want to risk it."

"Is there any chance of reconciliation?"

"Pastor Broussard . . . I'd rather not talk about this."

"Why don't we go grab some coffee? We can do a Bible study or just talk, whatever you want. You have grown so much over the past year, and I want to make sure you keep moving forward."

Jonathan really needed some guidance. He had been so despondent. The hope and faith he got from studying the Bible could be a powerful force to help him get out of the rut he was falling back into, he figured.

"Okay," he said. "Let's grab some coffee."

* * *

"I see a lot of potential in you, Jonathan," Ana said as the two of them sat in a crowded campus coffee shop. She reminded Jonathan of the words Professor Hoffpower said to him after he finished his final the year before. There was a stark difference between the two, though. Jim Hoffpower was old and boring while Ana Broussard was young and personable. "I don't want you to give up on Bible study," she continued. "And I won't give up on you."

"A lot of people have given up on me, Pastor Broussard. You wouldn't be the first by a long shot."

"A lot of people may have given up on you, Jonathan. But Jesus will always be there for you no matter what. He'll never give up on you. And neither will I."

"It's comforting to hear that, although I'm pretty sure I've given up on myself."

"What do you mean you've given up on yourself?"

"I don't know. I'm stuck in a wheelchair. The girl I loved doesn't love me anymore and abandoned me." Jonathan took a sip of his coffee and sadly cast his eyes downward. "Life is just beating me up. I'm a total underdog without a comeback in me. I'm not winning by any means."

Ana leaned forward and took his hand. "I know what it feels like to be an underdog. I also know the power of prayer when it comes to lifting yourself up. I've faced obstacles as a female pastor in an industry dominated by males. I pray every day that I can be a trailblazer for other women, and those prayers have been powerful enough to lift me up and motivate me to succeed. I also have a Caucasian husband—he's a lieutenant in the Army—and I face obstacles every day being in an interracial relationship and wondering whether my husband will come home safe. I pray every day that he is safe, and those prayers are powerful enough to remind me that God has a plan for him, and if He is to take his life, then there is a reason why."

Jonathan immediately thought about Gabby. He wondered whether God had a reason to take her life. "You really think God would take someone's life because it's a part of His plan?"

"God has a plan for everyone. Remember: for those who believe in Him there is everlasting life. They only pass to be accepted into His Kingdom." She opened up her Bible to read the verse Jonathan heard the first day he went to Bible study, the one he had thought about at Gabby's grave. "For God so loved the world, that He gave His only begotten Son, that whoever believes in Him shall not perish but have eternal life" John 3:16 (ESV).

"Amen," Jonathan murmured as he set a pensive gaze upon the table. "It's just hard for me to accept that all this could be part of God's plan for me. Sometimes, I feel like His plan for me is more of a punishment. You see, Pastor Broussard, I got into a really bad car accident quite a few years ago. I got into the accident because I was texting my girlfriend instead of paying attention to the road. My little sister, Gabby, was in the car with me and didn't make it. I lost my legs. I'll never forgive myself for texting and driving. It ruined my life and took Gabby's."

Ana nodded along as Jonathan spoke. She was still holding his hand. "I spoke at a texting and driving event a year ago. During my speech, I thought to myself that God must have spared my life so I could spread the word about texting and driving, honor my sister, and take advantage of my second chance at life. But now with Sam and me breaking up and everything, I'm losing hope all over again. Everything in my life seems to be going down . . . It all just seems like a punishment and that God won't forgive me until I've atoned for my sins somehow. I just don't *know* how to atone for my sins." Jonathan sighed. "I just wish I could control my own destiny. It seems everything is out of control. I wish I could be in control."

"Sometimes things *are* out of our control, Jonathan," Ana said after a brief pause. "Everything happens in accordance with God's ultimate plan. But know this: God isn't punishing you. God will always forgive you." Ana let go of Jonathan's hand, flipped to a page in her Bible, and put her index finger on a verse she had highlighted in yellow. She read aloud, "In Him we have redemption through His blood, the forgiveness of our trespasses, according to the riches of His grace" Ephesians 1:7 (ESV).

Ana smiled at Jonathan. "God forgives you even if your texting caused that horrific accident. You aren't a bad person, Jonathan. You did what any normal boy would have done. But it's up to you to forgive yourself for looking at the text. And that you *can* control. It's not easy, but it's something you *can* do. You don't have to wait for God to forgive you. You don't need to atone for your sins. God has been here for you this entire time. He's just waiting for you to accept Him."

"Thanks, Pastor Broussard," Jonathan said. "I've been wondering for a long time if God is punishing me for some reason. I guess I've been the one punishing myself."

"I'm always here for you, Jonathan." Ana took a long sip of her coffee, placed her cup down gently, and furrowed her eyebrows contemplatively. "You said a lot of people have given up on you. You said I wouldn't be the first to give up on you by a long shot. Do you feel as though Samantha has given up on you?"

"No. When we broke up, I thought she didn't make me a priority. But I think I was the one who gave up on her. I think I was wrong to get angry at her for spending so much time trying to get into med school. I thought she loved me as much as I loved her. I would have dropped anything just to spend time with her. She had her priorities straight, I think. I regret challenging her for putting med school first. I should have been more patient. She was just chasing her dreams, and I was just so scared of being abandoned again."

"You say 'loved,'" Ana observed. "Do you not love her anymore?"

"I don't know. How do I know if I loved her? What if I just thought I loved her?"

"Have you ever felt love before, Jonathan?"

"I don't know. What does love feel like, Pastor Broussard?"

"I think love is best summarized in the Bible." Ana flipped to another page in her Bible she had highlighted in yellow. She read it aloud. "Love is patient and kind; love does not envy or boast; it is not arrogant or rude. It does not insist on its own way; it is not irritable or resentful; it does not rejoice at wrongdoing but rejoices with the truth. Love bears all things, believes all things, hopes all things, endures all things. Love never ends. As for prophecies, they will pass away; as for tongues, they will cease; as for knowledge, it will pass away" 1 Corinthians 13:4–8 (ESV).

"By that definition, I loved her. But our love didn't endure. It ended. In that case, we weren't in love."

"You don't think your love endured? You don't think you still have the same feelings for her in your heart?"

"I do. And I know she felt similar to me. But I don't know if she *still* does."

"Who's to say she doesn't? If it was love, it endured. If it was love, then it is love now. It doesn't just *go away*. The Bible tells us that."

"You really think she might still love me?"

"If she loved you then, she loves you now.'"

"Even if I broke her heart?"

"You might have to take some measures to repair her broken heart, to be fair, but deep down, my bet is she loved you then and still loves you now. With a little effort, you can absolutely reconcile and repair your relationship."

Jonathan and Ana finished their coffees and made arrangements to meet at the same coffee shop every Thursday morning to study the Bible together. Jonathan was happy to have her guidance. He had never felt as good about himself since the accident than he did when he was regularly going to Bible study. After he strayed from God and the Bible, he started falling back into a rut. He was comforted to know God wouldn't stray from him. He felt better knowing God would never abandon him.

Jonathan went back to his apartment and tried to read the Bible to himself. He still had the Bible Samantha had given him. He had never opened it because Pastor Broussard always had printouts of the parts of the Bible they were studying during Bible study. It had been stashed in his writing cabinet. He opened his writing cabinet, pulled it out, and opened it to the inside cover. There was a note there from Samantha. It read, "This book changed my life for the better. I hope it will do the same for you. Love, Sam."

Jonathan teared up as he read the note. He flipped through the pages and noticed Sam had highlighted her favorite passages. Jonathan opened to a random page and read the first highlighted portion he saw.

"Trust in the LORD with all your heart, and do not lean on your own understanding. In all your ways acknowledge Him, and He will make straight your paths" Proverbs 3:5–6 (ESV).

Jonathan thought about what Ana had said to him. He had to stop trying to understand why God's plan seemed to make him into a victim. He would never understand, so he had to stop leaning on his own understanding. He just had to have faith that God would make Jonathan's path straight.

The conversation he had with Ana earlier that day, more than anything, motivated Jonathan to win Samantha back. It would take some effort to win her back and regain her trust—that much he knew—but he was willing to do whatever he had to do. He was determined to do something extraordinary to let Sam know how much she meant to him, so he decided to go back to physical therapy with Dr. Jackson Bui and get prosthetics. Then, he'd surprise Samantha with a dance under the stars.

CHAPTER 37

—————— ··•●●●•·· ——————

More than two months had passed since Samantha and Jonathan broke up. December had gone by painfully slowly for both of them. While they both harbored residual anger and stubbornness during November, by that point, they were both just sad. And they both hoped they might get back together someday.

Samantha was still stressed as ever awaiting decision letters from medical schools, which had started to trickle in. The pain of not having Jonathan in her life anymore made the suspense harder to cope with. She often found comfort from calling Scarlett and talking with her about how she missed Jonathan. The two sisters grew closer as the wedding approached.

Jonathan found companionship in Tom and Elijah, who often came to keep him company. Jonathan figured out ways to take care of himself but still needed rides to the grocery store every now and then.

Jonathan had been back in his rut for a month. He was drowning in his sorrows. He hadn't even told his parents that he and Samantha had broken up and was not looking forward to that conversation. He took a handicap-accessible taxi service home to Katy to spend Christmas Break with them and dreaded knocking on the door because he knew they would ask about Samantha. His parents would open the door at any minute. Jonathan sat in his wheelchair, feeling utter apathy, when he heard their footsteps approaching. He didn't want to talk about Samantha. The door opened, and Jeff and Rose were both standing behind it, smiling, happy to see him.

"Hey, Mom. Hey, Dad."

"Hi, Jon," his mom said with a big smile. Her smile turned into a frown when she noticed he hadn't shaved or cut his hair in months and wasn't wearing proper clothes. Rose could tell something was wrong.

Jeff, however, had no clue. He just shook Jonathan's hand, patted him on the shoulder, and joked around. "Samantha can't be too thrilled about kissing you with that gnarly beard on your chin!"

"She's not kissing me anytime soon, Dad," Jonathan said dejectedly. "We broke up a couple of months ago."

"Oh. I'm sorry, Jon," Jeff said with a concerned expression on his face. "What happened?"

"I don't know," Jonathan bluffed. "She had to focus on medical school, and we just grew apart, I suppose."

"I'm so sorry, honey," Rose said. "She was a lovely girl."

"There are plenty of fish in the sea," Jeff added in an attempt to raise Jonathan's spirits.

"Yeah, true," Jonathan replied. "But I really had high hopes for this one."

"You'll find another girl just as lovely," Rose assured him. "And if it was meant to be, it would have been. We'll always be here for you, Jon. We're happy you're home."

"Thanks, Mom."

"I've been through my fair share of breakups," Jeff said. "And I *know* the best thing you can do is stay busy so you don't dwell on things."

"Yeah, I've been trying to stay busy," Jonathan replied. "I think I'm going to start working with Dr. Bui again. I think I'm going to try to get prosthetics and learn to walk."

"That's a great idea!" Rose said happily. "I've been wanting you to do that for a long time."

"Jon," Jeff said, "come this way." He motioned for Jonathan to follow him as he walked into his study. Jonathan wheeled in after him to find him holding an old photo album in his hands. Jeff beckoned Jonathan to come closer. He flipped open the album to the first page. It was an old Polaroid picture of his mother and father at the beach.

"Wow . . . look at you two," Jonathan marveled. "Was that taken in Galveston Island?"

The McCalisters had gone to Galveston Island many times for family trips but hadn't been since the accident.

"It sure was," Jeff said with a nostalgic expression on his face. "Stewart Beach to be exact. That was the day I met your mother. It was one of the best and worst days of my life."

Jeff snickered, and Jonathan was confused.

How could it have been one of the worst days of his life? He found love. He met my mother.

Jeff noticed Jonathan's confusion. "Jon, the day that picture was taken, my heart was broken by a girl I was in love with. In fact, we took a trip down to Galveston so I could propose to her. But before I could ask for her hand in marriage, she broke up with me. I was devastated."

Jeff put the photo album back down on his desk and took a seat. "So, I moped around the beach the rest of the day. That's when I met your mother. She was there with her girlfriends and asked me to take a picture of them." A whimsical smile crept across Jeff's face. "The rest is history."

"Wow, what an amazing story," Jonathan said. "I know you guys met at the beach, but whenever you told the story of how you met, you left out the part about getting dumped by your girlfriend."

"Yeah, I know." Jeff shook his head and laughed. "But the point here is I met your mother—the true love of my life—after a heartbreak. A lot of times, heartbreak will lead you to your one true love."

Jonathan nodded approvingly as Jeff spoke.

"Keep your chin up, son," Jeff continued, "and don't ever settle for second best. You do that, and you'll find the one for you. Now, are you hungry? I'm ready for some Chuy's."

"My favorite restaurant," Jonathan said as he began to choke up over the thought of Gabby. "Yeah. I could eat."

Jonathan, Jeff, and Rose headed out to Chuy's and, although no one said it, they were all thinking of Gabby on the drive over. Sitting at their favorite table, the three of them reminisced about how Gabby would take the Chuy's decorative sombrero off the wall and wear it while engaging in an impromptu salsa dance. As their laughter filled the room, Jonathan felt grateful to finally have his family back again, even if Gabby was still missing.

CHAPTER 38

•••••••

Samantha eagerly stuck the key into the mailbox by the entrance to her apartment. Decision letters from medical school had been arriving over the previous few days. Every time she got home, she rushed to see whether she had a decision letter from UT Southwestern Medical School in Dallas. She twisted the key, opened the mailbox, and felt a flurry of nerves dancing in the pit of her stomach when she noticed an envelope from UT Southwestern Medical School on top of the mail. She grabbed the stack of mail, rushed up to her room, and swung the door open.

"Kylie!" Samantha called out. "It's here!"

Kylie was washing dishes in the kitchen, so Samantha ran into the kitchen holding the letter in her hand like it was a golden ticket from *Charlie and the Chocolate Factory*. She dumped the pile of mail onto the kitchen table and grabbed the letter from UT Southwestern Medical School. Kylie turned the faucet off, dried her hands, walked over to the kitchen table, and stood next to Samantha.

Kylie had already been accepted to veterinary school and knew UT Southwestern Medical School was Samantha's first choice. Samantha was holding the decision letter in her hands, with Kylie over her shoulder. For a moment, she didn't want to open it. She didn't want to be let down if she was rejected. She had done well in the interview. She met the qualifications academically. So, she knew the likelihood that she would get in was very high. Nonetheless, she feared rejection.

"Well, open it, Samantha!" Kylie shouted. "It's not going to open itself."

Samantha wedged her finger into the flap at the top of the envelope to tear it open. As she slid her finger across, she felt a huge rush of anxiety and sadness. She had worked so hard for this but, until two months before, she pictured herself sharing the moment with Jonathan. But there she was, with Kylie by her side, about to find out whether her hard work had paid off.

With the envelope torn open, Samantha paused, took a deep breath, pulled out the letter, and unfolded it.

She began to read it aloud. "Dear Ms. Reid, I am—" Samantha squealed and began to jump up and down in joy. "I am delighted to inform you that you have been accepted to UT Southwestern Medical School in Dallas!"

"Congratulations, Sam!" Kylie shouted.

Samantha hugged Kylie, still jumping up and down. She was ecstatic. "I'm so happy!"

"I can tell," Kylie said in response, laughingly. "I'm so happy for you, too!"

Samantha's happiness dwindled as she thought of Jonathan again. She stopped jumping up and down and sighed.

"I wish I could tell Jonathan," she said sadly.

"Aw, Sam," Kylie murmured sympathetically. "You *can* tell him. Why *couldn't* you?"

"How?"

"Email him. Send him a message on Facebook. Or text him."

Samantha pulled out her phone. "What should I say?"

"Just say that you thought he'd like to know that you got into UT Southwestern Medical School, or something like that. I don't know. Keep it simple."

"Okay." Samantha sent Jonathan an email saying just what Kylie suggested, adding that she hoped he was doing well and that she's been thinking of him. Samantha was desperate to talk to Jonathan again. She missed him dearly.

She sent him a similar message on Facebook right after she emailed him but decided not to text him.

She was crestfallen when he responded on Facebook with only "Congrats." It was an insincere commendation, and she was sad to see that he hadn't responded to the more personal part of the message

CHAPTER 39

onathan sat on his parents' couch staring at the TV but thinking about the Facebook message Samantha sent. While he was happy for her, it scared him to know her life was so great without him in it. She clearly didn't need him to achieve her dreams. And, he thought, she was clearly doing much better than he was.

Suddenly, a knock sounded at the door. For the first time he could remember, Jonathan thought about how much *he* wanted to get prosthetics so he could just get up off the couch and open the door. Instead, he reached for his wheelchair, wheeled it next to him, and lifted himself into it to go open the door. As he was wheeling to the door, it creaked open. It was Rose. Someone was behind her. He couldn't tell who it was because the door obstructed his view.

"Hey, Jon!"

He immediately recognized the voice.

Dominic.

"It's been way too long," Dominic said enthusiastically as Jonathan made his way to the door.

"Dom?" Jonathan said as he wheeled behind Rose. "What are you doing here?"

"Jon . . ." Dominic looked nervous, as though Jonathan would just tell him to turn around and leave. "What's up?"

"I invited Dominic," Rose explained to Jonathan. "I thought you could use a friend right now."

"You came all the way from Boston?" Jonathan asked. "What about school?"

"I'm on Christmas Break too, man."

Dominic gave Jonathan a big hug like nothing had ever happened between them.

"How've you been?" Jonathan said. "How's law school going?"

"It's pretty stressful, actually. There's a whole lot of reading. I spend more time in the library and in class than I do sleeping. What about you? Have you taken your LSAT yet?"

"Nah, man, I might take it in the summer. I'm actually thinking about coaching football instead. I don't know, my life's kinda complicated right now. Come take a seat, man." Jonathan led Dominic to the couch, and Dominic sat down.

"What's complicated about your life, man?" Dominic asked as he sunk into the couch cushions.

"Well, when you resigned as my personal assistant, I had to get a new one. A girl named Samantha took the job, and we fell in love. But two months ago, we broke up."

"I'm sorry, man. You okay?"

"At first I was angry. Then I was sad. Now I want to get back together with her. But I screwed things up big time. I'm not sure if I could win her back, but I want to."

"You've got to follow your heart, Jon. If you want to win her back, you've got to take the chance. You know that old saying? You miss 100% of the shots you don't take. The sting of 'what if' will last a lot longer than any kind of rejection ever will. You don't want her to be the one who got away."

"True."

Jonathan mused over what Dominic said for a moment.

"What else is complicated? You say you want to be a coach?"

"Yeah. I've gotten closer with Tom since you left and have been helping him coach a quarterback named Elijah for the past year and a half. Tom said I could become a graduate assistant, and he'd help me get a coaching gig with the Stallions. I'm still not sure about it, though."

"You'd be a great coach. You have a knack for making complicated things seem simple."

"Thanks, Dom." Jonathan smiled as he felt a wave of nostalgia wash over him, remembering his time working with Elijah.

"Have you gone back to Dr. Bui? Last time we saw each other, you had just stormed out of his training center."

"I haven't, no, but I want to. I wanna try to walk with prosthetics again."

"Then what are you waiting for?"

"I don't know how I'd get there or anything. I have no personal assistant anymore to drive me around."

Dominic smiled. "You've got me."

"What do you mean, man? We're like three hours away from Waco."

"Dr. Bui told me to be a good friend and get you to come back so you can move forward with recovery. He said it would change your life, so I promised him I'd be there for you if you ever became ready. I want to be a good friend to you, Jon. I want to help you change your life."

"Then let's go."

A few days later, Jonathan and Dominic got into Dominic's car and started the long drive up to the Calvary Performance Institute in Waco. Rose offered to rent them a handicap-accessible van since Jonathan's van was back at school, but Jonathan decided he wanted to turn over a new leaf, so he lifted himself into the passenger seat, and Dominic put his folded-up wheelchair into the trunk. Jonathan called Dr. Bui in the car and told him they were on their way.

The building looked the same as Jonathan had remembered. This time, however, Jonathan wasn't nervous or apprehensive about going in. He was motivated to start the process of getting prosthetics. He wasn't doing it for himself. He was doing it for Samantha. He wanted to show her he could change for the better. He wanted to share that dance with Samantha under the stars.

The same lady who ushered them around the first time led them up to Dr. Bui's consultation room as soon as they arrived. No more than a minute later, Dr. Bui opened the door, delighted to see them.

"Jonathan McCalister," he said. "Are you ready to change your life? Are you ready to walk again? Are you ready to become a new man?"

"I'm ready, Dr. Bui," Jonathan replied, smiling.

Dr. Bui smiled back and nodded in approval. "Please, call me Jackson."

CHAPTER 40

S pring had arrived. Nostalgia flooded through Samantha as she drove up the long driveway of her childhood home. She was back in Southlake and about to move back with her family. She had missed them during college but wasn't excited to tell them she and Jonathan had broken up.

She knew they'd ask about him, as they expected to see him at her sister's wedding in a few months. She knew she'd have to break the news to them, and they wouldn't see him at the wedding.

Samantha parked her car in front of the large five-car garage next to the house. She looked to the porch. In front of it, there was a myriad of colors from a variety of flowers Samantha's mother had planted to enhance the front of the house. There were tulips, pink and delicate. There were hyacinths, white and bright, that swayed in the spring breeze. There were daffodils, yellow and perfectly symmetrical. Samantha always admired her mother's green thumb. Sara took great care in making sure the house always had an assortment of flowers to greet anyone who approached their door.

Samantha took a moment to feel grateful for her family and for having such a beautiful home to live in. She hadn't seen her family in quite some time, although she had been in constant communication with Scarlett about the wedding since she agreed to be the maid of honor. Scarlett knew all about Jonathan and was always available to comfort Samantha when she needed to confide in someone about the sadness she had been feeling about the breakup. Although her mother was often hard on her, Samantha was excited to reconnect with Sara, too. She was especially excited to tell her she got into her top choice for medical school. Maybe Sara would be as proud of her as she had been of Scarlett each time she won a beauty pageant.

Samantha popped open her trunk, grabbed a piece of her luggage, and made her way up the steps to the front porch. She sniffed in the familiar yet ineffable scent of home as she opened the door. *Home sweet home*, she thought to herself.

* * *

After Samantha greeted her family, she headed to her room to unpack. It took about an hour to unpack everything, and then she went downstairs to help her mom prepare dinner. They were going to have fried chicken with mashed potatoes, biscuits, and gravy. It was Samantha's favorite meal, a recipe from her grandma who lived a few hours away, and Samantha had offered to help her mom cook it.

While it felt good to be home, Samantha couldn't help but feel sadness over her breakup with Jonathan. It had been months, but she remained brokenhearted. His reply of "Congrats" to her message about getting into medical school made her feel as if he didn't even want to be on speaking terms with her. She still loved him, and it was hard to move on.

Samantha didn't know how long it would take for her broken heart to mend, but she hoped it would mend soon. The pain was almost unbearable. It was like she could physically feel it in her chest. It was like her heart was slowly tearing apart.

Everyone in her family could sense something was wrong, but Scarlett was the only one who knew why she was so depressed. As Samantha helped her mother prepare the meal, Sara asked Samantha what was on her mind.

"Is everything all right, Sam?"

"Yeah. I'm fine," Samantha lied. "I'm great, actually. I got into medical school at UT Southwestern Medical School in Dallas, my top choice. Everything is going great!"

Sara stopped peeling the potatoes she had been peeling and looked at Samantha joyously. "I'm so proud of you, honey, that's amazing!"

"You're proud of me?" Samantha was surprised to hear those words. She never expected her mom to be proud of her unless she followed in her or Scarlett's footsteps by winning a beauty pageant or getting engaged to a good-looking rich man like William.

"Of course I am, sweetie. I've always been proud of you."

Samantha was even more surprised to hear her say that. "That means a lot, Mom," she said. "I always thought you wanted me to be more like you and Scarlett. I never knew you've been proud of me all along."

Sara sighed. "I don't want you to be like me or Scarlett. The only reason I ever pushed you to do beauty pageants is because that's the only thing I could give you good advice about. I know nothing about medicine. I know how to be a southern belle, a socialite, and a beauty pageant queen. That's all I'm good at. You're special, Sam. Don't let anyone ever tell you you're not. You're so much smarter than I ever was."

"Really?"

"Oh, Sam," Sara said as she put the peeler and the potato down on a cutting board resting on the countertop. She walked over to Samantha and opened her arms as though she wanted to hug her. Samantha didn't know what to do. She couldn't remember the last time she had hugged her mother. She couldn't remember the last time that her mother said she was proud of her. She couldn't remember the last time her mother had said something that loving to her. She had always told Samantha to be more like Scarlett or her. Tentatively, Samantha embraced her mother and they hugged each other tightly.

"I want you to just be you. You're perfect the way you are. You're more than perfect. I love you, Sam. I'll always be your biggest fan."

For a moment, Samantha forgot all about Jonathan. All of her problems momentarily disappeared. Tears of joy formed in her eyes. It felt good to connect with her mother. It was such a foreign feeling that, until that moment, she hadn't known she'd longed for. It was like an empty space was being filled inside her that she never knew was empty. She hadn't felt so good in a long time. She had never really understood her mother or felt accepted by her. After what Sara had just said, everything changed.

"Thanks, Mom."

"Of course, sweetheart! You two girls are the best things that ever happened to me!" Sara went back to peeling the potatoes as Scarlett walked in. She saw Samantha had tears in her eyes and immediately felt concerned.

"Are you alright, Sam?"

Samantha wiped the tears from her eyes. "I'm fine, it's just the onions we're cutting up for the gravy." The onions hadn't even been cut yet. Samantha realized this right after she said that. Scarlett did, too.

"The onions aren't even being cut yet, silly." She got closer to Samantha and said, in a whisper, "Is it about Jon?" Sara overheard her whisper this and looked over at them quizzically.

"What happened to Jon?"

Ugh, Samantha thought, *here goes.*

"We broke up," Samantha said. "We've been broken up for a while."

"Oh no!" Sara replied. "I was looking forward to seeing him at the wedding. That's too bad. Is that why you seem so sad today? Are you thinking of Jon?"

"A bit." Samantha didn't want to talk about Jonathan.

"How are you feeling?" Scarlett asked.

"I don't know." Samantha reached for an onion and started to cut it. "I've got to cut the onions."

Scarlett didn't accept Samantha's attempt to blow off her question. She pressed on. "Sam . . . love is not logical. It's actually irrational. It's not meant to be easy, and it'll pair you with the people you least expect. You know, my fiancé is really not the type of guy I generally date. But . . . I fell for him because of how he makes me feel. William makes me feel truly special, and he makes me want to be a better person. I am lucky to have that with him, and I see the same thing with you and Jon."

"What am I supposed to do about it?"

"When two people are truly in love, they find a way to make it work. You can make it work. When you find someone that inspires you, who truly connects with you, you have to fight for him. Do you think he's worth it?"

"I totally think he's worth it, but I don't know how to approach him. I sent him a message on Facebook letting him know I got into med school and had been thinking about him, but he only replied with 'Congrats.' He's probably already moved on and too bitter to come back." The tears that had been forming in Samantha's eyes began to pour down her cheeks. "Maybe he doesn't care about me anymore."

Scarlett hugged her and rubbed her back. "It'll be okay, Sam," she said. She had listened to Samantha talk about how much she missed Jonathan ever since they broke up. She couldn't bear to see her still so upset about the breakup. She had to do something. She knew exactly what she would do. She would invite Jonathan to the wedding.

* * *

After dinner, Samantha sat in her room and turned on the TV. She wanted to watch something that would distract her from thinking about Jonathan. As she flipped through the channels, she saw that the movie version of *Pride and Prejudice* was playing, so she put it on. It was at a scene where Mr. Darcy—played by Matthew Macfadyen—was confessing his love to Elizabeth Bennet—played by Kiera Knightley—in the pouring rain.

Samantha thought of Jonathan, and how he had given her *Pride and Prejudice* and told her she reminded him of Elizabeth Bennet. She had read the book a few times over. Kiera Knightley and Matthew Macfadyen played their roles perfectly. She had started watching the TV to forget about Jonathan, but Mr. Darcy made her think of him. She was glad she found *Pride and Prejudice*, even if it ruined her plan to watch TV to stop thinking of Jonathan. She sat there and watched the rest of the movie with a nostalgic smile on her face.

CHAPTER 41

· · • • • · ·

"**K**eep that balance, Jon! That's it!" Dr. Bui was behind Jonathan, nudging and pushing him in every direction trying to knock him over. "I'm gonna keep pushing, pulling, and shoving until you can't stay up!"

"I can do this all day!" Jonathan responded. He was strong from the many hours he had spent at the gym. It was challenging, but it was nothing he couldn't handle. Dr. Bui tried to knock him off balance for a few more minutes and then stood up and grabbed a medicine ball.

"Stay where you are, Jon," Dr. Bui said. "I'm gonna throw this ball at you. Try to catch it. But here's the thing: I'm gonna purposely throw it far away from you so you have to reach for it. This is another test of your balance. The goal is to catch each throw without falling over."

"Let's do this!" Jonathan put his hands up. Dr. Bui threw the medicine ball high and to the right of Jonathan, and Jonathan extended his reach to catch it.

"Nice catch!"

Jonathan caught pass after pass for a few more minutes without losing his balance, until Dr. Bui was ready to move on to some strength and resistance workouts. He had Jonathan lie down on a table with a gap in the middle of it and turn to his side. Dr. Bui then hooked up a pulley to Jonathan's leg through the gap in the table and asked Jonathan to lift his leg into the air, pulling against the resistance. After a few reps on one leg, he rolled over to his other side and repeated the exercise with the other leg. Dr. Bui then asked Jonathan to lie on his stomach. He applied the pulley to each leg again, and Jonathan lifted each leg into the air, pulling against the resistance.

Every other day, Jonathan and Dr. Bui went through the same exercises together to improve Jonathan's balance, strength, and flexibility. After a handful of sessions, Dr. Bui surprised him with his new long-term prosthetics. Dr. Bui had gotten Jonathan fitted at a prosthetist before they started their training, and they had just come in. The first session with his new prosthetics was spent practicing putting them on, taking them off, and trying to balance on them. Once he was able to balance came the hard part: he had to learn how to walk with them. He had failed before, with Dr. Austin, but he refused to fail again. He didn't care how challenging it would be. He was doing this for Samantha.

"Before we get you walking, let's have you work on your balance with the prosthetics a bit more," Dr. Bui said as he pulled a flat platform over to Jonathan with a railing on each side. "Stand in the middle of this, and sway back and forth until you can balance on one leg at a time."

Jonathan reached out his hand, grabbed the railings, and used them to support himself as he walked into the middle of the platform. He started to sway until he could balance on one leg at a time.

"Good, Jon, well done. Now I want you to swing your leg so your knee extends fully as your heel touches the ground."

It took a few attempts, but eventually Jonathan successfully swung his leg so his knee fully extended as his heel touched the ground.

"Alright, now let's get back to your balance. I'm going to throw this medicine ball at you—don't worry, you won't have to reach for it; I'm going to throw it right at you. But you have to catch it without falling over. If you feel like you're gonna fall, just grab the railing."

Dr. Bui softly tossed the medicine ball at Jonathan, straight to his chest. Jonathan successfully caught it and tossed it back each time.

"I'm impressed, Jon. You're doing really well."

"I guess I've had some experience already," Jonathan said. "I did some of these exercises right after the accident, but I gave up before I got any good at walking."

"Well, let's get you good at walking then. We're gonna start with a level surface," Dr. Bui instructed. "Let's just walk across the floor of my studio. You'll have this crutch in one hand," Dr. Bui handed an elbow crutch to Jonathan. "I'll hold your other hand as we walk across the floor together."

"Okay."

Jonathan used the railing to get off of the platform. He took Dr. Bui's hand with his left hand and used his right hand to support himself with the elbow crutch. Slowly, they started to inch their way across the floor, step by step. It was about twenty feet of walking.

"You're doing great, Jon," Dr. Bui said encouragingly. "Just make sure you aren't tripping over yourself with that left leg." They went back and forth across the office floor until Dr. Bui was able to let go of Jonathan's hand and Jonathan was able to walk with the crutch.

Months of training passed. Jonathan made tremendous progress. First, he walked on the prosthetics with the crutch. He eventually became able to walk on them without one. He could walk up ramps and stairs, sit down in a chair, and stand up from a seated position. He could get up on his own if he fell. He learned everything he needed to learn about his prosthetics. By May, Jonathan no longer used his wheelchair at all. His time with Dr. Bui was coming to an end. On their last session, Dr. Bui praised Jonathan's progress.

"I'm really impressed, Jon. You've come so far."

"Thanks, Dr. Bui. I really appreciate all the help you've given me."

"I've been wondering, Jon. Why the change of heart? What finally made you want to get out of your wheelchair?"

Jonathan smiled whimsically. "I've got a dance I need to get to."

CHAPTER 42

—————————— •·•●●●●·•· ——————————

Shortly before summer was about to start, Jonathan was taking a walk in his prosthetics. As he walked by the building that Dr. Johanssen's zoology lab was in, he thought of Samantha and Kylie. He hadn't seen them since he broke up with Samantha.

Maybe they're in there.

Jonathan walked into the building and down the dimly lit corridor that led to Dr. Johanssen's zoology lab. At the end of the corridor was the metal door that read "Authorized Personnel Only." He didn't have the lanyard Samantha gave him when he covered for Kylie, but he didn't care. If Samantha was in there, he could try to win her back. He opened the door, turned into the hallway, and walked through the door that read "Lab Animals."

He was disappointed to see two strangers dressed up in PPE gear. One of them—a girl with red hair and pale skin—was holding a water bottle for the mice and shaking it. The other one—a boy with freckles, glasses, and thick blond hair—turned to look at Jonathan as he walked in.

"Hey there," the boy said. "Are you looking for Dr. Johanssen?"

"Nah," Jonathan said glumly, "I was just looking for two friends of mine who used to work here."

"What are their names?" The girl asked.

"Samantha and Kylie."

"Never heard of them," the boy said.

"Me neither," the girl said. "Do you know the trick to getting the bubbles to appear on the water bottle? Dr. Johanssen said we need to make the bubbles appear."

Jonathan thought of the time when Samantha had taught him how to do that. He still remembered it like it was yesterday. "You've got to fasten the stopper and make sure the water has entered the water-delivery tube."

"Oh, okay," the girl said. "Thanks."

Jonathan turned around, walked out, and started back toward his apartment with his head down. He had done enough walking for the day. As he walked along the sidewalk with his head down, he heard a familiar voice rasp his name.

"Jonathan."

Professor Hoffpower.

Jonathan looked up to see Professor Hoffpower standing in front of him. His back was a bit more hunched than it had been the last time Jonathan had seen him almost two years before. He was wearing khaki pants and a sweater vest with a collared shirt and tie under it.

"Hey, Professor–"

"What'd I say when I saw you last, Jon? Call me Jim." He had a genuine smile on his face. "Did you grow some new legs?"

Jonathan let out a laugh. "I've been seeing a physical therapist. He's helped me walk again using prosthetics."

"I'm glad you're taking steps both figuratively and literally. You look great, Jon."

Jonathan appreciated his words. He could tell that Jim was sincerely happy for him. "Thanks, Jim."

"Why don't you come to my office? It's right in this building over here." Professor Hoffpower pointed at a building about twenty feet to the left of them. "We ought to catch up."

Jonathan quickly felt creeped out—and just as quickly felt guilty for feeling creeped out.

Why am I so creeped out by him? He's a good guy. I should give him a chance. I probably won't see him again, and he's the only professor who has ever really cared about me.

Jonathan took a deep breath and managed to smile. "Sure, Jim."

Together they walked into the building. Each step seemed difficult to Jim as he shambled along. Jonathan actually had to walk slower to keep pace. It seemed to Jonathan that a crutch like the one he used when he learned to walk with his prosthetics would benefit Jim. Eventually, they reached his office. The office was nothing special—it was a small room with just a desk and a bookcase full of dusty tomes—but the walls were full of pictures. They were all pictures of Jim with random people. Some of the pictures looked older than Jonathan, and it was weird to see Jim as a youthful man. His caterpillar eyebrows were less wild, and he looked energetic.

"What are these pictures? Who did you take them with?"

Jim shuffled over to the chair behind his desk and took a seat. "Those are former students of mine," he explained. "They're my trophies, if you will. I pride myself on being a mentor to each and every one of those students. I even stay in contact with some of them."

Jonathan nodded and took a seat. He felt bad that he hadn't let Jim be a mentor to him. "I'm sorry I didn't confide in you as much as I should have."

"Nonsense, Jon. It's never too late. Why not confide in me now? Where do you see your studies taking you? How do you envision your journey after leaving Central Texas University?"

"I'm actually quite confused on that front," Jonathan admitted. "I'm torn between becoming an attorney and pursuing a football coaching career for the Stallions."

Jim rubbed his chin and contemplated for a moment. "Those are two very different career paths. I know you'd be an amazing attorney. You were one of my brightest students. You'd have no trouble completing law school and becoming successful. But do you want to become an attorney for the money or because that's what you're passionate about?"

"I don't know, Jim. I can't say that hasn't crossed my mind, though. Becoming a coach would mean making a lot less money, but I know I'd be happier."

Jim nodded slowly. "Jon, I was in a similar situation when I was your age. I was torn between becoming an attorney and becoming a professor. I knew I'd make more money as an attorney, but I also knew I wouldn't be as happy."

"You chose to be a professor, I take it?"

"I chose to be an attorney. I was miserable for years until I finally quit and became a professor. From that day forward, not a day passed when I wasn't excited to get out of bed in the morning. It feels like I haven't worked a day in my life ever since. What I love most about being a professor, though, is helping students like you. I love being a mentor. If becoming a coach is what will make you happier, I think you should pursue that. That said, I'd be glad to write you a letter of recommendation if you want to pursue law school."

"Thanks, Jim. It means a lot." Jonathan smiled and pulled out his phone. "Shall we add another photo to your wall?"

Jim leaned in and reached over his desk to wrap his arm around Jonathan's shoulder. He smiled and put a thumbs up with his other hand as Jonathan snapped a selfie.

"Whatever you decide to do in your life, make sure it's something you are passionate about and helps you make the biggest impact," Professor Hoffpower said.

Jonathan nodded and studied his face. His words rang in Jonathan's head. *Make the biggest impact.*

Jim held out his hand and Jonathan shook it. Jim then reached into his desk, pulled out a business card, and handed it to Jonathan. It had his name inscribed at the top with his phone number and email address.

"Let's keep in touch, Jon."

"Sure thing, Jim." Jonathan smiled and tucked the card into his pocket before turning around and leaving the office.

* * *

When Jonathan got back to his apartment, he noticed an envelope sticking out of his apartment mailbox. Curious, Jonathan grabbed it. It was from a house in Southlake.

Samantha.

He walked down into his apartment and ripped the envelope open. It was a letter with a card underneath it. It was an invitation to Scarlett and William's wedding on July 18th. Excitement brewed inside Jonathan as he unfolded the letter.

Jonathan,

I saw you and Samantha during Spring Break more than a year ago. It was as if Samantha was a completely different person when she was with you. She was happy and free.

Ever since she came home, she's been depressed and moping around the house. I don't want to see my sister like this.

You and Samantha are meant for each other.

I'm putting the ball in your court. This is a formal invitation to my wedding. This might be your last chance to win Samantha back, if you're interested.

I hope you are.

Scarlett

Jonathan was more than interested. This was his chance to share that dance with Samantha under the stars. He was so excited he didn't know what to do. But then he did. He knew what would help him express his feelings. As fast as he could, he hobbled over to his room, opened his writing cabinet, pulled out a journal, and began to write. His thoughts of excitement didn't translate into giddy sentiments as he thought they would:

All these years, I felt so alone.

All these years, I thought no one was looking out for me. I thought I was abandoned. Like the burden was mine to bear. Mine only. And God was punishing me the whole time. I was at the end of my burning wick.

But I've been wrong.

God has always been here for me.

Mom has been here for me.

Life is but a candle that burns as slow as you let it. I just wanted it to melt. I just wanted to burn.

Dom was here for me. I was just too burnt to face the flame.

People have added wax to my candle to help this flame burn slower. To help me live life in the moment instead of burning up in the past.

Pastor Broussard. Professor Hoffpower. Dr. Bui . . . Samantha . . .

Jonathan flinched as he wrote her name.

ACT VI

CHAPTER 43

———— ·•◦•●•◦•· ————

I t was a beautiful day for a wedding. The altar was situated on a cliff by the water overlooking the southern coastline of Texas. It was decorated with white roses that matched the white seats arranged for attendees. Samantha felt happy for her sister, but her smile felt insincere as she posed with the bridesmaids for pictures. They were in a clubhouse overlooking where the ceremony would take place.

William was on his way to get a first look at Scarlett before the ceremony began. Scarlett was in the bride's room waiting for him as Samantha and the other bridesmaids posed for their pictures. Samantha barely knew any of the bridesmaids—they were all Scarlett's friends—and she felt lonely even though she thought, as the maid of honor, she would feel at the top of the world. She couldn't stop thinking about Jonathan. If he were there, she would have felt a whole lot better. She wondered what he was doing at that moment and what he was thinking about. She couldn't help but feel a little disappointed wondering how things would have been if he had been there with her—how perfect the day would have been.

Soon enough, the bridesmaids and groomsmen were standing at the altar waiting for Scarlett. The bridesmaids stood on the left side with Samantha, as the maid of honor, standing closest to the center aisle. The groomsmen stood on the right side, next to William. As the organ played in the background, Samantha thought about how joyful and hopeful the atmosphere was. She had heard the phrase "love is in the air" before but never paid much mind to it. That phrase seemed to make total sense at that moment. As she looked at William waiting at the altar, she thought about Jonathan. She fantasized about him standing at a wedding altar, like William, waiting for her to walk down the aisle to marry him.

"Here Comes the Bride" began to play as Scarlett appeared, walking out of the clubhouse, dressed in a beautiful white gown with a bouquet of flowers in her hands. Dan was walking alongside her with their arms linked together. Everyone stood and turned to watch Scarlett as she walked down the aisle. Some had tears in their eyes. Everyone was smiling. Samantha's legs began to feel weak. Scarlett looked so beautiful. Dan looked so proud. William looked as though he felt like the luckiest man alive.

Scarlett reached the altar and faced William. The pastor began to speak. "William and Scarlett, today, you enter as individuals, but will leave here as husband and wife, blending your lives, expanding your family ties, and embarking upon the grandest adventure of human interaction. The story of your life together is still yours to write. All those present have come to witness and celebrate your love and commitment this day, eager to be a part of the story not yet told."

William and Scarlett smiled at each other. Both looked ready to cry. "True marriage is more than simply joining two persons together through the bonds of matrimony," the pastor went on. "It is also the union of two hearts and the blending of two families. It lives on the love you give each other and never grows old but also thrives on the joy of each new day. Marriage is, and should be, an expression of love. May you always be able to talk things over, to confide in each other, to laugh with each other, to enjoy life together, and to also share those moments of quiet and peace, when the day is done. May you be blessed with a lifetime of happiness and a home of warmth and understanding."

The pastor turned to William. "Do you, William, take Scarlett to be your lawfully wedded wife, promising to love and cherish, through joy and sorrow, sickness and health, and whatever challenges you may face, for as long as you both shall live?"

William nodded his head. "I do."

The pastor turned to Scarlett. "Do you Scarlett, take William to be your lawfully wedded husband, promising to love and cherish, through joy and sorrow, sickness and health, and whatever challenges you may face, for as long as you both shall live?"

Scarlett nodded her head. "I do."

Scarlett handed her flowers to Samantha, and William put a ring on Scarlett's finger.

"By the power invested in me by the state of Texas," the pastor said, "I now pronounce you husband and wife. You may now kiss the bride."

* * *

Samantha swayed back and forth with her father as they danced at the evening reception. Her chin rested on his shoulder, her left hand wrapped around his back, and her right hand entwined with his. Next to them, Scarlett and William danced together. The sappy romantic song playing as they danced made Samantha feel lonely despite her father's company. She still couldn't stop thinking about Jonathan.

After the dance, Samantha sat down at the bridal party table all alone and watched everyone else dancing. She had enjoyed watching Scarlett and William share their first dance, but now watching everyone dance just made her feel lonely and bored. She took a sip of champagne, and then another, and another. She wanted the effects of the alcohol to kick in so she could stop feeling so sad about Jonathan. *A Thousand Years* by Christina Perri began to play as Samantha rolled her eyes.

Great, Samantha thought, *another sappy song to make me even sadder*.

With her eyes fixed on the bottom of the champagne glass as she took sip after sip, she didn't notice everyone turn and look at the tall handsome man who had just entered the wedding tent. She overheard a few ladies whisper to each other excitedly.

"Who is *that*?" One of them said.

"I don't know, but I want to find out," another responded.

Curious, Samantha looked up to see both ladies staring in the same direction. Samantha followed their gaze to see none other than Jonathan. He was looking directly at her. They stared into each other's eyes for a few seconds. Samantha wore an expression of shock while Jonathan wore an expression of joy. She couldn't believe he wasn't in a wheelchair. He was *standing*. Not only was he standing, but he was *walking* toward her. She couldn't help but gasp and put her hand over her mouth as butterflies roiled inside her belly, tingles shot up her spine, and tears of joy poured down her cheeks.

Scarlett saw Jonathan walking over, too. She was in the midst of dancing with William and excitedly whispered into William's ear, "Let's let them share this dance." William wasn't sure what she meant but just nodded, put his hand upon her back, and led her off the dance floor. He curiously watched the man with the peculiar gait. Scarlett's eyes were fixed on Jonathan, too. The eyes that had been upon the newlywed couple followed their gaze to watch Jonathan approach Samantha.

Jonathan walked directly up to Samantha, looked her in the eyes, and smiled. He reached out his hand. "Sam," he said, "Can I have this dance?"

"Jon? How'd you get here? Of—" Samantha fumbled over her words, "—of course, Jon."

The two took to the dance floor with the eyes of Dan, Sara, Scarlett, William, and dozens of others locked on them. Tears came to Scarlett's eyes as she saw her plan come to fruition.

Neither Jonathan nor Samantha had ever felt so complete as they did in that moment. Samantha absorbed Jonathan's scent as she rested her head on his shoulder and they swayed back and forth. The music was perfect. The moment was perfect. Everything was perfect to her. And, for Jonathan, nothing could have been better either. He was having the dance he had been fighting for.

As the song ended, Jonathan leaned into Samantha's ear and whispered, "I missed you, Sam." He held her tighter, his mouth still next to her ear. "I'm never letting—"

Sam placed her finger on Jonathan's mouth, stopping him midsentence. She smiled and kissed Jonathan as Scarlett and the wedding party looked on in adoration and approval. Scarlett's wedding had just become as legendary as she had dreamed it would be.

EPILOGUE

· · · ● ● ● · · ·

Samantha sat in the bleachers, watching the Central Texas University Stallions take the field. She had made it just in time. She had been working in her practice all day and was still dressed in her scrubs. Next to her were Jeff and Rose. In between Jeff and Rose was a little girl wearing a cheerleader outfit.

"Let's go, Stallions!" The girl called out. She strained to see above the people sitting in the row in front of her, so Jeff picked her up and placed her on his shoulders to get a better view. She shook a pair of pom poms and stuck them high up in the air.

Jonathan walked down the sideline wearing a headset and a CTU Stallions hat. He walked up to the quarterback as the offense took the field. It had been a long time since Elijah filled that role, and now it was a young man named Ethan Prett. Jonathan stood next to Ethan, pointed at the clipboard in his hands, and started to instruct him on what he was to do. Ethan nodded, ran onto the field, and Tom came to stand beside Jonathan. Tom nudged Jonathan, showed him some plays on his clipboard, and the two went over the offensive plan for the Stallions' next drive.

"Gabby," Samantha said to the little girl in the cheerleader outfit. "There's Daddy walking down the sideline! Say, 'Hi!'"

"HI, DAD!" Gabby screamed out at the top of her lungs. Jonathan turned to look at Gabby and blew a kiss. He looked at Samantha, smiled, and mouthed

"I love you" as well. Samantha mouthed it back with a big smile on her face. As he focused on her smile, the memories of their first two years together came over Jonathan. He took it in and marveled at the sight of the present day.

God is great.

Deep inside, he believed his sister was watching from above. And, at that very moment, everything in Jonathan McCalister's life was perfect.

ABOUT THE AUTHOR

— • • ● ● ● • • —

lenn Vo is a practicing Dentist who moonlights as a writer. When he is not battling tooth decay and gingivitis, Glenn likes to create romantic stories that warms the heart and soothes the soul. His love for writing came from reading and then creating his own "Choose Your Own Adventure" type of stories. This led to forays into journalism at his high school and culminated in a column for his college newspaper. Initially an English major in college, Glenn received an ultimatum from his father to switch his major to the health sciences. Despite this change, he continued to pursue writing while working toward becoming a dentist.

2612 Cherryhill Lane is the result of many years of hard work and dedication. Many of the plot points and characters were jotted down between studying the various anatomical structures in Dental Anatomy. And as a dentist, he would work on the novel in between patients, drafting important plot points on patient bibs and sticky notes. But in all seriousness, this novel represents what is possible if you have a dream and never give up.

Glenn currently lives in Flower Mound, Texas, with his lovely wife, two rambunctious kids, and a feisty beta fish named Dory. He attends Northwest Bible Church and Gateway Church.

CPSIA information can be obtained
at www.ICGtesting.com
Printed in the USA
JSHW011506010920
7543JS00001BA/89